Linda Regan is a successful a
from television to film, radio
eight crime novels, all criti
set in London, where she was born and brought up.

Praise for Linda Regan:

'Regan exhibits enviable control over her characters
in this skilful and fascinating WhoDunnit'
Colin Dexter

'One of the best up-and-coming writers'
Peter Gutteridge, *Sunday Observer*

'Regan continues her sure-footed walk on the noir side.
Entertaining stuff, but not for the faint-hearted'
Kirkus Reviews

'A sound debut; I look forward to
Linda Regan's next book'
Tangled Web

'Extremely well written'
Encore Magazine

'This is a book you can't put down'
Eastbourne Herald

Also by Linda Regan and available from Headline

The DCI Banham series

Behind You (*previously published as* Staged Death)
Secret Remains (*previously published as* Soho Killers)
Killer Looks (*previously published as* Monroe Murders)
The Terror Within
The Burning Question

The DI Johnson and DS Green series

Brotherhood of Blades
Street Girls

The DI Johnson series

Guts for Garters
Sisterhoods

LINDA REGAN
SECRET REMAINS

Copyright © 2007 Linda Regan

The right of Linda Regan to be identified as the Author of
the Work has been asserted by her in accordance with the
Copyright, Designs and Patents Act 1988.

First published in 2007 as *Soho Killers* by Accent Press

First published in 2023 by Headline Accent
An imprint of HEADLINE PUBLISHING GROUP

1

Apart from any use permitted under UK copyright law, this publication may
only be reproduced, stored, or transmitted, in any form, or by any means,
with prior permission in writing of the publishers or, in the case of reprographic
production, in accordance with the terms of licences issued
by the Copyright Licensing Agency.

All characters in this publication are fictitious and any resemblance
to real persons, living or dead, is purely coincidental.

Cataloguing in Publication Data is available from the British Library

ISBN 978 1 0354 0583 1

Offset in 11.04/15.2pt Times New Roman by Jouve (UK), Milton Keynes

Printed and bound in Great Britain by Clays Ltd, Elcograf S.p.A.

Headline's policy is to use papers that are natural, renewable and recyclable
products and made from wood grown in well-managed forests and other
controlled sources. The logging and manufacturing processes are expected
to conform to the environmental regulations of the country of origin.

HEADLINE PUBLISHING GROUP
An Hachette UK Company
Carmelite House
50 Victoria Embankment
London
EC4Y 0DZ

www.headline.co.uk
www.hachette.co.uk

ACKNOWLEDGEMENTS

In no particular order, I am indebted to:

Everyone at Accent, for being so lovely to work with. A special big 'thank you' to my editor Greg Rees for endless patience, and his patience with my computer illiteracy!

DC Paul Steed for all his advice with police procedure and protocol. I truly don't know where I'd be without that help.

For the supply of artistic Elastoplasts and endless pep talks, I thank my wonderful husband Brian Murphy – not least because he looks better in a dress than any woman I know! And if that seems a bit of a puzzle in itself, check out his acting credits – I think he's played more women's parts than I have!

I am lucky enough to have been blessed in life with a bunch of wild but wonderful girlfriends, who have stood by me through thick and thin. (And I don't just mean my waistline.)
Some of you I met through the Grand Order of Lady Ratlings, the showbusiness charity, who, besides helping anyone in need, stand by each other. Others I have known since our schooldays, and others I met on theatre

engagements or television shows.

You all know who you are; I call you my PinC friends (Partners in Chablis!). We have laughed, cried, eaten chocolate, and drunk our way through life – and this book is dedicated to you.

And finally, millions, billions, and trillions of 'thank yous' to everyone who read the first book in the DCI Banham series, and for all the uplifting letters you sent me – because without you, this book wouldn't have been commissioned.

NEARLY TWENTY YEARS AGO...

Shaheen lifted nervous fingers and touched the throbbing, delicate area under her left eye. The flesh was puffy, and its normal light brown colour had a mauve sheen. By tomorrow she'd have a whopper. *But this is nothing*, she thought, glancing in the mirror at the other five girls who were happily dressing behind her. A much bigger problem faced them all, and it was because of her.

She released the hook on the black and red lace suspender belt and peeled the sweaty black fishnet stockings down her shapely brown legs, leaving only the red satin G-string that was the uniform of the Scarlet Pussy Club strippers.

She tossed the stockings toward the grubby white plastic washing basket that overflowed in the corner. They missed. Susan, standing stark naked by the basket, picked them up and threw them in.

Shaheen smiled a 'thank you'. In the mirror she watched Olivia and Katie, sitting together as always, on a flimsy wooden bench. They were both tall, stunning blondes with perfect bodies, alike enough to pass for twins. Shaheen could see why Ahmed had chosen to use them as a double lesbian act. As solo strippers they were naturally sexy and scintillating, and the punters loved them; but the money-grabbing, perverted bastard was shrewd enough to know that together they would pack his seedy club to capacity. Not that they *were* lesbians – not even close.

Olivia's enormous bosom welled over the edge of the strawberry pink boob tube she was now wearing. Katie was dressed in an almost identical top, in pastel blue, and although her boobs were not large, they were in proportion to her tiny little waist and snug bottom.

The other three girls were all naked and sharing the single towel Ahmed provided. They took turns to wipe the sweat from their overheated bodies before clambering into their street clothes. Shaheen knew they were all looking forward to being paid and having Sunday off before another week of hard work and degradation began.

None of them had any idea.

She dabbed brown powder over her bruised and aching eye, then reached for her short white rah-rah skirt and broderie anglaise top. She despised herself for what she was doing. She liked the girls, and they were kind to her and seemed to accept her. She didn't think badly of them, but she'd had a different upbringing and she was still a virgin. Now Ahmed was going to take it out on them, and they didn't deserve it. They needed their jobs here a lot more than she did.

Shaheen's parents had been good to her, put food in her mouth and given her a good education; they were even willing to pay for her to go to college. So why had she been so stupid? They had shown her love, and she had repaid them by running from their suffocating ways to work in a Soho strip club. Three of these girls were students, trying to work their way through college. They needed their wages. They'd had to learn to strip in a way that turned the punters on, and made them pant all the way to the bar to purchase the over-priced drinks – and give in to Ahmed's disgusting sexual demands. Shaheen was a virgin, and because he needed a brown-skinned girl, she had been excused the sex.

Or so she thought. Now Ahmed had gone back on his word. He had told her the only pay she would get if he didn't get his perks was another black eye, and this one really hurt. But worse still, he had said the other girls wouldn't get their wages if she didn't give in to him. The money wasn't important to her; she could walk out and go home to her parents. But the girls *had* been kind to her, and she didn't want to drop them in it like that. She just didn't know what to do.

'Thank the Lord it's Saturday,' Theresa said in her soft Dublin accent, flinging her nun's costume in the washing basket. 'Money in my purse, and a day in bed.'

Shaheen wanted to cry. How could she tell them it wasn't going to happen?

Kim was standing nude in the middle of the room, using the grubby towel to wipe the sweat that ran from the edge of her short brown hair down her long slender back.

'It's like an oven in here,' she said, fanning herself with the towel. 'Shall I open the window and risk the stale curry from the gents' urinal next door?'

Theresa was now sitting on the floor, wearing nothing but her red uniform G-string and zipping scuffed red boots over her skinny, freckled legs. She tossed her mane of red hair out of her face. 'Go on, the smell of my feet is probably worse,' she joked.

Susan bent forward, and her heavily peroxided, waist-length hair nearly touched the floor as she pulled a nylon brush through it. At twenty-one, Susan was the oldest of the girls. She had been stripping all her working life, and had become a mother-figure to the others, guiding and protecting them. She lifted her head and grinned. 'I *thought* I could smell cheese.'

The other girls laughed, but Shaheen couldn't.

'What's wrong, love?' Susan asked her. 'You're not yourself tonight.'

She shook her head, but suddenly everything was too much. Covering her mouth with her hand, she burst into tears.

Kim moved from the window and rubbed Shaheen gently on the back. 'What is it?'

'I didn't do the sex bit for Ahmed,' Shaheen said. 'He said as long as I stripped all the way and the punters liked me, he'd let me off because I'm a virgin.'

'The punters *love* you,' Susan said, slipping an arm round her.

Their concern made her feel worse. 'Well, he's gone back on his word. He hit me again when I pushed him away.' She gingerly stroked her swollen eye, and started to cry again. 'I don't know how to do a blow job, I'm a virgin,' she sobbed.

'Perverted bastard,' Susan said. 'I never fuckin' gave him a blow job. That's a wind-up.'

The room went quiet.

After a few seconds Katie said, 'Olivia and I had to.'

'He made us,' Olivia agreed.

'I said I wanted to earn enough to go to drama school,' Katie told them, 'and Olivia said she needed quick money to go to college too, to be a lawyer. Ahmed said it boiled down to the same thing – we both wanted to tell lies for a living. He said we'd be great as a double act. Then he said we had to prove ourselves and do the full lesbian job, as a sort of private audition, just for him.'

Olivia giggled with embarrassment.

'He knows we aren't really lesbians,' Katie said. 'He *is* a perv, though. He was getting his rocks off while we did it.'

Shaheen noticed Kim blush and look at the floor.

Olivia nodded. 'He was wanking while we were pretending to have it off. We couldn't stop giggling. We only agreed because we needed the job so desperately.'

'He shoved a big dildo up me,' Katie added. 'It really hurt.'

Olivia winced and nodded.

The room fell silent again. Shaheen felt even worse.

Kim said, 'He wanted me to give him a blow job but I told him I was gay. I said I desperately needed money to go to ballet school and do a choreography course. So he made me masturbate to ballet music.' She shrugged. 'I did it. I stripped off and spread my legs over a chair.' She flicked an embarrassed glance to Olivia and Katie. 'I thought it was quite funny, till he stuck a rubber penis up my back passage and called me Dusty Springfield.'

Shaheen was shocked. Suddenly she wanted to run

home to her parents. But she was determined not to let these girls down.

'Filthy fucker,' Susan spat.

Theresa's pale, freckled face suddenly turned pink. Against the red of her hair, Shaheen thought she looked like a Belisha beacon. 'I did the full works,' she admitted in a whisper. 'The electric bill was way overdue, and me mam's off licence was refusing to give us any more on tick. Life with me mam without gin is unthinkable, so I just did it. Then the next night he made me give him a blow job. It was stinky and floppy and I'd rather not remember it, if it's all the same to you.'

Theresa slipped a cotton dress over her thin, freckled body, bare apart from the red satin G-string. As she reached behind her to pull the zip up, she said quietly, 'If you don't know how to do one, wait till someone you love shows you, that's my advice.'

Olivia smiled. 'You've met that someone now.'

'Good for you,' Katie added.

Theresa blushed scarlet again, looking at Olivia. 'You don't mind me having him, do you?'

Olivia shook her head. 'If he makes you happy, I'm delighted. It's the least you deserve.'

'He's great,' Theresa said dreamily. 'I'm really glad you ditched him for Fat Kenneth.'

Olivia pulled a white blouse around her shoulders and over the pink boob tube. 'Brian's too nice for me,' she said.

'That's not true,' Katie protested. 'You deserve someone nice too.'

'I can't cope with nice people,' Olivia said. 'Anyway, Fat Kenneth is quite nice really.' She leaned in to the mirror to check the mascara around her wide violet eyes wasn't smudged, then gave Shaheen a saucy smile. 'He's *also* stinking filthy rich. That's a big turn-on for me. So you're very welcome to nice Brian, Theresa.'

'Sensible girl,' Susan said.

'I'm going to make my own money,' Katie said. 'That's the only reason I'm doing this crap. I'm going to be a famous film star. Then I'll love 'em and leave 'em, until I meet Mr Right. Then I'll marry for love.'

The atmosphere had lightened again, and Shaheen felt another surge of guilt. 'Ahmed's making threats,' she blurted out.

'He's always making threats.' Kim had been tying the strings of Shaheen's wraparound bodice; she stopped as she caught the other girl's eye. 'What do you mean?' she asked warily.

'Money threats,' Shaheen said weakly.

The girls exchanged glances. 'Why didn't you say so before?' Susan said, an edge creeping into her voice.

'What threats, exactly?' Kim asked.

'He says if I don't let him have my virginity, he … he won't pay any of you either. I … I'm sorry. I didn't want to make trouble.'

Five sets of eyes burned into her. Theresa shouted, 'I've got to have that money tonight. Mam owes over two hundred pounds to different off-licences, and we've no food for the weekend, and …'

'Oh, 'e'll fucking pay us.' Susan's tone was steely.

'We've earned it, and we ain't going to beg that fucker for nothing.'

At first Shaheen had been shocked by Susan's constant use of the F-word; before coming to the club she had barely heard it twice in her life, but now she heard it a few dozen times every night. It had taken some getting used to, but she had grown to like Susan, and trust her, as they all did.

Katie looked up from her seat on the bench. 'I'll remember this,' she said. 'When I'm a famous actress, I'll use it for my motivation. How it felt to be afraid and desperate for the money I worked all week for in a poxy Soho strip club.'

Olivia looked surprised. 'I don't think you should ever admit you did it. This is the pits.'

'I'm not ashamed,' Kim said. 'It's all a form of art.'

Susan's dirty laugh was famous. 'A blow job on Ahmed Abdullah ain't fucking art!'

'Don't remind me,' Theresa said with a giggle. 'It was like a mouldy chipolata sausage, and I thought he'd never come.'

'We've all more than earned our wages,' Susan declared. ''E ain't pulling that one.'

'Didn't you have to do anything for him?' Shaheen asked.

Susan picked up the G-strings and oddments of clothing that littered the floor and threw them into the wash basket. 'I used to be 'is bit on the side. I used to lie there and think of the money. I'm too old for 'im now, but that suits me fine.' She turned back to face them, looking first at Olivia, then at Theresa. 'You don't think this has got anything to do with Theresa and Brian, do you?'

Theresa frowned. 'Why should it have? He didn't say anything when Olivia was with Brian.'

Shaheen shook her head vehemently. 'No, it's all because of me. He said he'd withhold all our money until I did it with him.' Her hand went back to her cheek. 'I'm so sorry.'

'That's it, then.' Katie picked up her satchel bag. 'I'm going to confront him. Who's coming?'

'Me.' Olivia grabbed her small holdall.

Susan raised a hand. 'Let's all go. There's just one of him and six of us. Brian, too, if we have to.'

Theresa nodded. 'I've got to have my money tonight. If he refuses, we'll take him hostage and just grab it. He keeps it in his top drawer. It's ours, we've earned it – it wouldn't be stealing.' She looked at Shaheen and shook her head sadly. 'I don't know why you don't just go home to your parents. We all need our wages; you don't.'

Shaheen started to cry again. 'But I do. I need to stand on my own two feet, I really do.'

'If you needed it like we do, you'd have agreed to Ahmed's terms and humiliated yourself like we've all had to,' said Olivia with a touch of acid.

'To get enough money to make something of our lives,' Katie added.

'Or even just to pay our way out of poverty,' Theresa added quietly.

Shaheen looked at the floor. Her eye hurt even more as tears flowed out of it.

'Don't let's argue,' Kim pleaded. 'Susan's right, we've earned it, and we're six against one. Let's stick together and go and get it. I want to go home.'

'Is all the washing in?' Susan asked in her motherly tone. 'Check you've initialled your G-strings, then we know we won't get anyone else's.'

'I wash my own,' Shaheen said. 'At least then I know they're clean.'

'And he hasn't been sniffing them,' said Theresa with a snort of laughter.

They walked two by two along the narrow corridor, Shaheen behind the other girls. She still felt dreadful; this was all her fault.

'I'm glad you're OK about me and Brian,' she heard Theresa say over Olivia's shoulder.

'Oh, that was just a fling,' Olivia answered. 'He always fancied you, but you used to dash off to look after your mum. And Ken's more my type.'

'Sports car, and rich parents,' Theresa giggled.

'And he's already at law school, so we've got lots in common.'

'You've a good future after going through all this shit,' Theresa said. 'Enjoy it, and don't settle down until you're really ready.'

'I'll be ready,' Olivia answered with a little laugh. 'If he's rich enough.'

'You won't need to marry,' Katie chipped in. 'You'll make it for yourself. The richest lawyers are the ones with no scruples.'

'Suits me,' Olivia laughed.

'She'll be a great lawyer,' Kim said. 'She's got it all – brains *and* beauty.'

'I haven't got anything,' Katie said. 'That's why I want to be an actress – so I can pretend to be somebody else.'

'What?' exclaimed Kim. 'You have the face of an angel and a beautiful figure. Every man who comes to the club is in love with you.'

'*And* every woman,' Olivia teased.

Listening to their banter, Shaheen longed to be one of the crowd. Whatever their backgrounds, they cared for and supported each other. All she had done was make their tough lives tougher. There was only one thing she could do: offer to give Ahmed what he wanted. She opened her mouth to speak, but Susan put a finger to her lips to quieten them all. They were outside Ahmed's office door.

Susan flung it open and marched inside. 'We've come to get our money,' she said.

The other girls followed her in and stood in a line behind her. Ahmed was sitting in his black leather chair, counting a pile of grubby notes on the desk in front of him. He swiftly put the notes away in the top drawer, locked the drawer and pocketed the key, then lifted a glass of brandy and took a large sip. His dark eyes swept along the line of girls, coming to rest on Shaheen.

'Tell her to fulfil her contract and I'll pay you,' he said, waving the glass in her direction.

Susan took a deep breath. 'You gave her the job 'cause you needed a brown-skinned stripper …'

'I did.' He lifted the glass again. 'But I taste all the girls.'

'We're strippers, not whores,' Kim said sourly.

'Same thing. Call it manager's perks. Those are my rules. Either she gives out or no one gets paid. Choice is hers.'

Tears stung Shaheen's eyes again. This was all her fault. She felt Kim's arm slide around her.

'Why do you stroke her?' Ahmed's voice was silky. 'Ah, is it because she is also a lesbian?'

'She's upset, Ahmed.' Susan's tone was placating.

'So she should be. She's let you all down.'

'No!' Olivia shouted. 'It's you – you've let us all down.'

His ugly mouth twisted with amusement; he was obviously enjoying the power he had over them.

'Yes,' Katie butted in. 'You said …'

'I'll do it with you.' Shaheen was acutely aware of the tremble in her voice, but she braved it out. 'As long as you promise to pay them. Theresa needs it to pay the gas bill and…'

But Ahmed wasn't listening. He stood up, moved swiftly round the desk and grabbed her. She gagged as his mouth bruised hers, then shrieked as he lowered his head to her cleavage and bit her. He reached up behind him and pressed a switch; a video recorder mounted on the wall clicked on. Then he was unbuckling his belt and pulling his zip down. 'Come on then,' he invited. 'Anyone want to join in?'

Olivia looked at Katie in horror. 'That's a camera. He videoed us all. When we did it with him. When we performed for him. Didn't you? Didn't you!' she yelled at

Ahmed.

'Of course.' He slid his hand up and down his swollen dick. 'Hey, let's have a party.'

Shaheen tried to back away but he grabbed her by both arms. She clenched her teeth, too terrified to scream.

Kim forced her way between them. 'Leave her alone,' she shouted.

Olivia pushed her aside and backed Ahmed towards the wall. 'Where are they?' she snarled. 'I want those tapes. We'll have a life after this – I'm not having mine wrecked by some sleazy pervert.'

Shaheen was sobbing hysterically. Ahmed pushed Olivia and sent her flying, then seized Shaheen and pulled her towards him. 'Never mind her, darling.' He put her hand on his swollen dick. 'Here, feel. That's just for you.'

Shaheen let out a loud shriek, and Kim intervened again. She was taller than Ahmed, slim and muscular, and in good shape from her dance training. She elbowed him in the ribs and pushed him sideways, winding him a little. 'Leave her alone!' she yelled again. 'That's rape!'

'That cupboard,' Susan shouted to Katie and Olivia. 'All 'is private stuff's in there.'

Ahmed was forcing Shaheen back against the wall. Susan waded in to help Kim pull him off; he flailed at them and pulled her towards him, but was distracted as Olivia and Katie opened the cupboard and began to fling its contents on the floor. 'Oi, you two! Pack it in!' he shouted.

Shaheen slumped against the wall as Susan followed Ahmed across the room.

'There's whips and handcuffs and God knows what in here,' she exclaimed.

'And videos!' That was Olivia. 'They've got our names on them. The bastard's even labelled them.'

Something fell to the floor with a loud clatter, then Shaheen watched in horror as Ahmed reached over the girls' heads and grabbed a whip from a high shelf. She held her breath – but he only cracked it against the floor to get their attention.

He cracked it again, and this time it landed on Kim's back. Kim gasped with shock, then grabbed the glass from his desk and waved it close to his greasy face. 'Come on then, big man,' she goaded. 'You gonna take me on?'

He grabbed her wrist and twisted it viciously. The glass dropped and smashed on the floor. At the same moment his trousers slipped and fell below his knees, exposing shabby blue Y-fronts. Shaheen felt her sobs turn to hysterical laughter, and the other girls joined in.

He dropped the whip, turned back to Shaheen and pushed her against the wall again. She froze rigid as he pressed himself against her and reached down into his underpants. 'You'll like this,' he said with a leer. 'You and I will have some fun and all the nice girlies will get their money. Everyone goes home happy.'

She felt him fumble with her waistband, then her skirt slipped down her legs to the floor. Only the red G-string remained; one tug on the leather ribbon and it fell to the floor too, leaving her exposed for whatever vileness he had in mind. 'What a lovely pussy,' he said pawing at her.

Shaheen started yelling. It seemed to arouse him even

more, and he pushed his erection against her.

'Kick him, Shaheen,' Olivia shouted.

Susan was on the desk, reaching for the video recorder. 'Quick,' she called to Olivia and Katie, who were scrabbling on the floor. 'Find your tapes, quick as you can, or he'll bloody do it to her.'

Shaheen struggled as Ahmed rubbed his body lasciviously against hers. Why didn't they come to her aid instead of messing with those tapes?

Then Kim lunged at him. 'Stop it. You're an animal.'

Ahmed pulled back from Shaheen and reached down for the whip, but Kim was quicker. She kicked at his hand, and suddenly Katie was there, handcuffs dangling from her hand.

As she clicked one cuff around his wrist, he pulled his hand away to avoid the second. Then, quick as a flash, he pushed his head down Shaheen's bodice, biting her spitefully on the nipple and holding it between his teeth. She screamed, and Kim tugged at his hair, shouting, 'Let go of her!'

He lifted his head and spat in Kim's face. Shaheen seized the moment, bringing her knee up sharply into his balls. He reeled and staggered into the wall, mouth open, sucking in air. Kim grabbed the opportunity to click the second handcuff on him, and he slumped, crippled with pain but muttering a stream of abuse.

'Oh, gag him,' Olivia shouted from the floor by the cupboard, where she and Katie were still desperately searching through the video tapes.

'What with?' Shaheen's brief burst of confidence had

drained away; she looked around helplessly.

'Your G-string.' Katie waved a hand at the discarded red scrap lying on the floor. 'Then find the key to his desk and let's get our wages.'

Susan picked up the scarlet knickers and held them out in front of her. 'For Chrissake get a move on,' she urged, advancing on Ahmed with bared teeth.

His head whipped from side to side as she tried to tie the gag. Shaheen grabbed his hair and Kim and Theresa held his legs down, but he resisted and fought like a caged animal. He jerked his head, banging it over and over against the wall, and as he sucked in air to relieve the pain, he sucked the G-string in too. Suddenly his eyes bulged and his limbs thrashed as the flimsy fabric lodged in his throat. The girls all released their grip on him, and then the only sound in the room was the cracking of Ahmed's knees as he slipped into a heap, trousers round his ankles and his penis shrunken like an old mushroom.

The girls all stared in horror.

Olivia stepped away from the pile of videos. 'Fucking hell,' she whispered. 'He's not dead, is he?'

'It might be a wind-up,' Susan said, putting a hand out to stop the girls going any nearer.

Kim knelt beside Ahmed and felt his pulse, then put her ear to his chest. With a grimace she prised his mouth open; the end of the leather ribbon lay on his tongue.

'He's all but swallowed the G-string, and he doesn't seem to be breathing,' she said tentatively. 'Theresa, go and get Brian.'

'For sure.' Theresa scrambled towards the door.

The tape in Olivia's hand clattered to the floor. 'I'll come with you.'

The other girls looked at each other, and without a word Kim picked up Shaheen's skirt and handed it to her.

Theresa and Olivia were back in minutes with Brian. He stared at Ahmed's inert body on the floor.

'Is he dead?' Katie asked in a shaky voice.

But Brian's gaze had moved to the bleeding teeth marks on Shaheen's cleavage. 'If he's not, I'll finish the job off meself.'

He knelt beside Ahmed and held his mouth open, exposing the end of the ribbon. He pulled on it and the g-string, dark with slime, dangled from his fingers.

'He's dead all right,' Brian said. 'He could have choked, or he may have hit his head. There's a mark here on his temple. That's the most vulnerable bit to bash – it can kill you instantly. That's what people aim for when they shoot you.'

No one said a word.

Brian stood up. He was a big bloke, well over six feet and exceptionally broad. He had earned his reputation as the best club bouncer in London; no man ever picked a fight with Brian Finn. But he treated women as gently as a newborn baby. He understood and cared for these girls, and felt a responsibility toward them; they came from poor backgrounds or broken homes and, like himself, they had to be survivors. At twenty-seven he was ten years older than most of them, but streetwise beyond his years. He knew what a crook Ahmed was, and how he took advantage of young and needy girls.

'Should we call an ambulance? Or the police?' Theresa asked faintly.

Brian thought for a moment, then took a deep breath. 'Neither,' he said decisively. 'I'm going to dump the body.'

The girls looked at each other nervously. 'He deserved everything he got,' Brian went on. 'I'm not gonna let you lot get into trouble. You could be done for manslaughter.'

The girls were shocked into silence. Finally Olivia spoke. 'Is he definitely dead? Are you really sure? Could he just be unconscious?'

'Sweetheart, he's dead,' Brian said gently. 'We've got to get rid of him.'

This time it was Susan who broke the silence. 'He's right,' she said dully.

'Just go home and act as if nothing happened,' Brian told them. He picked up one of the videos, frowning when he saw Kim's name on the label. 'What the hell are these?'

Susan explained.

'It gets better,' said Brian bitterly. 'Look, don't worry you about those neither – I'll bury them with him.' He began to gather up the scattered tapes, and Theresa handed him a plastic supermarket carrier she pulled from her shoulder bag.

'Have you got wages outstanding?' Brian asked when the tapes were dealt with.

'That's what we came for,' Susan said. 'Five hundred pounds each. The takings are locked in the drawer and the key's in his trouser pocket.'

'He owes ...' Kim stopped and corrected herself. 'He

owed Shaheen for three weeks. That's fifteen hundred pounds.'

'Bastard,' Brian spat. 'Grasping toe-rag. He ain't paid you for three weeks?' He groped around Ahmed's feet where his trousers were bunched, shaking his head as he dug in his pocket for the key to the drawer. There was a thick wad of notes; he counted out the right amount to each of the girls, then put the remainder back in the drawer and locked it, leaving the key in it.

'Go home,' he said.

'Where will you dump him?' Olivia asked nervously.

'Don't you worry about that. I've got an idea. You know that new office block they're building down at the docks?' The girls looked at each other, nodding dubiously. 'They'll be concreting the foundations in the next couple of days; I'll drop him in one of the trenches, and by Tuesday he'll be under ten feet of concrete. Then all this will be history.'

'But ... you're really sticking your neck out for us,' Kim said. 'How can we ever thank you?'

Brian shrugged, and slipped an arm round Theresa's shoulders. 'It's an easy one. He was an evil tosser. You're lovely girls, and you don't deserve trouble. Just go off home before the bar manager sees you and wonders why you're so late leaving. Go on. I'll sort it.'

Five minutes later they were outside in the cold night air, walking along the pavement, arms linked. Theresa and Shaheen both walked in the road, but only the occasional car or night bus passed them.

It was Olivia who broke the silence. 'He must really

love you, Theresa. That's one hell of a risk he's taken for us.'

'He hated Ahmed as much as we did,' Susan said. 'Hated the way he took advantage of you and then wouldn't give you what he owed you.'

'We've got it now,' Kim said. 'I just hope that's the end of it.'

'I still think it's wonderful of Brian to stick his neck out,' Olivia said again. 'You've got a good one there, Theresa. To think I dumped him for Fat Kenneth.'

'That's how he is,' Susan said. 'He believes women should be looked after.'

They came to a ragged halt as Shaheen buckled at the knees and started to cry. 'God, what have we done?' she sobbed.

'Nothing!' Olivia and Susan said in unison.

'We've done nothing,' Susan repeated.

'We've killed someone,' Shaheen howled.

'It was an accident,' Theresa said firmly, taking hold of Shaheen's elbow and giving her a little shake.

'It was self-defence,' Kim insisted.

Susan stepped to the front of the group and grasped Shaheen's shoulders. 'It doesn't matter what it was! Get a grip, Shaheen. It never happened, OK?'

Shaheen struggled to control her sobs and reluctantly nodded her head. The girls huddled round her, hugging each other for comfort.

Susan took a deep breath. 'We must never talk about this again. Not ever, not to no one. Agreed?'

Kim, Theresa, Katie and Olivia nodded. After a

moment Shaheen followed suit.

'We carry on as if it never happened,' Susan said. 'If we're questioned, we have to tell the same story. He was alive when we left the club. That's all we have to say. He paid us, and we left.'

'Questioned? Who by?' Shaheen sounded wary.

'The police, maybe. We have to come back on Monday night as if nothing has happened. With luck we'll just find the club closed, but in case…'

'Let's agree the story, then.' This was Katie. 'We did our last stripping spot at the usual time, got paid by Ahmed in our dressing room then all left the club together. He was alive when we left.'

'We stick to that story no matter what happens to us in the future,' Susan said firmly. 'Agreed?'

'Agreed.' They piled hands in a gesture of solidarity.

'Susan's right, Shaheen.' Theresa squeezed her arm, and the other girls nodded their agreement. 'What happened tonight must never be mentioned. Even amongst ourselves. You never know who might overhear.'

'So what happens on Monday?' Shaheen asked, still a little tearful.

Susan was still in charge. 'We come to work as usual. There'll be no job, probably no club – but we act surprised.'

'And after that, we go our separate ways,' added Olivia. 'But whatever happens, we keep the secret. We never tell a soul.'

Brian had found it a real struggle to get Ahmed's trousers back on, so getting the body into the car had seemed a doddle. Everyone had left the club except the bar manager; after seeing him off the premises, he had reversed his car to the back door, then slung one of Ahmed's arms around his neck as if he was drunk, and dragged him round to the passenger door. Ahmed's dead body slumped back in the seat, looking so lifelike it gave him the creeps.

Burying the body in the foundations of the office block was a great idea. The concreting would be finished in forty-eight hours and nobody would ever know what lay beneath it. He glanced over at the seat beside him; Ahmed could easily have been asleep. The red G-string protruded from his shirt pocket like a handkerchief.

It was then that Brian glanced in his mirror and noticed the police car behind him. *Don't panic*, he told himself; *just drive properly and stay within the speed limit*. They'd have no reason to stop him.

It was another couple of seconds before the flashing blue light reflected in his mirror. As the police car pulled alongside him and signalled for him to pull over, he realised that in his haste to get Ahmed in the car, he hadn't turned on the lights.

As the two policemen approached his car, one carrying a breathalyser kit and the other a torch, the irony hit him. He never touched alcohol; he was a lifelong teetotaller.

CHAPTER ONE

Detective Inspector Paul Banham was making good progress. In his eleven years as a detective in the murder squad he had, on many occasions, sought the help of psychological profilers, and he had enormous respect for them. But counselling, he had discovered, was psychology of a different colour.

Counselling was personal: in his case very personal indeed. For one thing it meant facing up to his reaction to – no, his all-consuming fear of – looking at certain corpses. It was common knowledge among his colleagues that he got the shakes, and sometimes even fainted or threw up, when he looked at a young, murdered woman.

But that wasn't the worst part. His counsellor was also helping him to deal with his sex life, or lack of it; and the prospect of his colleagues knowing about his inadequacy in that department didn't bear thinking about. If they found out, he'd be a laughing stock, and would never command the respect he needed to head a murder enquiry. He'd never be able to show his face in the incident room again.

Of course, Lottie knew. They were twins, and though he hadn't told her, she knew anyway, just as he knew things about her. She had been the one to suggest that he talk to someone; in fact she had begged him to seek counselling, and once or twice they had almost quarrelled about it. He had argued that it wouldn't help, that the only thing that would solve the problem would be if the police finally caught the bastard who had murdered his wife and their eleven-month-old daughter, and ensure that bastard suffered as terrifying an ordeal as the one he'd inflicted on Diane and baby Elizabeth. If that happened, Banham could put his life back together, perhaps even love again, physically as well as emotionally. But despite breakthroughs in forensics, after eleven years they were highly unlikely to catch the killer.

So Banham had given in to his sister's nagging and taken the bull by the horns. He had been having regular sessions with a counsellor for several weeks now. He had to admit it was a lot to do with Alison Grainger, the detective sergeant with unusual black-flecked, sludge-coloured eyes who had crept into his heart.

It was seven years since she had moved over to the murder division of CID to work with him, and from the start they had understood each other and worked well together. The squad's success rate was improving all the time. Recently he had realised how attracted he was to her. A few weeks ago he had invited her out for a candlelit supper, and she had asked him to her flat for coffee afterwards. In a blind panic, he refused, with the feeble excuse that business and pleasure didn't mix.

That had made Alison very angry, and no one wanted to be on the wrong side of Alison Grainger's temper. So Banham had decided it was time to do something. He'd made an appointment with Joan Deamer, a middle-aged, approachable counsellor his sister Lottie promised would change his life.

That was seven weeks ago, and already he was beginning to feel different. The physical feelings he'd believed he would never experience again had started to stir. At one counselling session they had talked about blue films, and Joan had given him a couple to take home. The effect had been like a door bursting open; after eleven celibate years, he found he could function physically again. He had a sexual future, and the person he wanted in it was Alison Grainger.

Joan had urged him not to give up on a relationship with Alison. She had assured him he could always ask her out again; Alison was quite bright enough to see past his excuse about not mixing business with pleasure, and if she felt as he did, she wouldn't hold his moment of panic against him.

But he wasn't sure; his confidence was still on the low side. As he walked down the steps from Joan Deamer's office, the thought of that temper brought a smile to his face. He knew the signs: the black flecks in her eyes seemed to expand, then the verbals began to flow within seconds. Those eyes were beautiful: so much so that he even looked forward to her losing her temper.

He flicked his wrist to check the time. It was seven thirty, nearly bedtime for his six-year-old niece Madeleine. He decided to head for his sister's; he could ring for a pizza for himself and Lottie, and while they waited for it, he could read Madeleine another chapter of the book of stories he had bought her the previous week. He loved watching her angelic little face as she listened to the goings-on of the Flower Fairies' daily duties. Tonight it was the turn of the Cowslip Fairy.

The drive took him twenty minutes, including a quick stop at the garage for a couple of cans of lager, a bunch of flowers for Lottie and far too many bars of chocolate for Bobby and Madeleine.

He made it as far as the doorway; a beautiful, excited six-year-old princess ran down the stairs announcing to the doll on her arm, 'It's Uncle Paul. He brings us chocolate, Barbie.'

Then his mobile began its urgent chirp.

Half a dozen police cars, blue lights flashing silently, signalled the spot as Banham drove down the road.

A uniformed officer stood in front of the blue and white plastic cordon, redirecting cars down the next side road. Banham flashed his warrant card and the officer waved him through. Alison was already there, bending over the boot of a car with a torch in her gloved hand.

She looked around as Banham approached. No one ever described Alison as pretty, or even striking; in fact DC Colin Crowther, the team's self-styled expert on women, had once said she was pretty average. But Banham thought she was beautiful. She reminded him of a red squirrel; she often wore her long, naturally curly, mouse-coloured hair tied back in a pony-tail resembling a bushy squirrel tail.

Heather Draper the police pathologist was peering into the car boot alongside Alison. When she saw Banham she moved to block his view.

'She's been dead about two weeks, we think, guv,'

Alison said. She was dressed from head to toe in black, a woolly hood up to keep out the bitter February cold. Only her face peeped out, with one escaping curl balanced on her forehead. Banham found her wide-set eyes more captivating than ever with her curly hair covered. He stared into her serious face and read the concern in her eyes.

'It's not a pretty sight,' she warned.

He nodded, and took a deep breath as he moved toward the boot. Alison shone the torch on the contents.

The dead woman was curled in a foetal position, her bloated face angled and facing him. Blood from the wounds in her head had slid down her forehead and congealed, to be overrun by a colony of maggots in the holes that once were her eyes. Other overfed insects that had feasted on her now lay dead in the rotting remains of her open throat.

Bulging from her disintegrated mouth was a piece of rotting, discoloured fabric. A thin, blood-drenched ribbon hung from one side of the blackened lip, making her look almost vampire-like. Even in the winter gloom Banham could see she looked Asian; her hair, now grey with dirt, had been black and her skin light brown.

After a few seconds he turned to Heather Draper, who was dressed in the usual blue plastic overall. 'Her nose was broken too?' he said.

She nodded.

He rubbed his fingers across his mouth, a habit he had when he was thinking. He hoped neither Heather nor Alison realised how much of an effort it was to hold himself together and not throw up.

'She obviously put up one hell of a fight. I hope she was dead before he closed the boot,' he added quietly.

'I wouldn't want to say until I've done a full examination,' Heather said, 'but that's the way it looks. I think the legs were broken afterwards, to fit her into the space.'

'He was either very strong or very angry,' Banham said, turning his head to keep the smell at bay. 'Any signs of sexual assault?'

'No.' Alison and Heather spoke in unison.

'But this?' He indicated the G-string bulging from her mouth. 'It's underwear, isn't it?'

'Not hers. She's still wearing her knickers.' Alison Grainger pointed her torch on the body. The stink of excrement from her black skirt made Banham turn away to grab a lungful of fresh air.

Heather Draper lifted the skirt with blue latex-gloved hands, revealing warm, unglamorous thermal knickers.

'There,' said Alison. 'A bit different from what's jammed in her mouth.' She too turned away from the stench and inhaled fresh icy air.

'He broke both her legs to get her in there,' Banham said thoughtfully. 'So he was in a hurry. But he made time to force those things in her mouth.'

'You mean, you don't think it was an afterthought?' Alison asked.

Banham shook his head. 'No. Something tells me she was in the car with him.'

'She's a bit old to be a tom, guv.'

'Some men like them older.'

'Not even older toms wear knickers like that, though. So, if she was in the car, she knew her killer.'

Banham walked round to the front of the car. A group of SOCOs were busy with their swabs, tweezers and tiny polythene evidence bags. Max Pettifer, head of forensics and Banham's bête noir, was sliding a brush around the steering wheel. He heaved his bulk out of the car and smirked at Banham. 'Not throwing up in a bucket?' he said, lifting a thick, wiry eyebrow.

One of these days, Banham thought, *I'm going to take a pair of forensic tweezers and pluck those eyebrows right off Max's face.* He waved at the air in front of the other man's face. 'I'm surprised you're not, after the amount of garlic you ate last night.' He stepped back. 'Have you got anything of interest to tell me, like was she a passenger in the car?'

'Urine on the headrest of the passenger seat,' Max said flatly. 'With luck that'll be your killer's DNA. He probably got over-excited and pissed in her face. She's been there a good couple of weeks from the state of the maggots,' he added.

Banham muttered reluctant thanks and returned to the waiting Alison. 'Who found the body?' he asked her.

'Uniform,' she told him. 'Look at the way the car's parked. It looked abandoned, so they radioed it in. Turns out it was reported stolen two weeks ago. The woman who owns that house said she first noticed it four days ago. Uniform checked the boot and …'

'Right, get the car to the pound,' Banham interrupted.

'How soon can I have your first report?' he called to Max Pettifer.

'As usual, guv'nor. As soon as I get it done.'

'And yours?'

Heather Draper was a lot less irritating. 'I'll work as quickly as I can,' she told him.

He started back towards his own car, the gruesome image of his own wife and baby on that fateful night flooding his mind. But he shook away the memory before it consumed him. He had to focus. This woman was probably a wife and mother. Her family would be relying on him, and he wasn't going to disappoint them.

Alison called after him, 'Where are you going, guv?'

He looked over his shoulder. 'To the station, to make a start.'

She caught him up. 'Do you want some company?'

He found himself staring into those sludgy eyes. 'Haven't you anything better to do?'

She shook her head and shrugged.

She had no idea how much pleasure that gave him. 'Come on, then. Leave your car. I'll drive.'

CHAPTER TWO

Olivia Stone was attempting to butter bread for sandwiches. She had promised to make them with banana and sandwich spread for her thirteen-year-old daughter's gymkhana day, and was regretting it. She flung the knife on the granite worktop, wishing she hadn't given her daily help the day off. Her nerves were in shreds and the bread kept tearing. Since Brian Finn had been released from prison, she could hardly think straight. It wasn't that she hadn't known it was coming.; he'd always said he'd be out after nineteen years with good behaviour, and now he was.

It was the blackmail note that she hadn't expected.

It was true that the girls had got away scot-free while he'd served that nineteen-year stretch, but they had done everything they could to help him. Well, she had, courtesy of Kenneth's millions, and Katie too, since she started earning big money in the number one TV soap. They had supported Bernadette, the child Theresa had with him just after he went down. And surely he knew he could still rely on them, now he was out. But here it was: a demand for a hundred grand, or he would send the pornographic videos from the Scarlet Pussy Club to the press.

What none of them had understood at first was why he was turning against them after serving all those years to help them. He had the power to destroy Kenneth's career as a government minister, and Katie Faye's as the nation's favourite soap star, but none of them ever dreamed he would use it. But the note said he wouldn't return the tapes until that cash was in his hands.

Olivia had been pregnant at the same time as Theresa, and had married 'Fat Kenneth' Stone. He was filthy rich, so she was able to make sure Theresa and Brian's daughter had everything she needed. Poor Bernadette was born brain-damaged, and all the club girls had rallied around to help – all, that was, except Shaheen. *What a cow*, Olivia thought, sending another wad of butter flying across the marble surface. Bloody Shaheen had done nothing at all – except causing the problem in the first place.

She opened the nearest of the three fridges in the large kitchen and pulled out a bottle of gin. She placed it on the granite surface in front of her; it took less than a second before she gave in and poured a small measure, topping it up with slimline tonic. It was only ten thirty in the morning, but today she needed it. She swallowed a mouthful and assured herself everything was going to be just fine. Five out of the six had agreed that Brian should be paid; only Shaheen disagreed, and Olivia wasn't about to let her get in their way. She and Katie had raised the hundred grand between them – well, Katie had, and Olivia was going to pay back half of it as soon as the bank draft came through. Brian deserved a new start, and they'd get all the pornographic videos back. The lid could be sealed on the whole embarrassing affair, and finally they could move on.

None of them wanted any reminder of their summer at

the Scarlet Pussy Club, or of what happened on that sweltering night. In any case, it was she and Katie who had the most to lose, and they were the ones who were paying up. If those videos got into the wrong hands, her marriage would be ruined, along with Kenneth's career. And Katie, after years of struggling for a break as an actress, had just been voted the nation's favourite small-screen character: the naïve, innocent staff nurse Penelope. The tabloids would have a field day.

The kitchen door suddenly opened. She hastily pushed the glass of gin behind the spaghetti jar as her nineteen-year-old son Kevin walked in the kitchen.

'We're ready to go, Mum. Have you made Ianthe's sandwiches?'

'Two minutes,' she snapped.

'Who rattled your cage?'

Olivia closed her eyes. No point taking it out on the kids – it would only backfire if Kevin threw one of his teenage strops and refused to drive Ianthe to the stables. 'Sorry. You're still OK for the gymkhana, aren't you, Kev?'

He sighed heavily. 'Yes, Mother dearest. I'll sit and watch the pretty horses all day, and bring her home safe. Just do the bloody sandwiches!'

He loped off into the hall, and she felt like throwing the breadknife at him, her nerves were so frazzled. But somehow she held herself together. It had taken a lot of planning to get all the girls together and the house to herself for the day, but she had managed it. Kevin would take his sister to pony club, Kenneth was in meetings in the House till late, and she'd given the daily woman the day off.

All that remained now was for the girls to decide which of them should meet Brian and hand over the money. At least Shaheen wouldn't be there. They had all told her what they thought of her half-arsed suggestion about going to the bloody police with the blackmail letter and, since then, no one had heard from her. She was supposed to meet Susan in London two weeks ago; Susan had offered to talk her round. But Shaheen hadn't turned up, and hadn't been answering her mobile ever since. And none of them was allowed to phone her home in Leicester, so end of story. *Good*, Olivia thought. Shaheen hadn't even been in an embarrassing porno video.

She opened her packet of menthol cigarettes and lit one up, and sliced a banana onto a hunk of badly buttered bread. The vinegary smell of the sandwich spread made her gag; *how can Ianthe eat this stuff?* She emptied half the jar over the banana and pressed a second thick slice of white bread over it. *That's enough*, she decided; her feet were aching and she needed to sit down and calm herself before the girls arrived. She threw the sandwiches in a paper bag, opened her purse and took out a twenty-pound note; *let them buy burgers*, she thought, slipping it into the bag with the sandwich.

The video played through her mind as it seemed to a hundred times a day: Katie lying across a wooden chair, not a stitch on and legs in the air; Olivia standing astride her, bending to suck her nipples. *How could I have been that naïve?* Her face burned; what would the prime minister say if he saw them? Or Katie's television producer? A hundred thousand pounds was a small price to avoid embarrassment of that order.

The children were clattering around in the hall, gathering Ianthe's riding things together. She called to Kevin and threw him the sandwich bag. 'There's money in there,' she said. 'Buy McDonald's for lunch and keep the change for petrol.'

'Cheers, Mum.'

'Just look after your sister.'

'Will do.'

'And, Kevin? I could really do with a day to myself.'

'Toyboy on his way over, is he?'

She could never tell how serious he was. 'Is that what you think of me?'

'Chill, Mum. Just kidding.'

Ianthe hugged her goodbye, and Kevin took the car keys off the hook. They left, squabbling good-naturedly, and Olivia sighed with relief. She massaged her temple points with her fingers, promising herself that, after today, she too could make a new start. It wasn't as if it would be hard to decide which of them would take the money to Brian; it had to be Susan. Both she and Katie had to protect their public profiles; Kim's other half was a copper; Theresa was too angry with Brian. Susan was the only one left.

Susan had visited him often in prison, and she still worked in the sex industry. Olivia had visited too, but more out of duty than friendship – she had married Kenneth as soon as she found out she was pregnant, and when he became an MP, she had to be careful. Then, when poor Theresa's baby was born, just a month after Kevin, and they learned she was brain-damaged, the guilt kicked in. As if letting Brian serve a life sentence for their crime wasn't bad enough, they had deprived that little girl of a father when she needed one so badly.

So she, Katie and Susan had done everything they could to help; they kept in close touch with Theresa and supported little Bernadette financially, and even kept Theresa's mother in gin, one thing guaranteed to make life easier for Theresa. Not that bitch Shaheen, though. She had moved back home to Leicester, married a plumber and had three healthy children. The only contact they had with her was birthday cards. Yet she thought *she* had the right to tell them they should go to the police with Brian's demand for money. Not that anyone listened. It was her fault in the first place, and they had been clearing up her mess for the last nineteen years.

Suddenly Olivia wanted to cry. That video kept playing through her mind: standing naked, stroking Katie's nipples, then the agonising pain as Ahmed unexpectedly shoved that dildo into her. And all for a demeaning job in a filthy strip club, to make quick money to pay her way through college.

Instead of crying, she burst out laughing. After all that she hadn't even gone to law school. She'd got pregnant and married Kenneth instead. Not that she regretted it – well, not much. She had everything money could buy: a lovely house; designer clothes; two wonderful kids – both healthy, if a bit unruly. Ken had a terrible temper and sometimes took it out on her, but she knew she annoyed him. He'd taught her the difference between politician's wife and footballer's wife, and worked hard to give her the polish a junior minister's wife needed; she did her best not to let him down, but the other wives' posh style didn't come naturally to her.

All the same, whatever his faults, Ken had never been mean with money. Just as well, since she had none of her own, and without his she wouldn't have been able to help Theresa.

But when Brian had told them he was being released, and she had asked for one final lump sum, Kenneth had drawn the line. Enough was enough, he'd said; Theresa and her brat had had thousands out of him already. Why he should have to cough up yet another large sum just to give a pair of losers a new start?

Olivia hadn't lived with him for nineteen years without learning a thing or two; she'd be able to lay her hands on her share of the hundred grand and by the time he found out it would be too late. It would just take a couple of weeks.

He wouldn't be pleased, but the alternative was unthinkable. She sipped her drink and tried not to imagine what he'd do to her if those videos got in the wrong hands. He'd probably kill her, even though it was his own fault for not parting willingly with the money and driving Brian to desperate measures.

So she was sorting it. For all their sakes.

Katie Faye fed coins into the studio coffee machine, and

absentmindedly pressed the button marked 'Coffee Black No Sugar'. Her figure was still reed-slim and her face still line-free; no one would guess she was thirty-seven and counting. She had to work at it, watching what she ate and getting a full quota of sleep at night – which, with early morning calls when they were filming on location, sometimes meant going to bed at eight o'clock. But she was the nation's pin-up, the much-loved Staff Nurse Penelope Diamond in the hospital soap *Screened*. She had climbed to the top of the ladder, and was determined to stay there.

She pulled out her coffee from the machine and took a welcome mouthful. She had been up since five filming, and had lain awake most of the night. But today everything would be sorted.

She was more than happy to pay the hundred thousand pounds Brian was demanding. If Olivia wasn't able to come up with her half, she certainly wouldn't hold it against her; poor Liv hadn't said why it was going to take a while, but then she never did say a word against Kenneth. They all knew what went on, though, and Katie was pretty sure it was fat Ken who had pulled the plug.

Olivia had already done her share. At first it had been mostly her money – well, Kenneth's – which supported Bernadette; it wasn't until the last five years Katie had been able to help out. Her life had completely changed when, after struggling for eleven years as a bit-part actress, she had landed the role of Penelope.

Since she had been in *Screened* she had never been happier. Penelope's popularity had grown and, everywhere she went, people flocked around her for autographs. When she drove along in her newly acquired BMW, other drivers shouted, 'Hello, Penelope.' Fans came up to her in the street, requesting plasters, or asking her to diagnose their aches and pains. She loved it; the job was everything she had worked for, everything she had ever dared dream of. Her world had come up roses.

But how she regretted the weeks in that seedy Soho strip club – and what had happened on that fateful Saturday night. Katie had never stopped feeling guilty about letting Brian go to prison – all the more so because Theresa'd had to bring up a disabled child alone. No amount of money could make up for that. There was no question but that Brian should have the money; it was just sad that it had to be like this. Still, she had to have those videos back, no matter what the cost.

It was the guilt that had kept them together, the girls from the Scarlet Pussy Club. They'd remained friends ever since that dreadful night, supporting each other through all their ups and downs. All except Shaheen Hakhti. She was the only one of them that had a decent start in life, yet she had done nothing to help either Theresa or Kim.

Poor Kim had gone into a depression and become addicted to tranquillisers; one thing led to another, and she finished up injecting heroin. It took three attempts at rehab to get her off the drug, and she was still fragile and in poor health.

Not only did Shaheen ignore Kim's plight as well as Theresa's; she didn't even write to Brian in prison. She just got on with her life and behaved as if the whole appalling business was nothing to do with her. And now she had the cheek to suggest they should go to the police. It wasn't as if the selfish cow had anything to lose; she had made sure there was no video of her. She had really shown her true colours over this.

Katie eyed the chocolate biscuits beside the coffee machine and debated allowing herself something sweet to keep her energy up. But she really had no appetite.

Her thoughts ranged back over the past few years. After the drug phase, when Kim met her girlfriend Judy and made a supreme effort to stay clean, she had started a dancing school. It soon became successful – unsurprising, as Kim was a great dancer and really knew how to motivate youngsters – and, as soon as she had money to spare, she started to contribute to Bernadette's upkeep.

Susan, too, had done her bit. She hadn't changed one iota; she had put some weight on, but she was still the same cockney girl with a heart of gold. She had even carried on stripping right up until six months ago, when she was offered a job managing a sex shop in Soho, with a flat above it for her and her cat Tara. Not only had Susan visited Brian regularly; she also helped Theresa and Bernadette financially, and babysat so Theresa could have something of a life. Katie had a lot of time for Susan.

She tossed her coffee in the bin, unable to swallow another mouthful. Her nerves felt like filed teeth. There were five more scenes to smile her way through before the meeting at Olivia's with the other girls.

As she headed for her dressing room to change for the next scene she took deep breaths to calm her nerves.

Shaheen wasn't a problem, nor was the money. They just had to get it to him and make sure he gave those videos back, then it would all be in the past.

Susan would do it. They could all rely on her. Katie took out her mobile phone and began to dial.

The sign outside the shop door flashed red in a steady rhythm. It read 'SEX AND THE TITTIES'.

Susan kept the door wide open, to let any passing trade know they were welcome to come in and browse around the sex aids. She reckoned it helped to sell a few extra bits each week; she worked on commission and needed to boost the takings in any way she could.

It was a cold morning in Soho. Susan had the heating on, and Barry White blared out of the radio. She was standing just inside the open doorway, dusting the mannequin dolls that displayed crotchless knickers in a variety of colours and designs.

Her long, over-bleached hair used to hang to her waist, but had recently been cut short and permed, giving her a poodle-like appearance. She wore a short red imitation leather jacket with the collar turned up, and fluffy grey earmuffs with matching gloves. Under the jacket she had on two jumpers, neither of which reached the imitation snakeskin belt around her hipster jeans; the snake and rose tattoo decorating the base of her spine was in full view. She held a cigarette in one hand and dusted with the other, happily singing along out of key with Barry's deep bass tones, totally oblivious to the expressions of the passers-by as they stared at her bare skin, tattoo and the edge of her purple thong.

The phone started ringing. She threw the stub of her cigarette down and ground it with the toe of her shabby red stiletto before walking back to the counter. 'Sex and the Titties,' she said in her best upmarket accent.

She relaxed back into her native cockney when she heard Katie's familiar voice. 'You sound worried, darlin'. Shaheen ain't rung, 'as she?'

She listened as Katie explained. Brian could have the money, but she wanted Susan to be the one to take it to him. Susan was flattered. She adored Katie; fame hadn't changed her a bit, and no matter how busy she was, Katie was as generous with her time now as when she was working as a waitress and touting for small breaks.

''Course, darlin', that ain't a problem. 'E's back living with 'is mum. I'll give 'im a bell and drop it round there. I won't ask for a receipt, under the circumstances.' She roared with laughter, and was relieved to hear Katie giggle. 'It'll be over soon,' she reassured her.

'You don't think Shaheen will *really* go to the police?' Katie asked.

'I don't think bloody Shaheen is even gonna turn up,' Susan said quickly. 'I've left messages and messages on 'er mobile, and she ain't so much as rang back.'

There was no response from Katie.

'Look, she don't want to know, she told me so 'erself. If she didn't turn up two weeks ago to meet me, she won't come today. It's not as if we need her permission.'

She pulled a cigarette free of the packet on the counter and struggled to light it with a green throwaway lighter.

The flame wavered and died in the icy breeze blowing through the open door; Susan stretched the phone cord as far as it would go and toed the door shut.

Over the phone she heard the tannoy in Katie's dressing room.

'It's gonna be OK, mate,' she assured her again. 'You go off and shine like the star you are, and I'll see you at Livvy's later.' As an afterthought she added, 'How about a present for Bernadette?'

'Good idea.'

'Theresa said a toy would be good. What d'you think about a Roger Rabbit vibrator? She is over eighteen after all ...' Katie's famous giggle sounded down the phone. 'That's better. You sound like your old self again.' She tapped ash into the cheap saucer by the till. 'It'll all be over in no time and life'll be back to normal, you'll see. Brian's not a bad bloke. I'll give 'im the money, get the videos back, and that'll be an end to it.'

'I just hope you're right.' Katie sounded despondent.

'He ain't a grass,' Susan pointed out. ''E proved that by doing nineteen years and saying nothing. 'E wouldn't give them videos to the press.' She stubbed her cigarette out. 'Yes, I agree, prison does change people. But if he was gonna stitch us up, why wait till he'd served 'is time?'

Katie said nothing.

'I'm just glad you and Liv have got the money,' Susan went on. 'I sure as fuck couldn't get a hundred K together. Listen, mate, I can hear you being called again. I'll see you later.' She paused. 'And don't worry about Shaheen. She's not going to make any trouble.'

Theresa McGann was dressed in a worn grey tracksuit and shabby trainers that owed nobody a thing. She walked from the kitchen through to the tiny lounge and turned on the television.

Bernadette gurgled happily as the colours and movement appeared on the screen. Theresa heaved her daughter up from the floor, manoeuvred her into the chair and tied a bib around her thick neck.

'Lunchtime,' she said cheerfully, pulled a stool in close to the chair.

'Ung-hi,' Bernadette echoed.

She ate noisily, spraying half-chewed cauliflower cheese all over Theresa and the threadbare carpet. 'Was that good?' Theresa asked.

Bernadette gurgled her approval. Cauli cheese was one of her favourites.

'Just you wait. Things are going to get even better. Your daddy's coming home and we're getting out of here.' She gave her daughter a kiss on the top of her head and used the bib to wipe her cheeks and chin.

Nearly nineteen years of caring for a handicapped child and a violent alcoholic mother had taken its toll. Theresa's hands were covered in red rings of psoriasis that crept up her arms like a map of the world. Her nails were short and bitten, the skin around them raw.

She took the bowl back to the kitchen and poured milky tea for her daughter and black coffee for her mother. *What would it be like*, she wondered, *to have a dishwasher*? Could they find one to fit this tiny kitchen? Maybe when this business was sorted out and Brian came home they would move out of the high-rise council flat. There wasn't really room for four of them, and it was time he got to know his daughter.

She picked up the coffee to take it through to her mother, and caught sight of her reflection in the glass panel on the kitchen door. She wore no make-up and her face was a network of lines.

Things are going to change.

Her mother's voice booming from the bedroom brought her back to reality. 'Theresa! Has my giro arrived?'

Theresa closed her eyes and didn't answer.

'Bring it in here if it's come. I can sign it, and ye can cash for us both and pick up me shopping.'

Theresa still didn't reply. She put the coffee down on the table and went to the front door. A few envelopes lay on the mat. Thank goodness, the giros were there. But so was the gas bill: a red one.

'Theresa, a woman could be dying in here of a thirst. Have you made the coffee?'

The flat was cold; the heating was set to come on for a couple of hours in the morning and the same in the evening. Yet she still dreaded the gas bill. And she hated having to ask Olivia to pay it. *Well, not for much longer.*

'THERESA, FOR THE LOVE OF CHRIST, ARE YOU DEAF?' Her mother's voice boomed so loudly the entire flat seemed to vibrate. 'Will ye tell me, do we have our giros yet? Or is it to be another dry day for your poor pain-ridden mother?'

Theresa's voice stuck in her throat.

'THERESA! Theresa, if I have to get out to ye now, I'll give ye such a fucking slap, you'll not know if it's Christmas or Easter.'

Theresa swallowed hard. 'It's OK, Mother, the giros are here. One minute now and I'll be there.'

She walked back into the lounge and picked up the phone. She thought for a moment, then punched some numbers into the keypad. After another second, she changed her mind and put the phone back on its cradle.

PC Judy Gardener stooped over the work surface in the small kitchen she shared with Kim Davis. Her large hands held a flat knife, smoothing butter back and forth across thick slices of bread. 'Kim,' she called, 'do you want hummus in both your sandwiches?'

There was no answer. Judy put the knife down and walked out of the neat kitchen into the dining area, then up the narrow stairway to the bedroom.

Kim was there, packing a large holdall with her dance gear. She was thinner than nineteen years ago, tall and willowy, and her dark brown hair was cut short in a boyish crop.

She opened drawers and threw tights and leg warmers into the bag, took a couple of leotards and a pink nylon dance bodice from another drawer, and bundled them in all in.

Judy watched her for a few seconds. 'Kim, this is the first issue we've disagreed over in eight years. And much as I admire your loyalty to those girls...'

But Kim wasn't listening. She tugged angrily at the zip,

which refused to close.

Judy folded her arms across her chest. 'Do you want some help?'

Kim carried on pulling at the zip, almost in tears. 'No, it's fine.'

'Is it? Then it's the only thing in this house that is.' Judy turned away and walked back down the stairs.

As she expected, Kim followed her. 'I should never have told you,' she said, fighting back the tears. 'I've broken a nineteen-year-old promise, and I've put you in a split loyalty situation because of your job.'

'Stop it, Kim. You know I can't handle it when you cry.' Judy sat on the sofa and dropped her head into her hands. She'd really thought Kim had turned the corner. When they first met eight years ago, she had been a mess: not long out of her second attempt at rehab, up on a charge of possession which she strenuously denied. Judy had believed her. For one thing, the drug in question was cocaine, which Kim had never used; but more importantly, Judy trusted her instincts and there was something in Kim's eyes.

They fell completely and unexpectedly in love and, against all the warnings of her fellow police officers, Judy took Kim home to live with her. Kim was still in withdrawal; Judy helped her through it, and supported her when she backslid a couple of years later and went into rehab again.

That time Kim succeeded. She had been clean of drugs for six years now. Her strength and confidence had slowly returned under Judy's tender care, and together they had set up a dance school in a rented room in a local community centre. As that prospered, so did Kim. The mood swings and self-harming had stopped. She started to take proper care of herself again, ate properly and put herself through an exercise regime every day. She said she had never been happier, and Judy had what she'd always wanted: to love and cherish someone who loved her in return.

But then Kim had dropped this bombshell. It wasn't that Judy blamed her at all; in fact it helped her to understand where the drug abuse and self-harming came from. It wasn't Kim's fault, it wasn't the fault of any of the girls – but it was threatening their relationship, and Judy wouldn't stand by and let that happen. That was why she was angry.

'Yes, of course you should have told me,' she said a little too sharply, looking into Kim's unhappy brown eyes. The dark circles under them looked almost like bruises. 'We agreed we'd tell each other everything.' She put out a hand, and after a moment Kim took it and sat down beside her. Judy took her in her arms and rubbed the back of her head like a mother would a frightened child.

'I broke my promise to the other girls,' Kim said flatly.

'I know.' Judy kissed the top of her head. 'But what happened at that club has affected you very deeply. I'm on your side, and I'll look after you. That's my promise.'

'It could affect your job.'

'It won't.'

'But if Shaheen…'

Judy put her finger over Kim's mouth. 'She won't. It's

not going to happen. Trust me.'

'OK.' Kim stood up and hefted the gaping bag on to her shoulder. 'I have to go. I'm late.'

Judy followed her to the door, zipping the bag closed as she walked. 'Best not to invite crime,' she said with a small smile.

Kim smiled back, and Judy stroked her cheek lightly. 'After today we start again. Problems over, everything behind you. And no more secrets. OK?'

'OK.'

'I love you and I'll look after you.'

'I just don't want you to put your career on the line because of me.' Kim's eyes searched Judy's face. 'I've already been enough trouble.'

'You haven't, and my career's fine.'

'Suppose he comes back for more money? Olivia and Katie aren't bottomless pits.'

'Just make sure you get the videos back,' Judy said. 'I'll sort anything else.'

CHAPTER THREE

The team was gathered, all solemn-faced, some perching on the desks next to computers or stacked files, others making use of the stools and chairs.

Banham walked in and cast his eyes around the room. He was pleased to see Colin Crowther, the young, ambitious cockney DC; he always requested him for his team. Crowther was in his late twenties, and only about five feet four, with a mass of curly dark hair. Either the young DC couldn't find clothes small enough to fit his diminutive frame or he had no idea what size to buy. Alison Grainger had once told Banham she had seen Crowther purchasing clothes in a children's shop. This morning the brown velvet sleeves of his jacket were turned over so many times he looked as if he was wearing rolls of carpet around his wrists. He had matched the jacket with a red shirt and a tie that looked like some leftover school uniform, in diagonal stripes of blue, green and red.

Banham really liked Crowther, who had a hit rate with women that even Johnny Depp would find hard to beat. The lad was hardworking and shrewd, and put in far more hours than his shifts demanded. He was the front-runner for promotion next time a sergeant's post was available; though he wasn't the most experienced detective on the team, he was by far the most streetwise. The son of a known villain, he had a lot of useful contacts and wasn't afraid to use them. And Banham knew he could trust him with his life.

Next to Crowther sat DC Isabelle Walsh. She resembled a young Vivien Leigh, and attracted men like Crowther attracted women – at least until she opened her mouth. She was outspoken and vulgar, and had a knack of rubbing people up the wrong way.

She too was after promotion – but rumour had it that Isabelle Walsh had made it into CID on her back. She had been a beat copper until someone high up in CID took a shine to her. Two months later she was promoted into CID murder division. Banham didn't care; to him it proved she would stop at nothing to further her career, and that meant she would get results. And, apart from Alison Grainger, solving murders was all that interested him.

He stared at the photo of the murdered woman on the whiteboard. Her face was yellowed and bloated, her eyes covered in congealed, maggot-infested blood. The head hung at an angle, leaving the wide knife wound in her neck in clear view. A pair of satin knickers had been forced into her open mouth, leaving a thin ribbon dangling from her lips like a child's strand of liquorice.

Banham picked up the marker pen and wrote under the photo: 'UNNAMED FEMALE. AROUND MIDDLE-AGE. PROBABLY EASTERN EUROPEAN OR ASIAN.'

The team sat silent, looking at him expectantly.

'Who is she?' he asked. 'Someone's mother? Someone's wife?' He swallowed as his throat thickened with emotion. His own ghosts were never far from his mind. 'Was she dead when she was put there? If so, where was she killed? Who is looking for her? Someone must be.'

He moved aside to give them all a clear view of the picture. Everyone stared in silence for a few seconds.

Banham looked round the room. 'What do we have on the car?' he asked a middle-aged ginger-haired detective who was leaning against the wall with his notebook balanced on his bent knee.

Ginger Pete looked up. 'Reported stolen twelve days ago in central London,' he said. 'Uniform are checking CCTV around the area. We already know there was no congestion charge paid or due; that probably means it was stolen at night.'

'That's something, I suppose. What about Missing Persons?'

'Being checked, guv.' This was Crowther. 'She could have come in on a train. Nothing on HOLMES so far.'

Banham turned back to the board. He wrote 'WEAPON?' by the side of the picture, then 'ITEM OF UNDERWEAR IN MOUTH?'

He interlocked his fingers and rubbed his mouth thoughtfully, staring at the distorted features in the photograph. *Did she feel the knife carving into her neck*, he wondered. *Did she have a husband*? And would he feel the same as Banham, for the rest of his life? An image of his own wife, bludgeoned and dying, reaching out to help her baby daughter, jumped into his mind, and he wrenched his focus back to the woman in the picture.

Alison Grainger knew him well. Suddenly she was beside him, facing the room full of waiting detectives as he pulled himself together.

'Interesting that the car was reported missing in the middle of London,' she said. 'How did it end up all the way out here? Why did she get in the car? She wasn't a tom, not wearing chain store thermal knickers and a warm vest. I think she knew her killer.'

Alison looked across at Isabelle Walsh, challenging her with her eyes. The mention of knickers was a cue for one of her tasteless remarks, but Isabelle obviously got the message; she said nothing.

'OK, let's start with the underwear,' Banham said, turning to face the room. 'The red G-thing is down with Penny in forensics. The leather ribbon makes it quite distinctive.' He shifted uncomfortably from foot to foot. 'I'm not an expert on women's underwear, but Alison thinks that sort of fabric and design goes back twenty-odd years. Modern G-strings only have a thin piece at the back.' He couldn't look Alison in the eye. 'Isn't that what you said?' he asked the top of her head.

'That's because more women wear trousers now,' Alison agreed.

'Some women don't wear *any* knickers,' Isabelle announced, uncrossing her legs in her tight-fitting jeans. Crowther gave Isabelle a speculative look. She responded with a broad smile.

'You're obviously an expert, Isabelle,' Banham said. 'See if you can track down its origin, manufacturer, year, how many were made, all of that.'

'Guv.'

'I'm willing to help with that,' Crowther said loudly.

'Good.' Isabelle's heavily painted mouth curved into a mocking smile. 'You can model the knickers for us when they come back from forensics.'

'Maybe our killer has had them for twenty years,' Crowther said. 'Or maybe they were the victim's. She could have been a tom twenty years ago.'

'And maybe someone has been waiting all this time,' Banham added. 'The question is, why?'

'Perhaps he's been in prison?' Alison suggested.

Banham nodded. 'Good thinking. Crowther, I think Isabelle can manage on her own. Check if anyone's been released lately for a crime that could tie up.' He looked round the room. 'Do we have anything else? Anything at all?'

No one said anything.

'OK. So if Crowther's right and someone *has* kept those knickers for twenty years, she wasn't a random victim; she was targeted. So once we find out who she is, we need to delve into her background. Where *was* she twenty years ago, and what was she doing?'

'She'd have been in her teens,' Alison said.

Banham nodded. 'So where did she go to school? Did she go to college, perhaps? And were the knickers hers?'

'They might come from somewhere in Asia,' Crowther said. 'She might have, originally at least.'

'Guv?' One of the other detectives raised a hand. 'What about the weapon?'

'Uniform are still going door to door where she was

found,' Alison said.

'Better expand it,' Banham said. 'Someone must have heard something. Put up an appeal board. Maybe a passing driver noticed something. Keep digging until you get something.'

PC Judy Gardener was on duty at the front desk in the station. She hurried in, carrying the beef and tomato sandwich she had made herself for lunch. Her usually large appetite had diminished; she was too worried about Kim to feel like eating. She brought the sandwich with her anyway; it was still lunchtime, and with an eight-hour shift ahead, she might well feel like it in an hour or two. She threw the Tupperware container under the counter and took over the paperwork from her colleague.

An hour later she was filling in forms for two young shoplifters when a middle-aged woman walked in.

'It's about my dog,' she told Judy.

With a sigh, the constable put down her pen and invited the woman to tell her what the problem was. It appeared she walked her dog on the same route every day; a couple of days ago the mutt had gone sniffing around under a bush in a long driveway and when the woman went to investigate she'd found a handbag.

'I was going to bring it in yesterday, but it was my day at the hospital and they kept me waiting even longer than usual. I'll tell you what, though – the owner of that handbag is very lucky it was me who found it. Her wallet and credit cards are still in there, and there's money in the purse, and a return ticket from St Pancras to Leicester, *and* house keys.'

Judy took the bag from the woman and opened it. The name on the credit card was Shaheen Hakhti-Watkins.

It took her a few seconds to compose herself. The woman was staring at her; she replaced the wallet in the bag and closed it, thanked her for being a good citizen and noted down her details. 'Someone will be in touch,' she told her, and suppressed a smile as the woman straightened her shoulders proudly and marched towards the door.

Judy opened the bag again, and stood very still, staring back at Shaheen Hakhti smiling at her from the photograph in her hand.

An aroma of freshly brewed coffee mixed with stale cigarette smoke wafted through the ground floor of Olivia Stone's enormous house. The five women were all in the sitting room, seated on the elegant chairs placed around the room, except Kim, who was in her favourite position curled up on the thick Turkish rug on the floor. The two onyx ashtrays on the stylish glass table overflowed with dog-ends. An empty wine bottle and a half-full bottle of gin stood beside them, surrounded by dirty glasses and clean coffee cups.

Katie Faye had just made fresh coffee. She poured a cup for Olivia, who had begun to slur her words. Katie wanted her to stay sober until they had finally sorted things out. Besides, if Kevin and Ianthe came home and told their dad that Olivia had been drunk, Ken would fly into one of his rages, and maybe even ban Olivia's friends from the house. And whatever Olivia said – or mostly didn't say – Katie knew she was terrified of his violent temper.

Susan sat up straight in a pale leather armchair, scribbling with a chewed biro in a tattered notebook. She took a sip of her third large gin and tonic; unlike Olivia she was still completely sober. 'All agreed then, cockles?' she said, dotting the pen on the paper and looking round at the other four. Her badly permed hair bobbed as she spoke.

Katie nodded.

'I'll bell Brian when I get home,' Susan said. 'If 'e can't meet me till tomorrow, I'll lock the money in me till overnight. I'll be sure to get all the tapes off 'im and check they're the right ones before I 'and over the money.'

The girls murmured their agreement as Katie handed her the envelope. Susan pushed it into the pocket of her jeans. 'Done and dusted then. End of a chapter. Thanks to Katie and Olivia, we can all move on.'

Olivia had wanted to tell the girls about Kenneth's sudden attack of stinginess, but Katie had persuaded her to keep it between the two of them. She glanced at Olivia, but the other woman was staring at the carpet.

'And no thanks to Shaheen Hakhti-Watkins,' Kim said, waving her glass in the air.

Katie grimaced. 'She isn't one of us now. She doesn't exist any more.'

'Shaheen who?' Theresa raised her glass, smiling sadly before putting it down and picking up one of her thin roll-up cigarettes and lighting it with a disposable lighter.

'She could at least have let us know she wasn't coming,' Kim said, wiggling her ankles nervously.

'She could have done loads of things, darlin',' Susan replied dryly. 'But she's done fuck all in nineteen years.'

'But now it's all over,' Katie said.

'We just need to get those videos back,' Olivia said, hardly slurring at all, 'then it will be.'

'I still don't understand why he did this.' Kim slipped off a shoe and wriggled her bare toes. 'He knew we had every intention of helping him when he came out.'

'Don't look at me,' Theresa said defensively. 'He hasn't been near since he got out of prison. I'm pretty annoyed with him, I can tell you.'

'We're paying up,' Katie said, with a warning look in Olivia's direction. 'Let that be an end to it.'

'I suppose prison changes people,' Kim said thoughtfully. 'And I suppose there's Bernadette to look out for too.'

'I just wish we could turn the clock back,' Katie said, attempting to steer the conversation away from Brian's motives.

'Don't we all?' Susan agreed.

'We were young and stupid, and it was an accident,' Kim reasoned. 'But we'll always have to live with what we did.'

'What Shaheen did,' Katie corrected.

'What Shaheen *didn't*,' Olivia said loudly.

'If she did go to the police,' Susan said slowly, 'I wouldn't be responsible for my actions.'

'You'd have to get in line behind Ju …' Kim stopped with a gasp as she realised what she had almost said.

Too late. Katie looked at Olivia, then at Susan and

Theresa and back at Kim. 'You haven't told Judy about this? Please don't tell me you've told Judy that we killed Ahmed Abdullah?'

Kim turned away and closed her eyes.

'Kim?' Susan clenched her fists. 'Kim, she's a cop. They have a code of practice ...'

'I haven't, right?' Kim looked at the carpet.

'We have a pact going back nineteen years, to keep Ahmed's death between ourselves.' Susan's voice rose several tones. 'Please don't tell me you've broken your word.'

Kim fiddled nervously with the fringe of the rug. 'No ... I was only saying ...'

The front door opened and slammed shut.

'Either Ken's meeting finished early or it's the kids,' Olivia said in a strained whisper.

Katie jumped up and grabbed the gin bottle from the table. 'Say we're having a meeting about a charity bazaar,' she said to the others, shutting the bottle in the drinks cabinet just as the door opened and Ianthe burst in.

'What's for tea, Mum?' Ianthe asked rudely. 'I'm starving.'

Olivia ignored her.

'Nothing,' Kevin answered from behind his sister. 'Mum's too pissed to get us any tea. So what's new?'

If they only knew the half of it, Katie thought. She picked up her handbag and took out her purse.

'Hello, Auntie Katie. How nice to see you,' she said pointedly to Ianthe.

'Hello, Auntie Katie. Hello, Mummy's other friends,'

Ianthe sing-songed back.

Katie handed Kevin a fifty-pound note. *He really has grown into the most handsome young man*, she thought. 'Let's have takeaway for tea. Take Ianthe to the Chinese and get what you want. I'm staying too. Your mum and I will have garlic prawns and noodles. And get duck pancakes for your dad.'

Kevin snatched the fifty. 'No problem,' he said with a grin.

'Can we have McDonald's instead?' Ianthe suggested.

'No,' Katie said firmly, looking at Olivia for support.

Olivia shrugged. 'Whatever, eat cow's arse for all I care.'

'She's already had a burger for lunch,' Kevin said. 'She'd eat them for breakfast and tea as well, given half a chance.'

'No wonder your dad won't allow them in the house,' Katie said, half-laughing. 'We'll have Chinese. Anyway, you like Singapore fried noodles.'

After they left the room, Katie started clearing the empties. Olivia sagged back in her chair with her eyes closed, and the other three gathered their things.

'Just let us all know when you've got the videos,' Katie said to Susan. 'I think we'd all like a hand in destroying them.'

Susan dropped her chewed biro into a red plastic handbag with a picture of a kitten on the front. 'Will do.'

Kim buttoned up her long military-style coat, and Theresa packed her tobacco tin and cigarette papers in her backpack. As they were about to leave, Kim turned to

Katie. 'What about Shaheen?'

Katie looked at Olivia, still slumped in the chair. Olivia shrugged.

'She doesn't exist,' Theresa said firmly, struggling to hold her backpack and the stuffed elephant Susan had given her for Bernadette.

'Shouldn't we at least let her know we've given Brian the money?' Kim asked.

Olivia straightened up a little and shook her head. 'No. There's no video of her, and she's already said she isn't interested. There's no need to contact her ever again. Once Brian has the money, it's over.'

'Is it, though?' said Kim. 'Are we sure there can't still be a comeback for us?'

'Only if your Judy knows.' Susan looked closely at Kim's face. 'She's a cop. You can never completely trust a cop.'

Katie watched as Kim struggled to school her expression. 'You wouldn't break our promise, Kim, would you?'

'Course she wouldn't,' Olivia said. 'After all we've all been through? Don't be silly.'

'If you did tell Judy, it'll *never* be over,' Susan said coldly.

'You just don't like the police,' Kim snapped.

'No, Kim. What I don't like is a grass.'

Kim stumbled through the front door, pushing it almost closed in Susan's face.

Susan caught it and set off after her. Katie put out a hand to stop her. 'Let her go.'

Theresa and Olivia nodded in agreement.

Susan sighed. 'Well, let's just hope she ain't that stupid.'

There are no secrets in a police station. When the woman with the dog came in, news of the body in the car boot had already reached the front desk.

Judy Gardener and Paul Banham had trained together at the Police Cadet College in Hendon, and had become good friends. She had been at his wedding, but after Diane's murder and Banham's transfer into CID, he had become withdrawn and something of a loner, so they'd lost touch.

Judy waited until the reception area was quiet before opening the handbag again. She knew what had to be done. She took out the mobile phone, scrolled down the address book and deleted Kim and her phone number from it. She checked the 'recent call' history for the one they'd made to her two weeks ago, and deleted Kim's name. It didn't matter that her prints were on the bag or its contents; the woman had handed it to her on the front desk after all.

Then, heart beating heavily against her ribcage, she made her way along the corridor to the incident room.

CHAPTER FOUR

The Chinese meal was laid out on the family-sized kitchen table. Kenneth sat between his son and daughter, and Katie and Olivia opposite. There wasn't much conversation; the only sound came from Kenneth, crunching noisily on his crispy duck. Olivia passed him a paper napkin to wipe the plum sauce that dripped from his chin. He took it, dabbed his chin, then wrapped more duck in a thin pancake.

Kenneth had lived well throughout his forty years. When Olivia patted his paunch and teased him about the extra three stone of weight he carried, he always flew into a rage and told her a tart without a brain would have no idea of the pressures that a senior post in the government brought him. But Olivia knew that the main cause was alcohol, and the expensive dinners he bought his constant stream of lady friends.

He had a broad, chubby face and was acquiring an extra chin. His large brown eyes could have been attractive, but his frightening temper had given them an air of cruelty. All the same, Olivia and Ken had stayed married for nineteen years, and in her own way she loved him, and often lay awake at night while he snored into his pillow, wondering how she could get him to love her back.

'Ianthe chose the duck for you,' Olivia said to him.

'Auntie Katie paid for it,' Kevin said.

'But Ianthe chose the menu,' Katie said quickly. 'How is it? Is it good?'

Ken had his mouth full. He gazed coldly at Katie before turning back to Olivia. 'You should be cooking your family's dinner,' he said to her. 'You spend more time worrying about Theresa's bloody child than you do your own.'

Olivia flicked a nervous glance at Katie. 'Please don't swear in front of the children,' she said, topping up her wine glass.

Katie came to her aid. 'It's my fault,' she said. 'I asked Olivia if we could have a meeting here. Theresa told me they were holding a fundraising bazaar for disabled children, and we were discussing how we could make it even bigger, and make more money this year.'

Kevin looked at his mother and burst out laughing. Ken crunched loudly on his duck, but made no comment.

'So I bought the supper as a "thank-you",' Katie added.

Ken wiped his mouth with the napkin then lifted a spare rib to his lips and sucked the juice off it.

'"Bloody" isn't swearing,' Kevin said to Olivia. 'Everyone says "bloody".'

'If that's the kind of company you keep, no wonder you failed all your bloody exams last year,' Ken snapped. 'That's why you're bloody well having to sit them again, at my bloody expense.'

Ianthe banged her fork noisily on the table and burst into tears.

'Ken ...' Olivia wavered between crying and losing her temper. 'Please don't start all that again.' She lifted

Ianthe's hand and stroked it. 'It's all right, darling. Daddy's just tired.'

Ken threw his half-eaten spare rib into the fingerbowl. The warm water splashed over the sides and into Ianthe's noodles. She snatched her hand away from Olivia and burst into tears again.

'This food's disgusting. I'm going out.' Ken stood up and headed for the door. 'I hope your charity meeting was successful,' he said over his shoulder to Katie. 'My wife is very generous with my money.'

'One of us has to be!' Olivia shouted after him.

Ianthe's sobbing grew louder, and Katie put an arm around her. 'Finish your noodles, they're delicious,' she said.

Kevin jumped up and ran after his father. 'Dad, you have no right to shout like that. Look how you've upset Ianthe.'

'Kevin, leave it!' Olivia called after him.

A loud ring at the front door cut her off.

'I'll go,' Kevin said, pushing past his father. 'It's probably for me anyway. I can't believe anyone would want to visit you. Or aren't I allowed to have friends?'

'Not if they're bringing drugs, you're not.'

'You should have been a comic, not an MP.' When he'd put a few yards between himself and his father, he added, 'Oh no, sorry – it's the same thing.'

Banham, Grainger and Judy Gardener stood on the doorstep, holding up their ID. The door opened to reveal a tall, strikingly good-looking young man.

'Who is it, Kevin?' called a woman's voice inside the

house.

Two women appeared behind him, one well-built and handsome, the other small-boned and fragile, with clear, wide-set blue eyes. Banham gazed at the smaller woman, mesmerised. Those eyes were huge and so blue he wanted to dive into them and drown. He hadn't seen eyes like that for more than eleven years.

Both the women were looking at Judy Gardener.

'Kim's gone home, Judy,' said the well-built one. 'She left with Susan Rogers, a couple of hours ago.'

Judy opened her mouth, then closed it again and looked at Banham. With a huge effort he dragged his eyes away from the smaller woman's beautiful face and held out his ID.

'I'm Detective Inspector Paul Banham,' he said, 'and this is Sergeant Alison Grainger. We work with Judy. Can we come inside, please?'

'Has something happened?' the small woman asked, an anxious note creeping into her voice.

A man's voice boomed out from the hallway. 'Get them in here, for Chrissake. Do you want the whole of Fleet Street to know the police are at our door?' It sounded familiar, but Banham wasn't sure where he'd heard it before.

The two women stepped back to allow Banham and Alison inside. Judy didn't move. 'I only came to show them the way,' she said to the women. 'Olivia, I'm sorry. I have to go home to Kim. Something has happened to Shaheen. I had to tell them about ... I'm really sorry...'

'Kevin,' Olivia said sharply. 'Go and clear the dishes,

please. And take Ianthe upstairs.'

'Oh, I think I'd rather stay and listen.' Kevin folded his arms and leaned against the wall, a grin spreading over his face.

'Kevin, please!'

The boy made a show of peeling himself away from the wall, and swaggered away down the hall. 'If you insist, Mother dearest. Ianthe? Come on, duckie, we have to make ourselves scarce so the grown-ups can talk.'

Judy waited until he had gone before whispering, 'Shaheen has been murdered.'

Olivia flinched, and looked across at Katie, who stood open-mouthed.

'Come in off the doorstep,' the man's voice sounded again.

No one moved. Banham stood just inside the doorway, watching the women's reactions.

'I must go,' Judy said. She lowered her voice. 'Look, you have to tell DI Banham everything you know. I had to tell him about Brian. The note. And the tapes.' She paused. 'And about the club. Everything. I had no choice. I'm sorry, really I am.'

Judy turned away and began to walk rapidly down the drive. Olivia called after her, 'What on earth has Kim been telling you?'

'I'm sorry,' Judy repeated without turning round. 'I have to go to Kim. She needs me.'

In the thirty-foot sitting room it looked like the night after a party. Used glasses and littered ashtrays still cluttered up the coffee tables and stale smoke clung to the air.

The two women were clearly on edge. 'I suppose we'd better introduce ourselves,' Olivia said brusquely, 'though I expect you know who we are. I'm Olivia Stone, and this is…'

'Nurse Penelope,' Alison chipped in.

'Who?' Banham was properly confused now. As if limpid blue eyes the image of Diane's weren't enough to throw him off balance.

'Sorry, guv. It's Katie Faye, isn't it? The actress? Off *Screened*?' Alison held out a hand and Katie shook it.

'What's happened to Shaheen?' Olivia asked before Banham had time to ask for an explanation.

A stocky man with a paunch and receding hairline appeared in the doorway of the sitting room. Banham recognised the government minister Kenneth Stone, who made frequent appearances on current affairs programmes. In the car on the way over, Judy Gardener had told him Stone had a violent temper and Olivia was often on the receiving end of it; this didn't seem to chime with the charm and perfect manners now on display, but Banham was well aware that appearances counted for nothing when it came to domestic violence.

'Detective Inspector, do sit down.' Stone indicated a deep armchair upholstered in soft caramel-coloured leather. 'And, sergeant, perhaps you'd like the sofa. Now, can I offer anyone a drink, or are you on duty?'

'Nothing, thank you,' said Banham, careful to keep his tone formal. He sat down in the leather chair, and Alison perched herself on the arm of the sofa next to it.

Stone sat down too, but the two women remained standing.

'Please tell us what's happened to Shaheen,' Katie Faye said urgently. 'Judy said...'

Judy had told Banham about the pornographic videos, and that Brian Finn, who had murdered Ahmed Abdullah, was newly out of prison and blackmailing the women for the return of the tapes. Crowther was on his way to bring Finn in for questioning; Banham had decided to talk to Olivia Stone himself. That Katie Faye was here too was bonus; Judy had said that these two women were paying the blackmail between them, and that Shaheen Hakhti had disagreed with their decision.

Thanks to Judy, Banham also knew that the Right Honourable Kenneth Stone MP had met his wife at the Scarlet Pussy Club where she was working as a stripper. What he didn't know was exactly how much Stone was aware of.

'Mr Stone, I'll need to talk to you in a while, but for the moment can I ask you to wait in another room while I have a few words with your wife and Miss Faye?'

The smile left Kenneth Stone's face, and the eyes he turned on Olivia were like chips of granite.

'It's all right,' Olivia said apprehensively. 'There are no secrets between us.'

'All the same,' Banham said firmly, 'I'd like to talk to the ladies first.'

Ken nodded curtly and got to his feet. 'Are you sure I can't get you some tea or coffee?' he asked, his tone no longer silkily courteous.

'No, thank you,' Alison replied.

Ken left the room without another word.

The atmosphere in the room seemed to lighten as he pulled the door pointedly shut behind him. The two women sat down, close together on the sofa.

Banham was having trouble taking his eyes off Katie Faye. Her skin was flawless, and her eyes, so large and blue, were fearful. He knew Alison was watching him, but he couldn't help himself. He wanted nothing more than to wrap his arms around her and comfort her, then take her away from this whole sordid mess.

But he had a job to do, and he was nothing if not professional. He told them about the woman's body in the boot of the car, sparing none of the details: the broken legs, the bloodied face, the scarlet G-string in her mouth. Then he took out the photograph from the handbag belonging to Shaheen, and handed it to Katie.

Olivia looked away, biting her lip.

Katie covered her mouth with her hand. 'Yes, that's her,' she whispered. 'Who would want to do that to her?'

'We're having Brian Finn brought in for questioning,' Alison told them. 'We know what happened at the Scarlet Pussy Club.'

A look passed between Katie and Olivia. 'What about it?' Katie asked.

'That pornographic videos were made which Brian Finn still has in his possession. We also know he is blackmailing you for their return, and that Shaheen Hakhti disagreed with your decision to pay him.'

Olivia seemed to relax a little; her shoulders dropped,

and some of the tension cleared from her face. 'We were expecting Shaheen a couple of weeks ago,' she told them. 'She was coming down from Leicester to meet Susan Rogers, another member of our ... little group. She wanted to take Brian's note to the police, and Susan was going to try to persuade her to agree that we should pay him what he asked. But she didn't turn up.'

'We just assumed she didn't want to get involved,' Katie said. 'And, to be honest, we were rather glad. She wasn't even in the videos. We were, Olivia and I – you can imagine what it would do to both our lives if they got in the wrong hands.' She looked at Olivia and then back to Banham. 'Exactly what do you know, Inspector?'

Banham held her frightened blue eyes with his own. 'It sounds as if you'd better tell me everything,' he said.

'Not a lot more to tell,' Olivia chimed in, hunching forward in her chair. 'Brian needs money. He has pornographic videos of us. Katie and I said we'd pay him for their return.'

Katie coloured and looked at the carpet. 'We didn't do anything illegal,' she said. 'Just – terribly embarrassing. Especially now.'

'We're not judging you,' Alison said sharply. 'We're here to investigate Shaheen Hakhti's murder, that's all. So if she didn't turn up for your appointment two weeks ago, when did you last see or speak to her?'

'When Brian sent the letter, about three weeks ago,' Katie said looking at Olivia for agreement.

Olivia nodded reluctantly. 'There were six of us,' she said. 'We worked together in that club, twenty years ago.

The manager made videos of us all.'

'All except Shaheen.' Katie looked at Olivia again. She picked up her handbag from the floor beside her and took out a letter. 'That's what Brian sent us.' She held it out to Banham but pulled back before he could take it.

'Everything you tell us is confidential,' he assured her.

'Unless it becomes evidence in a murder enquiry,' Alison added, as Katie handed over the letter. 'Brian Finn was only blackmailing you two? Is that right?'

'Yes,' Katie and Olivia said almost in unison.

'So why the involvement of the other women?'

'We can afford to pay him,' Katie said. 'The others can't. There are tapes of them too.'

'But not of Shaheen?'

'No, but ...' Katie looked helplessly at Olivia.

'Shaheen was one of us. We all worked at the club together. We contacted her, but she didn't want to know. We left it at that – it was up to her. We never thought for a moment...'

'You've all stayed in touch? After a summer job twenty years ago?' Alison sounded incredulous.

The dark flecks in Alison's eyes were clearly visible. It was plain to Banham that she didn't like Katie. Since both women were being very co-operative, he had no idea why.

'Stripping is a strange job,' Olivia said thoughtfully. 'Strippers bond together; it's you against the world. We all got on, and we stayed friends.'

Katie's voice rose a couple of tones. 'We were young and stupid and we needed money for college. The manager made it sound as if those videos were a condition of the stripping job. We all regret it now and are deeply embarrassed, but it bonded us and we stayed in touch.'

'Tell me about the other women,' Banham said.

'Theresa and I both got pregnant that summer,' Olivia said. 'We had our babies within a few weeks of each other. Her little girl was born handicapped, and I had a healthy, clever son. I wanted to help her, especially since the baby's father was in prison.'

'Kim got involved with drugs when she was at college,' Katie went on. 'She studied dance, and I did drama. I did everything I could to help get her get clean.'

'I married into money,' Olivia said, 'so I helped them both. There were no grants for drama school or ballet, not even back then. And none of us had parents to help.'

'What about Shaheen Hakhti?' Banham asked.

Katie looked at him with those big blue eyes. 'She went home to her family in Leicester and got married. No one really stayed close to her. Only Christmas cards. But when Brian's note arrived, we asked her what she thought we should do. She was one of us back then, after all.'

'She was supposed to come down to stay with Susan,' Olivia said, 'but she didn't turn up. I can't say any of us were especially bothered.'

'Including Susan,' Katie added. 'We just assumed she didn't want to bring up the past.'

'She had nothing to lose,' Olivia said flatly.

'Except her life,' said Alison quietly.

This time the women didn't look at each other.

'We know the knickers found in her mouth were about twenty years old,' Alison said.

'We wore scarlet G-strings at the club,' Katie said, her voice hardly above a whisper. 'They were uniform for all the strippers.'

'Judy Gardener told us that,' Banham said.

There was a silence. Then Olivia asked, 'What else did she tell you?'

'Enough to show that you could be in danger,' Banham said gently. 'We're having Brian Finn brought in for questioning. He has killed once; we know he is capable of it.'

For some reason Banham couldn't quite grasp, a look of relief seemed to pass across both women's faces.

'When Finn was convicted,' Alison said, 'he refused to give any explanation of why he killed Ahmed Abdullah, the club owner. Have you any idea why he did it?'

'Ahmed was cruel,' Katie said quickly. 'He made us all do horrible, perverted things, and he videoed them. Theresa worked for Ahmed, and Brian loved Theresa. He probably stood up for her.'

'Ahmed was a horrible man. No one mourned him,' Olivia added.

'Does your husband know about the videos?' Alison asked Olivia.

'It was a secret that we six girls kept between ourselves,' Olivia said. 'We didn't tell anyone else at all.' She clasped and unclasped her hands. 'Theresa and I have children. And the others all have careers.'

'Kim obviously told Judy,' Katie said. The hard edge to her tone surprised Banham.

'Do you know how Brian killed Ahmed Abdullah?' he

asked, looking from Olivia to Katie and back again.

There was another moment of silence. Again Banham noticed the women didn't look at each other.

'I think they had a fight,' Katie said quietly.

'Everyone hated Ahmed,' Olivia said again.

'I don't expect he meant to kill him,' Katie said quickly.

'We weren't there, so how would we know what happened?' Olivia added almost as an afterthought.

'You should ask Theresa,' Katie said. 'He was her bloke. If he told anyone, it would be her.'

Banham looked speculatively at Katie. 'Why do you think he didn't mean to kill him?'

'Brian wasn't like that. He was gentle.' She threw Olivia a quick, nervous glance.

'He was a club bouncer,' Banham reminded her.

'And asking you for a hundred thousand pounds for your videos isn't too gentle,' Alison pointed out.

Neither answered.

'I'll ask again. Does your husband know about the videos?' Alison asked Olivia.

Another brief glance passed between the women. Then Olivia shrugged. 'He knows we were strippers. That's where we met. He was a law student and he used to come into the club and watch Katie and me doing our turn. We had a lot in common. I wanted to be a barrister too in those days. We had an affair, I got pregnant, and we got married. End of story.'

'Does he know about the videos?' Alison persisted.

Olivia looked at the floor. 'Yes, he does.'

Katie stared at Olivia, but said nothing.

Another silence fell, and Banham rubbed his mouth thoughtfully. *Perhaps best not to push Olivia too hard on that for the moment*, he thought. 'Let's go back to Shaheen,' he said, with a quick glance at Alison. 'What do you know about her family?'

'Hardly anything.' Katie shook her head.

'I told you, she didn't keep in touch,' Olivia said.

'You sent Christmas cards. Didn't you exchange news?'

'She married a plumber and had three sons,' Katie said doubtfully. 'I don't know what use that is to you.'

Olivia sat forward. 'Her parents were religious fanatics,' she said. 'We never met them – she told us. That's why she ran away from home and came to work at the club. She didn't need money. It was her way of rebelling.'

'She never really fitted in,' Katie added.

'So you didn't like her?' said Alison.

'I didn't say that,' Katie snapped.

'Have you any idea who might want to kill her?' Banham asked. 'Did she have any enemies as far as you knew?'

'Not that we know,' Olivia answered. 'But why would we?'

'Well, whoever did kill her had something to do with that club,' Alison said. 'What's more, they want us to know it. That's why they left the G-string.' She handed Olivia a photo of the knickers. 'They're with forensics at present.'

Olivia held the photograph by a corner; she and Katie both grimaced. 'The uniform G-strings were scarlet, with black leather ribbons,' Katie said, looking at Olivia. 'I can't be sure – that one looks such a mess. But it's certainly the right shape.'

A picture of Katie Faye wearing nothing but a scarlet G-string with black leather ribbons jumped into Banham's mind. The thought excited him, and he allowed himself a moment to enjoy the sensation. *Perhaps the counselling is working.*

Alison was drawing the interview to a close, a strange expression on her face. Banham shook away the mental image of Katie and took one of his cards from his pocket. He wrote his mobile number on it before handing it to Katie. 'If you think of anything else, just phone me,' he said, speaking directly to her. 'Meanwhile, we'll need you both to come to the station and make a formal statement.'

The women exchanged another worried glance.

'No one apart from my team will need to see them,' Banham reassured them.

'Unless they become vital evidence in Shaheen Hakhti's murder,' said Alison.

Olivia opened the door to reveal Kenneth Stone hovering in the hall with a worried expression. It was clear to Banham that he had been listening.

'May we have a few words now, sir?'

'Not possible, I'm afraid.' Ken jerked his head in the direction of the kitchen. The door was wide open, and his son and daughter sat at the table devouring the remnants of the Chinese supper. They were clearly listening in too.

Stone moved close Banham and lowered his voice. 'Inspector, I really don't want this getting into the papers. A man in my position can't afford adverse publicity.'

'I understand,' Banham said. 'Somewhere more private?'

Stone led the way upstairs. He unlocked a door at the end of the corridor and stood back to allow them inside.

It was a small office equipped with the usual phones, faxes, computer and printer. Banham noticed the whole of one wall was covered with pictures of naked women. Even the desk lamp was a nude.

Banham showed him the picture of Shaheen.

'I recognise her,' Stone said after a few moments. 'She was one of the strippers at that appalling club. I think. Mind you, it's been nearly twenty years, and the old memory isn't what it was…'

'I'm sure you're aware we're investigating a murder,' Banham said coldly.

Stone nodded. 'All a bit embarrassing for me, old chap. OK, so I met my wife in the Scarlet Pussy, but one hopes to leave one's wild youth in the past. Pity Olivia couldn't. She'll have told you about that damned video. You'll see why I can't afford for any of this to get out – my parliamentary career would hit the skids.'

'It won't,' Alison said, looking up from her pocket book. 'Not from us. So you know Brian Finn has been released from prison and is blackmailing your wife?'

Stone said nothing for a few moments. Then he sat down in his comfortable leather office chair and locked his hands behind his head. 'Yes, of course I know. And yes, I should have come straight to you people, but I decided to give Olivia the money and pay the bastard off. I can't take risks with my career.'

Alison and Banham exchanged a look, and he continued, 'When was the last time you saw Shaheen Hakhti?'

'Back then, in The Scarlet Pussy Club. I admit I was quite friendly with her then, with all the girls, but that soon came to an end. I married Olivia, and she didn't keep in touch. The other girls are still friends, but Shaheen moved back to Leicester.'

'What about Brian Finn? Did you know him well?' Banham asked.

Kenneth became noticeably agitated. He tapped his foot and sighed impatiently. 'No. Hardly at all.'

'So he never threw you out of the club when you were young and wild and carefree?' Alison asked with a lacing of sarcasm.

He gazed coolly at Alison. 'He wouldn't have dared. I was one of their best customers. And he was besotted with Olivia, even though she was my girl.'

'Then I'd lay odds you didn't like each other,' Banham said quickly.

'I don't know about him, but I had no feelings either way. He had a fling with the Irish girl, Theresa McGann. She has his daughter. Talk to her.'

'Oh, we intend to,' Banham said.

'Olivia can give you her address.'

'We already have it,' Alison said.

'Where from? Oh, of course. PC Judy. Kim's other

half.' He looked from Banham to Alison. 'Well, isn't that lucky? Inside information. Better get on with it then, hadn't you? Get the murder solved. I don't want Olivia getting in a state.'

Alison consulted her notes. 'What about Susan Rogers? Another stripper from that club. Do you know her too?'

He gave an embarrassed bark of laughter. 'Oh yes. She manages in a sex shop in Soho. *Sex and the Titties*. I try to keep my wife away from her.' He looked sharply at Banham. 'I'm sure you can see my point, Inspector. Imagine the pictures in the tabloids – minister's wife shops at erotica emporium!'

'Do you know if she kept in touch with Brian Finn?'

'I have no idea. I do know what *I'd* like to do to Brian bloody Finn ...'

Banham gave him a long look. 'Please leave it to us, Mr Stone. We're bringing him in for questioning.' He handed the MP a card. 'If you think of anything we should know about, please you give us a ring.'

Stone accepted the card. Banham thought he looked more than a little worried.

Alison stood up and took out a photograph. 'One last question. Do you recognise this?'

Kenneth Stone glanced at the photo. An unpleasant leer spread across his face. 'They're a bit of a mess, aren't they? But no man forgets knickers like that. I watched a lot of girls take them off.'

'Nasty, greasy upper-class lecher,' Alison Grainger spat as she fired up the car.

Banham clicked his seat belt shut. 'I think he fancies you,' he grinned.

She looked at him with a quick frown, unsure whether he was serious. Either way, it wasn't the kind of thing he usually came out with.

Banham's mobile chirped, saving her the need to comment. She reversed into a three-point turn and headed down the wide driveway.

'Good man,' Banham said into his phone. He flipped it off and put it back in his pocket. 'Crowther has interviewed Theresa McGann. She's coming to the station tomorrow. He's sitting outside Finn's mother's flat. The mother is on medication and can't be left too long; he'll have to come back soon.'

'Good. Bloody hell, who do all these belong to!' Gravel flew into the air on both sides of the car as Alison manoeuvred forward two inches and then back three, in an attempt to get around the three large cars parked in the Stones' drive. 'What's this doing to my exhaust?' she said, half to herself.

Banham checked the time. 'The post-mortem results won't be in till tomorrow,' he said. 'I'll be at the station later, but I've got a private appointment I want to keep first. Can you drop me *en route*?'

'A date?'

'An appointment.' Banham's lips twitched. 'A private appointment.'

Alison's eyes started to flare. Was she jealous? Perhaps there was a chance for him after all.

'You didn't exactly keep your feelings about Katie

Faye private,' she said pointedly, crunching the car into forward gear and heading for the gateway just a tad too fast.

He looked at her. What had he done? Katie Faye was gorgeous. Who wouldn't think so? And those eyes ... just like ... he swallowed hard as the memories flooded his mind. But it wasn't like that, whatever Alison was thinking.

'I thought work and pleasure didn't mix,' she said flatly.

'Just keep your eyes on the road.'

He loved it when the black specks shone in her eyes. If only he could tell her...

Alison turned into the road, wheels bouncing in and out of the potholes. 'I just hope she doesn't turn out to be a suspect,' she said.

'Alison, they're frightened women. If we can win their trust, things will be a hell of a lot easier.'

'Whatever you say, guv.' A stone flew up and hit the windscreen. 'You'd think the occupants of this road would club together and get it surfaced,' she said. 'They're the ones who use it.'

'I think that's the point,' he explained. 'They don't want all and sundry turning it into a short cut. It keeps it private.'

'Like your date tonight.'

'I'm not going on a date.'

'So where are you going?'

'Watch the road!'

The stench of putrefying fruit and vegetables filled the air in the market street in Soho, even though trading for the day had been over for a couple of hours. Some of the unsold stock still lay in the road, flattened by the wheels of the passing traffic, or sat rotting in nearby dustbins. And a few of the small shops in the road still remained open, hoping for some late business.

Sex and the Titties was one of them. Susan had re-opened when she arrived back from the meeting with the girls. Sex shops often did well in the early evening. Lonely men often came in to purchase a blow-up doll or a penis extender, or groups of girls on a night out wandered in to amuse themselves after a drink in the pub, and often bought the expensive underwear or sex toys.

Susan had just finished serving a gaggle of teenage girls who wanted to see the vibrators in action. She had lined them all up on the counter and demonstrated each one in turn, and the girls had giggled hysterically, then left the shop. Their laughter could still be heard fifty yards down the road. Susan was well aware they had only come in for some entertainment, and had no intention of buying anything, but, after such a tense day, she had needed some amusement herself. What was more, she fully understood their need to explore their new-found sexuality; they reminded her of herself at their age – raw, silly and anxious to know all about sex. None of them could have been more than sixteen; Susan wished very briefly that she could turn back time.

She decided to leave the shop open for another hour. She had lost this afternoon's trade and was hopeful of making it up. She had to make a success of this job. It meant she no longer had to display her ageing body to drunks and sad perverts each night, and she didn't have to worry about her cellulite and sagging boobs. She could finally throw away her tassels and fur G-strings and nipple-free bras, and stop fretting about the rapid approach of middle age.

She enjoyed not having to be out till two or three in the morning working in seedy, damp clubs. She could curl up in front of the television with Tara, her beloved cat, in the warmth of the flat over the shop. She had started to feel content. There had never been a regular man in her life; most blokes had been one-night stands, none ever seemed to want more. That was the way it was for strippers; they were regarded as an escape from reality, almost like prostitutes, and none of the men cared about the person inside.

Her body bore the scars of men's fetishes. A punter once stubbed his cigarette out on her backside when she turned away from him. Three of her back teeth were missing after an over-excited punter took a swing at her in the middle of her act. She no longer believed she would find a man to share her life. Her close male friends were all gay, and had often worked with her in the seedy clubs as drag acts. They were the ones who knew her name, or were there on the end of the phone when her shelving fell down or her car wouldn't start.

Her closest girlfriends were the girls from the early days at the Scarlet Pussy Club, the women with whom she shared a life-long secret. They had only worked together for those few weeks, but what happened had entwined their lives, and no matter where life took them, they would always be there for each other.

Susan's parents had died when she was only seventeen, so, in a way, those girls were her family. She had two cousins, but they never called or remembered her birthday; the Scarlet Pussy girls never forgot it.

Mostly she was happy with her lot. As long as she could keep this job until she retired, everything was going to work out fine – even this business with Brian Finn. He would be paid, as he well deserved, then they could all move on.

It was a freezing night, and if she was staying open for business, it meant leaving the street door wide open to invite passing trade. She decided she would make a hot mug of tea to get her through the hour.

As she walked from the shop to the tiny kitchenette at the back, she checked, for the third time since she had returned from the meeting, that the brown envelope containing the cash was in the cutlery drawer. She wanted Brian to have the money as soon as possible; keeping it in her kitchen was too much of a responsibility. She had phoned him twice since she'd returned, and would try again after she shut up business for the day and arrange to meet him first thing in the morning.

As she filled the kettle, she thought she heard someone walk into the shop. 'Be there in a flash,' she called, giggling to herself at the innuendo.

No one answered. Punters often wanted to remain anonymous, and she was used to it. She didn't speak again.

She plugged the kettle in, still giggling to herself, and turned to find herself face to face with a figure in black, blocking her exit to the shop. She let out a loud yelp, and only saw the knife as it swung towards her.

She didn't scream as it hit her. It happened too quickly. Blood and splinters of bone spurted high in the air as the razor-sharp edge ripped into the top of her head. She reeled backwards, and the next blow lodged in her temporal artery. Blood shot everywhere, staining the grubby walls and ceiling, and as her head hit the wall behind her she lost consciousness. Her body slid slowly down, gore clinging to the wall behind her. Her one remaining eye stared as Tara, back arched in fear, crept through from the shop.

The killer spotted the animal, and made a speedy swing, slicing the terrified animal's head from its body and batting it though the air like a cricket ball. It hit the wall, then seeped into the bloodied mess that a few seconds earlier was the bubbly Susan Rogers.

Finally, gloved hands prised open Susan's blood-filled mouth, forced a red G-string between her teeth and closed the mouth around it. The murderer turned quickly, opened the cutlery drawer, took the brown envelope and left.

CHAPTER FIVE

Banham was pleased he was able to keep his weekly appointment with Joan Deamer. She asked him how his physical problem was progressing, and looked slightly amused when he mentioned Katie Faye as well as Alison Grainger.

'Katie's so pretty,' he told her. 'Any man would be attracted to her. And ...' He looked down at his lap, and Joan said nothing, waiting for him to continue.

'And?' she prompted when he didn't.

'It's ... her eyes. They're so blue ...'

He closed his eyes as the nightmare images of his wife and daughter began to fill his mind again. His heart began to pound, and he had to fight to slow his breathing.

From a distance, Joan's calm voice penetrated the rushing sound in his ears. He couldn't make out what she was saying, but it seemed to soothe the panic all the same. He opened his eyes, and after a few moments the room stopped swaying, and he was able to look at Joan's concerned face.

'Are you OK now?' she asked. 'You had me worried for a minute there.'

Banham nodded, swallowing hard.

'Do you want to tell me about it?'

As happened so often during these sessions, it took a

minute or two to get started, but once he did, he found he couldn't stop talking. Joan listened patiently as he told her again about the worst night of his life, when he arrived home to find his wife and baby daughter brutally murdered, their bludgeoned bodies on the floor of Elizabeth's nursery. When the words stopped pouring out of him and he sat, breathless and drained, she covered his icy hand with her warm one and squeezed it gently, biting her lower lip.

Banham felt he'd been wrung dry. He was reminded of his first session with Joan, when the memory of that horrific night had come tumbling out for the first time. Slowly his heart rate calmed, and after a little while Joan spoke.

'What I don't understand is how what happened today connects to ... that night? There's clearly something – some kind of trigger.'

'It's ...' Banham breathed deeply. 'Katie Faye has ... her eyes are so ... so blue. Just like Diane's.'

'Ah.' Joan nodded. 'How does that make you feel, Paul?'

Banham struggled to find an answer. 'Scared,' he admitted. 'She's a main witness in the case I'm on, and I'm probably going to see a lot of her in the next few days.'

'So you're concerned you might not be able to handle it?'

'Partly, I suppose.'
'What else, then?'
'Well, I'm ...She's so...'

'You're attracted to her?'

'Of course. But then there's ... Alison. But that's different.'

Joan Deamer smiled. 'Paul, all I'm getting here is that you're a perfectly normal man, at least in the way you react to women. You have a problem, but you've come a long way since you first came to me. In fact, I'd say you've taken a second step forward.'

'What was the first?'

'Deciding to come for counselling in the first place. Now, where do we go from here? Do you think you're ready to move forward with Alison?'

He shook his head. 'I messed up big time there. I wouldn't dare.'

'How did she react when you showed an interest in Katie Faye?'

'I don't think she liked it, but...'

He was almost sure her small smile signalled genuine amusement. 'What does that tell you?'

He made no reply. Joan tried again.

'How do you think she'd react if you asked Katie Faye out?'

'That's a definite no-no. Katie's a witness in a current enquiry; it's out of the question.'

'And if she wasn't?'

He gave her a rueful smile. Joan Deamer could read him like a book. She knew he wouldn't have the courage. Why would the sexiest woman on television be interested in him?

He always left Joan's office exhausted but oddly

satisfied. After only eight sessions they had made a lot of progress. At least he'd begun to feel his life might eventually be more than work and loneliness, even if Katie Faye and her liquid blue eyes were way out of his league.

He felt a stab of sadness that he had blown his chance with Alison Grainger. As well as being attracted to her, he felt comfortable in her company, probably because they had work in common. At least they still had that. He pulled his mobile from his pocket and pressed her number.

'What news on Brian Finn?' he asked.

'We're still outside his mother's, guv. Crowther's keeping me entertained.'

With his endless fund of stories about his conquests, Banham thought. 'Good,' he replied. 'Keep me informed.'

He walked to his car mulling things over. The results of the post-mortem wouldn't be in until tomorrow, and Katie Faye and Olivia Stone had agreed to come to the station in the morning to make their statement. Finn would be brought in for interview tonight, but until that happened he still had time on his hands. He decided to pay his sister Lottie another call. He'd be in good time to tell Madeleine the story about the princess and the pea-fairy. He turned it over quickly in his mind. The princess was pricked by a needle from a spinning wheel and put to sleep in an ivory tower, but the pea-fairy was on duty under the mattress, and summoned a handsome prince to climb the tower and wake her with a kiss so they could live happily ever after. He would tell her the prince had a white pony; she loved ponies almost as much as Banham loved her.

It was dark, and the cold had really set in as he turned

into the small side road of Victorian semi-detached cottages where Lottie lived. His passenger seat was heaped with small chocolate bars for Maddy and Bobby, and a bottle of wine and a bunch of flowers for Lottie. He liked giving his twin sister treats; life wasn't great for her since her husband had upped and left.

Bobby was playing football against the outside wall. The boy ran to meet Banham as he drew up in his new dark blue Ford Mondeo.

'Hey, Uncle Paul, that's a new motor! Can I get a ride?'

Banham scooped up the gifts from the passenger seat and stepped out of the car. *What's Bobby doing in the street on such a cold night, playing on his own*? He held out a hand to his small nephew and pointed the key at the car. 'I'll have to clear that with your mum,' he said. 'If it's OK with her we'll bring Madeleine too.'

The front door of the tiny cottage opened into the lounge. As he pushed it, Bobby slid down his back, and Lottie looked up. She was sitting by the table talking on the phone, and brought the call to a swift end when she saw her brother and son. Her eyes were red as if she'd been crying.

An appetising aroma wafted through from her tiny kitchen. 'What's for supper?' he asked cheerfully. 'Is there enough for an overworked policeman?'

Bobby was jumping up and down beside him, trying to relieve him of the chocolate in his hand. 'Have you had your tea?' Banham asked the boy.

'Yep.'

Banham released his grip on the sweets, then put the

flowers and the wine on the table beside his sister.

'Pork chops, creamed swede and fried potatoes.' Lottie picked up the flowers and carried them through to the kitchen, looking everywhere but directly at her brother. 'And yes, there's loads, especially the swede. The kids won't touch it. Give me a few minutes.'

'You won't get your chocolate next time if I hear you didn't eat your swede,' Banham warned Bobby, who was kneeling on the floor rummaging through the assortment of sweets. He looked up at his uncle with a mischievous grin, which Banham found himself returning. Both Bobby and Madeleine could wrap him round their little fingers, and they knew it.

He called to Lottie, 'Take as long as you like. I'll take Bobby and Madeleine for a spin around the block in the new motor, then I'll put them to bed if you like.'

One bedtime story turned into three. At the end of each one, Madeleine asked if she was pretty enough to be a princess, and each time Banham told her she was. Finally she fell asleep, thumb in her mouth and arm around her white unicorn. Banham tucked her Barbie blanket around her and crept down the narrow staircase to join his sister.

'Drink, Paul?' Lottie held up the bottle of wine he had brought.

'Better not. I'm working tonight.' He sat down at the table, where she had laid a place for him. 'The swede smells great – the kids don't know what they're missing.'

'Cinnamon and butter, with a touch of black pepper.' She put the plate in front of him.

'What's on your mind, Lot?' he asked, picking up his

fork.

'Nothing.'

The answer came too quickly. He starting cutting his pork into very fine slices. 'I'm always ready to listen,' he said, 'and always at the other end of a phone.'

Lottie pulled her mouth into a smile, but it didn't reach her eyes. 'I know. You don't need to worry about me. It's all sorted now.'

He put a forkful of swede in his mouth and chewed slowly, turning his head to look at her. This time she didn't look away.

Brian Finn was only in his mid-forties, but the mass of dark curly hair from his youth had faded and thinned. He was still a big man, though the muscled physique from his earlier fighting days had turned to fat, and he looked like a middle-aged man who lived on junk food.

His shabby navy tracksuit looked as if it had been retrieved from a charity shop, and his trainers were grey with age and thick with mud. He was sweating heavily and breathing noisily as he jogged slowly toward the flats.

'He's coming,' Alison said, cutting Crowther off in mid-sentence.

Crowther opened the car door, ID his hand. Finn spotted him, froze momentarily, then made a dash for the graffiti-clad staircase that led to his mother's council flat.

'Brian Finn! Stop! Police!' Alison hit the pavement at a run.

But Brian had disappeared up the stairs.

Alison hotfooted her way up the stairs and caught Finn

before he reached the third flight. He tried to resist, but she held fast to his arm and pushed him against the wall. Crowther was right behind her, verbalising his disgust at the smell of stale urine.

Finn wrestled like a cornered wild animal. It took two of them to cuff his hands behind his back, and as they led the big man down the stairs, windows and doors all over the estate opened and curious heads popped out. A few kids leaned over a concrete balcony strewn with clothes. Alison looked up, momentarily distracted by a particularly inventive term of abuse, and Brian suddenly kicked out.

'This is a set-up,' he yelled. 'What the fuck am I supposed to have done?'

Crowther held on to him and hustled him into the back of Alison's car.

'We can start with resisting arrest,' she said calmly. 'If you carry on like this, we'll be adding assaulting a police officer.' She slid into the seat beside him. 'And then there's a small matter of blackmail.'

A stone came hurtling through the air and landed on the bonnet of her beloved car. 'And accessory to criminal damage,' she added.

Her famous temper was about to erupt. 'Leave it, sarge,' Crowther said abruptly. 'Let's go.'

Her fury subsided as fast as it had risen. He was right; this estate was dangerous enough; no need for them to make things worse for the local force.

Banham was at the station before Crowther and Alison arrived. Isabelle Walsh had left Brian Finn's file on his desk, and he had taken the chance to get up to speed on the man's history.

Finn had been caught red-handed with Ahmed Abdullah's dead body in his car. He confessed to his murder, but refused to answer any questions, and consequently served nineteen years of a life sentence, before being released a few weeks earlier. The cause of death was recorded as asphyxiation; the post-mortem revealed a satin thread in Abdullah's windpipe. The thread had been part of a red G-string found in the deceased's top pocket.

Banham rubbed his mouth, then picked up the papers and made his way to the interview room.

When he entered the room, Finn didn't look up. He sat motionless, head bent, staring at the table.

'He has refused legal representation, guv,' Alison said.

She turned the tape on and made the official statement. Banham tapped his chin with his fingers and looked at Finn. 'So you decided to blackmail Olivia Stone and Katie Faye?'

Finn lifted his head, but didn't answer. His eyes darted nervously from Banham to Alison and back again.

Banham sighed. 'OK. Let me remind you. You sent them a note demanding a hundred thousand pounds.'

Finn still said nothing.

Banham raised his voice slightly. 'One hundred thousand pounds. In exchange for video tapes you have in your possession. Tapes of both women, and three others, in intimate sexual situations with Ahmed Abdullah, the man you killed.'

Finn's gaze dropped back to the scarred table. 'Will I

go back to prison?' he asked quietly.

'Why did you kill Shaheen Hakhti?' Banham asked abruptly.

Alison threw him a quick glance, surprise in her eyes.

'What?' Finn looked astonished. 'I never ... Shaheen? Dead?' His brown eyes were wide and frightened now. 'I love them girls. I wouldn't hurt an 'air on their 'eads.'

'You killed Ahmed Abdullah,' Alison said. 'You admitted that.'

Finn looked her in the eye. 'And I've served my time,' he said, his voice firmer. 'I don't need to answer any questions about that. But I'm telling you, I wouldn't hurt them girls. I wouldn't. Shaheen, dead ...' His face dropped into his hands and he shook his head slowly.

'You'd blackmail them,' Alison said sharply. 'Isn't that hurting them?'

Finn looked up at her and his face crumpled. 'That's different. If they'd ...' His voice fell to a whisper. 'My kid's brain damaged.'

'We know,' Alison said. 'It's very sad. But blackmail is still a crime.'

Banham was watching him carefully. 'You choked Ahmed Abdullah with a red G-string,' he said. 'And Shaheen Hakhti was found with one in her mouth.' He paused. 'Only you cut Shaheen's throat as well.'

Brian looked terrified. 'I never did, guv.' He put his hands flat on the table and leaned towards Banham. 'I wouldn't do anything like that,' he said emotionally. 'Why would I want to kill her?'

'That's what we're asking you,' Banham said coldly.

There was a silence.

Alison looked Finn in the eyes. 'Shaheen wanted to take your blackmail demand to the police,' she said. 'She didn't want Olivia Stone and Katie Faye to pay you. And you knew that, didn't you?'

Finn made no reply.

'OK, let's go back to the beginning.' Banham was becoming irritated. 'There were six women working with you in the Scarlet Pussy Club nearly twenty years ago. Ahmed Abdullah made pornographic tapes of those women, which came into your possession. You knew they would pay handsomely to get them back. But Shaheen Hakhti wouldn't agree. She wanted to go to the police. So you killed her.'

Finn jumped up and banged his fist on the table. 'That's a lie! Till you said it just now, I didn't even know Shaheen was dead.'

'Sit down, Finn,' Banham said wearily.

Finn subsided into his chair, obviously still riled. 'You can't keep me here,' he said. 'I've committed no crime, and my mother needs me.'

'I can,' Banham said. 'I'm arresting you for blackmail, and you'll be held for further questioning in connection with the murder of Shaheen Hakhti. Caution him, sergeant.'

'We've got thirty-six hours to come up with something,' Alison said as they walked back to the incident room.

'I need the exhibits from the Abdullah case,' Banham said. 'If the G-strings were the same, we've got him.'

'Could it be a copycat?'

Banham shook his head. 'Abdullah was choked, and the G-string left in his top pocket. Shaheen Hakhti's throat was cut, and it was stuffed in her mouth. All the same, if the G-strings are the same, it's enough to get us into court.'

'But possibly not enough to get a murder charge to stick,' Alison pointed out. 'We need more. I'll chase up the CCTV. If we can track the car '

'It's connected to that strip club,' Banham broke in, rubbing his mouth in his habitual gesture. 'Why the G-strings, if it isn't?'

Alison nodded agreement. 'Who stood to lose if Shaheen Hakhti went to the police?'

Banham thought aloud. 'Kenneth Stone for one. His career's already on the line.'

'His wife too. And the vulnerable and gorgeous Katie Faye.' Alison wanted to bite the words back as soon as they were out; the wave of jealousy had taken her by surprise. But she decided not to back down; her opinion of the lovely Miss Faye was as much professional as personal. 'You don't watch *Screened*, do you, guv?'

'That hospital thing? You mentioned it before. I think my sister watches it. Why?'

'Katie Faye's the star. She plays a sweet, clean-living staff nurse. She's won awards – not for acting: people's favourite, nation's sweetheart, that kind of thing. That's the image she's built up. A pornographic video would ruin her. And it would probably cost Olivia Stone her marriage. The question is, how far would they go to protect themselves?'

'Ken Stone has a lot more to lose.' Banham pushed open a swing door and held it for her. 'He knows the tapes exist, remember.'

Alison flicked her long mouse-brown plait over one shoulder. 'That struck me as a tad strange,' she mused. 'He was young, rich and affluent yet he frequented a downmarket strip club like the Scarlet Pussy.'

'What's strange about that?' Banham turned to look her in the face. 'He was twenty-something and single; what was strange about liking to watch pretty girls undress? I'd call that pretty normal.'

Alison smiled to herself, but said nothing. Normally Banham would clam up and say zilch when this kind of subject came up; something had clearly changed.

'I think you should talk to Ken Stone again tomorrow,' he went on. 'He likes pretty women.'

'If it's all the same to you, I won't wear stockings and a thigh-length miniskirt, guv,' Alison replied dryly, delighted that Banham had hinted she was pretty.

'Take Isabelle with you. All the men fancy her.'

Typical! *He had to go and spoil it*. She swallowed down the sharp retort that sprang to her lips and marched swiftly through the next swing door.

Banham was completely oblivious to his lack of tact. 'With luck, something might turn up in the post-mortem report,' he went on. 'And we'll need to get a warrant to search Finn's flat. Let's try and retrieve the videos.'

'Crowther can do that,' Alison suggested. 'The residents won't give him so much grief. They dented the bonnet of my car with a brick today.'

'Better still if we could find more of those red G-strings,' he said.

'It would help if Crowther hadn't fallen out with Penny Starr,' Alison said acidly. Penny was the head forensic officer, and her relationship with Crowther had gone on so long people had only started gossiping about it when it came to an end. 'She was a great asset to us when they were an item; she used to work all hours if he was on duty too.'

'I didn't know it was over,' Banham said. 'Why have they fallen out?'

'It was yesterday's main gossip,' Alison said, as the door to the incident room swung open.

Crowther stood on the other side of it. 'Guv,' he said. 'I was just coming to find you. We've got another one.'

CHAPTER SIX

PC Judy Gardener was standing just behind Crowther, and beside her was an ashen-faced Kim Davis.

'Another what?' Banham demanded.

'Murdered woman,' Crowther said. 'With a red G-string in her mouth. This one's in Soho.'

Judy Gardener interrupted. 'Her name was Susan Rogers. She's another of Kim's ex-associates from that Scarlet Pussy Club. She's the one who was going to meet Brian Finn to hand over the blackmail money.' She paused. 'Olivia Stone and Katie Faye found her. They called me instead of 999.'

'Do we know what time she was killed?' Banham checked the time. It was a minute or so to half past ten.

'I don't know the exact time. A few hours ago.'

'How come it was Olivia and Katie who found her?' Alison asked.

'They went to her shop to see her. They rang Kim and me, and I put in the 999. That was a little after seven.'

'We've got Brian Finn in custody,' Banham told Judy.

'It was about eight fifteen when we picked him up,' Alison said quickly. 'Kim, why did Olivia Stone and Katie Faye go to the shop? I thought they'd already given Susan the money.'

'I don't know.' Kim took a step closer to Judy and

clutched her shoulder.

Judy slipped an arm around her lover. 'Sir, all these women are in a terrible state. Olivia and Katie are still at the murder scene. The place is surrounded with press. Bow Street police are there. I told them to expect you.'

'Crowther, go and get Finn's clothes off him and take them over to forensics.' Banham was already on his way down the corridor, Alison, Judy and Kim in his wake. Crowther skidded past him and set off at the run.

'Penny's on duty in forensics,' Alison called after him. 'Be nice to her – we need a quick return on the tests.'

The sex shop was surrounded by a blue police cordon and a crowd of journalists and photographers. The uniformed PCs guarding the cordon made Banham and Alison wait while they took their ID through to the officer in charge.

Because the murder had only happened a few hours ago, the details hadn't yet been put on the HOLMES computer; with nothing in the system to tie it to Banham's case, he found himself making a lengthy explanation to a skinny young detective sergeant with long, straggly hair tied back in a ponytail. Growing more and more impatient, he waited for the sergeant to check with his own superior officer, who was held up on another case; then even more precious time was wasted waiting for clearance from his own DCI. Meanwhile the sergeant was enjoying the power he wielded.

Cameras flashed nineteen to the dozen as they argued.

'Is it true that the actress Katie Faye is involved?' a journalist asked.

'Can you ask her to come out for a picture?' another shouted.

'Is it true that Ken Stone's wife is a customer in that shop?' This was a short, plump female reporter with mauve strands in the front of her gelled black hair.

The sergeant finally agreed to let them in, and Banham and Alison pushed their way through the crowd towards the entrance. When he reached the doorway, Banham turned to face the press.

'At the moment we have nothing to tell you,' he said. 'When we know more, I'll let you know. Meanwhile, please let us get on with our job.'

A young PC stood aside to let them through, her eyes widening as she turned to face the window display of crotchless knickers in a rainbow of colours and condoms in a fruitbowl of flavours.

Inside the shop, Banham took a good look at the young sergeant, who had introduced himself as Sid Philips. He was dressed in a worn brown leather jacket, and baggy jeans that sat on skinny hips revealing a little too much of his boxer shorts. His sparse ponytail was held by an elastic band at the nape of his neck.

The shop was a revelation. Banham noticed a large sign sellotaped to the wall above a display of contraptions like bicycle pumps with straps on either side. The sign said 'Penis Extenders'. Below the display was a fan of mauve faux tiger skin jockstraps.

He noticed Alison was staring at them in amusement; he only felt embarrassed, and wasn't sure where a pang of envy came from.

'Where are the women who found the body?' he asked Sid Philips.

'They're upstairs in the victim's flat at the moment,' the DS answered. 'They're very shaky, and have asked to be kept away from the press. They're both close friends of the victim, apparently.'

'Yes, we know,' Banham said.

'If I were you I'd leave them for a bit,' Philips said. His self-importance was annoying Banham. He fought an urge to remind Philips that he was the senior officer here; he had no wish to create friction between his team and the Bow Street murder squad. Neither inter-station politics nor one-upmanship interested him; he just wanted to catch the killer.

From the look Alison Grainger gave the scruffy sergeant, he deduced that she was as keen as he was to put him in his place, but she kept her mouth shut too. It was good to know they were thinking along similar lines.

'The victim's through there,' Philips told them, waving an arm towards a room at the back. 'Shall I take you through?' He led the way without waiting for an answer. 'You'd better take a deep breath, darling,' he added over his shoulder to Alison. 'It's not a pretty sight, even for us. If you're a bit…'

'A bit what?' she demanded.

'Female,' he smirked, looking her up and down.

Banham was feeling the pressure. If this was going to be a bad one, he didn't want to make a fool of himself in front of this cocky young sergeant. He weighed up whether to risk a look at the corpse, but Alison distracted him.

'Don't you dare come at me with your sexist remarks,' she snapped. 'And remember DI Banham is your senior officer.'

The lanky young sergeant fought to keep a smile off his face. 'Just thought I should warn you, darlin',' he said defensively.

'And I'm not your darling. Lead on.'

Banham stayed glued to the spot. Alison turned to face him, concern in her eyes.

'I'll be through in a minute,' he said quietly.

She nodded, understanding. 'Take your time. I can manage laughing boy.'

She followed Philips into the tiny kitchen, and the sight which met her stopped her in her tracks. She'd had nothing but black coffee all day in an attempt to shed a couple of pounds; it had been difficult, but at this moment she was glad her stomach was empty. She felt the coffee travel up into her gullet like a lift, then stop and drop all the way down again with a discernible thud. The relief that she wasn't going to vomit warmed her veins as she stared at the unrecognisable figure that once was Susan Rogers.

The remains of a ginger cat's head stuck to the dirty, flock-patterned wallpaper. Unimaginable body fluids had leaked down the wall on to the grubby, beige carpet with a great deal of blood; the headless torso of the cat lay stiff and blood-sodden beside the woman's body.

Alison knew Banham wouldn't cope with this. She walked back into the shop, where he was watching the blue-suited forensic officers moving carefully across the surfaces, tweezers or magnifying glasses in their latex-gloved hands, dusting surfaces for tiny particles which they carefully placed in little phials or plastic evidence bags for the lab. An exhibits officer was videoing from the doorway, pointing his recorder at the walls and floor and ceiling inside the shop, then following blood patterns into the kitchen where the victim lay.

Banham moved to take a closer look at a couple of blow-up dolls with red plastic mouths and no hair. They leaned by the glass counter that housed the till, 'Reduced' signs attached to their bottoms. He turned to look at two mannequins, one modelling matching bra and knickers in a purple and pink leopard-print, the other a bright blue pair of skimpy underpants with a penis-shaped vibrator peeking over the top.

A few months ago, she thought, *he would have been looking anywhere but at the displays, too embarrassed to admit he'd noticed them.* Was this a sudden interest in sex, or a way of avoiding looking at the victim? A sudden thought crossed her mind: had he met someone since their catastrophic date before Christmas? She felt a sharp stab of jealousy. His excuse for ending their embryonic relationship was that business and pleasure didn't mix; what if he'd met someone who wasn't connected to the police?

She pushed the thought from her mind; there was no time for it now. Another woman had been murdered, and they had to interview Katie Faye and Olivia Stone again. She needed her wits about her; to her great surprise, Banham was completely taken in by these women. Katie

Faye's long silky blonde hair and big blue eyes gave her an air of innocence as false as Olivia Stone's nails. And she couldn't fail to notice that Banham couldn't keep his eyes off Olivia's full bosom. It was demoralising for a girl who wore a 32A cup.

Banham peeled latex gloves over his hands and opened the till. He looked across at her. 'Forty pounds and some coins,' he said.

She took out her notebook and made a note.

'Guv?' She walked over to him, careful to keep her voice low. 'I think you should give the corpse a miss.'

He stared at her, then without saying a word, turned and walked the few steps to the back of the shop.

Alison closed her eyes, unable to bear it. When she opened them he was gazing at what was left of Susan's face and the mangled remains of her cat's head, horror all over his face.

He turned away quickly and made a dash for the door to outside. A crowd of journalists and photographers still hung around, but he couldn't help it; his body jerked violently and his stomach ejected what looked a pint of pig's swill. The photographers immediately started clicking and flashing, and as if for their benefit Banham threw up a second time over the window displaying the crotchless knickers and fruit-flavoured condoms.

Inside the shop, Alison went to the tap in the kitchen and filled a glass with water. Ponytailed DS Philips found it hard to keep the smile from his face. 'Don't you have many butchered bodies where you come from?' he asked, and burst out laughing.

'Don't they teach you respect for senior officers where you come from?' she snapped back.

'Not my senior officer, is he, darlin'?'

'And my name's not darlin!'

Banham was oblivious to the barrage of questions being fired at him. His mind was swimming with memories: his lovely wife, battered beyond recognition; his beautiful baby on her yellow bunny blanket, cold, dead and one blue eye staring.

'Guv.'

He blinked, and found Alison standing beside him holding out a glass of water.

He rinsed his mouth and spat, making a couple of reporters jump aside, then drank the rest in one swallow. Then he walked back into the shop. Philips stared at him, sucking in his cheeks. Banham looked him in the eye. 'Sergeant Grainger and I are going upstairs to talk to the women who found her, and then I'm going to get them out through the back door,' he said. 'I want you to call for more uniform back-up, and disperse that group of piranhas outside. And I want every detail of this murder scene kept confidential.'

Philips shifted uncomfortably. 'Will do,' he answered. To Banham's amusement Alison pinned her glare on the skinny DS. 'Sir,' he added.

Banham nodded, but the brief moment of goodwill melted as Philips said, 'Shall I ask them not to print the piccy of you throwing up? Sir?'

Olivia and Katie were waiting upstairs in Susan's bedroom. Someone had started to strip the old wallpaper from the walls but a few stubborn shreds remained and the wall behind it was grubby and grey. There were two uneven stripes of paint across one wall, one bright raspberry pink, the other violet. Susan had clearly been trying to choose between them. Olivia and Katie were sitting on the bed, which was covered with a lilac and white floral duvet. Both nursed glasses of brandy.

There were no chairs, but a small white dresser with a matching stool stood in the corner.

As he entered the room with Alison, Banham nodded to the uniformed officer inside the door. The officer left, and Banham sat beside Katie on the bed, leaving Alison to perch on the dressing table stool with her notebook.

'How are you feeling?' Banham asked.

'How do you think?' Olivia said sourly.

'Terrified,' Katie added, with a nervous stare from under her fringe.

Alison looked coldly at her. Katie needed to know that not everyone was taken in by her blue-eyed innocence.

'We'll need to ask you to account for the time from when you left home until you arrived here and found Susan,' Alison said, 'as precisely as you can.'

'I don't even know what time it is now,' Olivia answered. 'I think my brain stopped working when …' She gestured with the brandy glass.

Alison looked at her watch. 'Mine says the same as yours: ten minutes to twelve.' She pointed at the diamond Cartier on Olivia's wrist.

Banham's tone could have been meant for a sick child. 'In your own time, tell me what you remember, starting when we left your house, until the police arrived here.'

Katie gave Olivia a pleading look. 'Ken was in a terrible state after you told us about Shaheen,' Olivia said quickly. 'He's desperately worried – you know the effect bad publicity has on government ministers.'

Alison looked up from her notebook and caught Banham giving Katie a reassuring smile. Olivia carried on. 'Anyway it turned into a row, and he stormed out.'

'Olivia and I wanted to talk to Theresa and Susan about Shaheen,' Katie said, looking down into her lap. 'We were nervous for their safety. Judy had already told Kim. But …' Her voice faded and she looked at Olivia, who picked up the story.

'We couldn't get an answer from Susan on the phone…'

'What time was this?' Banham broke in.

'I've no idea. Have you?' Olivia asked Katie.

'I think it must have been between seven and eight. Perhaps earlier. We were worried about Susan meeting Brian alone,' Katie said, batting the blue eyes again. Alison carried on scribbling. 'She had the blackmail money, and she was going to phone him. We wanted to tell her to take someone else with her. It was too dangerous alone.'

'But then we were worried that if he didn't get the money he might hand those videos over to the press,' Olivia said anxiously. 'Imagine the headlines!'

'Oh, don't!' Katie shuddered.

Alison stared at them. If this was a nervous reaction, she understood and sympathised – but if it was an act, they were worse than Cannon and Ball.

'When we couldn't get an answer on the phone, we decided to come and see Susan,' Katie said. 'I'm going to stay with Olivia for a while, and needed to go home to pick up some things, so I popped home and we agreed to meet here.'

Alison looked at Banham. What was going on here?

'You arrived separately?' Banham asked.

Katie nodded.

'Where's home?' Alison asked her.

'Chelsea.'

'So how long did it take you?'

'About thirty minutes, I think.' She turned her big blue eyes appealingly on Banham. 'I changed, and I left home about half past eight. I had to find somewhere to park, so I arrived here, oh, about nine? I don't know exactly; I wasn't watching the time.' She looked from Alison to Banham and back at Alison with a lift of her eyebrows, then carried on more quietly. 'The door to the shop was wide open. I wasn't happy about it, so I rang Olivia on her mobile.'

'I was just up the road, parking,' Olivia said quickly. 'I told Katie to wait till I got here, and we went in together.'

Her long, brown imitation fur coat fell open, leaving her cleavage on show. She pulled the coat round her yellow T-shirt and jeans and pushed a long dark red nail into her shiny mouth.

'Had your husband gone out when you left?' Banham asked her.

'Yes, he stormed out not long after you went.'

There was a silence. *This isn't getting us anywhere*, Alison thought. Katie Faye was giving Banham that helpless look from under her fringe, and Alison could tell he was trying not to be taken in by it. He was failing miserably.

Tears suddenly spilled from Katie's eyes and the back of her hand flew up to catch them. 'We walked through to the kitchen calling Susan's name, and…'

Alison leaned forward. 'You mean when you got here?' Katie nodded. 'Miss Faye, this is very important. Did you touch anything when you came into the shop?'

Katie looked at Olivia. 'The till,' Olivia said. 'We opened the till, didn't we? Susan said she was going to lock the money in there.'

'Before going out to the back room?' Alison asked urgently. Now they were getting somewhere.

Olivia nodded. 'We were scared Brian might be here.' She looked from Alison to Banham, and Alison thought how hard her eyes were. But then Katie's were probably just as calculating. She was an actress, after all.

'You should have rung 999,' Alison said.

'When we found Susan, we panicked,' Olivia said. 'We rang Judy, and she said she would take care of it.'

'We weren't thinking straight.' This was Katie, and she spoke directly to Banham.

'You don't need to worry about Brian Finn,' Banham said gently. 'He's in custody. And tomorrow I'll get you both under police protection. But until I can put that in place, neither of you should go out alone, is that quite clear?'

Both women nodded nervously.

'I'm worried about the kids,' Olivia said anxiously. 'I'd like to get back. Ianthe was upset – she hates it when Ken drinks.'

'You could ring them,' Alison suggested a little too sharply.

'Both their mobiles are switched off.'

Banham stood up. Alison opened her mouth to speak, but thought better of it; judging by the way he kept looking at Katie Faye, he wouldn't take any notice of her anyway.

'OK,' Banham said. 'I think you've told us all you can for the moment. I'll need your clothes, though, for forensics.' His businesslike tone softened as he spoke to Katie. 'You say you picked some clothes up? Is there something you could lend Mrs Stone? I'll get forensics to bag what you're wearing, and you can both go home.'

'But you have to stay together, at your house, Mrs Stone,' Alison cut in. 'We need know where you are.'

'I'll send a female forensic officer up here to take your clothes,' Banham said.

'And we'll need your phones too,' Alison added.

'I don't feel safe without my phone,' Olivia said.

'You'll get them back in the morning.'

Banham handed Katie another of his cards. 'This is just in case you need me. Ring this number any time.'

Alison flicked her notebook closed. She had to admit he was being completely professional.

'We'll get you out the back way,' she said.

Alison and Banham walked back to her car in silence. Banham clicked his belt into place, saying, 'I'm not taking any chances. We'll get Judy Gardener compassionate leave, and tell her she's to stay with Kim twenty-four hours a day. The other three will need round-the-clock protection. Get that moving first thing in the morning, will you?'

'Guv.'

'And get someone to check on Theresa McGann now. I thought they'd be safe once we got Brian Finn banged up, but now ...' His voice trailed away, and Alison focused on the traffic. 'Can you lean on Isabelle?' he said suddenly. 'We need to find out where those knickers came from. Get on to Penny too – I need the results on this latest pair ASAP.'

'G-strings, guv,' Alison said. 'Not knickers.'

'Whatever.'

'We'll be lucky if Penny and Isabelle are even talking. Isabelle's the reason that Penny and Crowther fell out.'

'Why?'

'Isabelle and Crowther.' He could be so exasperating; didn't he take notice of what went on under his nose? 'They've been having a fling.'

He turned his blue eyes on her, and a horn blasted behind them as her hands shook on the wheel.

'I can't keep up,' he said with a shrug.

Then he turned away and stared out the window, in a world of his own again.

CHAPTER SEVEN

As Banham tacked the photograph on the whiteboard at the front of the room, a silence descended over the twenty-four detectives on the murder team. Now, beside Shaheen Hakhti on the board was Susan Rogers. Both photographs were horrifying, and both women had red G-strings protruding from what was left of their mouths.

Banham turned to face the room. 'These are savage killings,' he said. 'This murderer must ...' But his voice stuck in his throat as images of his dead wife and mutilated baby banged around his brain. *Thank goodness for Alison*, he thought; *she'll help me out*.

She did.

'We do have a lead,' she said. 'The same souvenir was left with both women.'

He found his voice and carried on. 'Nineteen years ago, both women worked in the club where a man called Ahmed Abdullah was murdered. An identical pair of G-strings was left in his pocket.'

'Not a pair, guv. It's singular,' Isabelle Walsh said loudly.

Banham frowned uncomprehendingly.

'It's G-string, singular,' Isabelle repeated. 'Not a pair of G-strings.'

'OK. G-string, singular. That's our link.' His hand

covered his mouth briefly, and he continued, 'Brian Finn, the club bouncer, who served nineteen years for Abdullah's murder, is in custody.' He looked over at DC Crowther. 'Penny is carrying out forensic tests on his clothes as we speak.'

He turned back to the whiteboard and stared at the pictures.

Alison broke the silence. 'Brian Finn has been blackmailing the women that worked in that club. He has videos of them having sex with Ahmed Abdullah. The actress Katie Faye is one of them; another is the wife of the government minister Kenneth Stone. Susan Rogers had arranged to meet Brian Finn to hand over the blackmail money – and that's missing.'

Banham took over. 'We have nothing solid on Finn. And if it isn't him, the killer is out there, and the other four women's lives are in grave danger. I have put in a request to the Super for twenty-four-hour protection and surveillance for them. I'll feel a lot happier when that's in place. PC Judy Gardener's other half is one of the four women. Gardener has been given compassionate leave and will be with Kim twenty-four seven until we have the murderer. The fourth woman, Theresa McGann, is the mother of Brian's child.'

'Guv, I don't think Finn is our murderer,' Isabelle Walsh said loudly from the back of the room where she was perched on the edge of a desk with three male detectives. 'Why would he? The women had agreed to pay up. He didn't need to steal the money.'

'We didn't find any money on him when we picked

him up,' Alison said. 'And I don't think he was expecting us.'

'We need to concentrate on that club and those ... G-strings.' He paused and glanced at Alison. 'Why would the murderer leave those?'

'The club closed down a few years back, and everything was sold off,' said a tall detective standing close to Isabelle Walsh.

'Any records left?' Banham asked.

'I'm on to that, guv.'

'Good work, Les. Can you also find out all you can about Abdullah, the club owner? Relatives, friends, anything you can.'

'Katie Faye and Olivia Stone found Susan's body,' Alison said. 'They claim they arrived at the murder scene, separately. They have to be suspects as well as potential victims.'

'Katie and Olivia were searched on the premises,' Banham reminded her. 'They didn't have the blackmail money on them. I believe they're innocent.'

Alison looked at him doubtfully.

The fax machine on a desk at the back suddenly started whirring, and Crowther went to put paper in it. He had been sitting on an adjacent desk to Isabelle Walsh. Today he wore a cheap, shiny grey suit, the jacket of which was more than a tad too large; the shoulders were heading toward his elbows and the cuffs were turned back so there was more striped lining than grey fabric on his lower arms. He had matched the suit with an earth-brown shirt and a wide tie nearly the same colour. The centre of the lad's hair was gelled into spikes and, to Banham, he looked like a cross between a cockatoo and a punk rocker.

Banham knew Crowther was conscious of his lack of height; he had obviously been told, mistakenly, that gelling his hair would make him look taller. *What does it matter how tall he is anyway?* Women seemed to love him regardless of his lack of inches. Banham didn't understand why, but he did understand the lad was a great worker, and a clever detective. Like Isabelle, he came from a tough background, and was determined to make something of himself in the force. The pair enjoyed scoring off each other, and it meant they got results.

Crowther pulled the paper out of the fax machine and scanned it. 'Forensics tests in from Penny.'

Alison and Banham exchanged glances. Forensics were only done this quickly when Crowther was pleasing the beautiful Caribbean forensic supervisor. It didn't take detective work to know his affair with Penny was back on. Banham was glad; not only was it a great help to the case, it also meant that Crowther's fling with Isabelle was over, and they were back in competition.

One of the older detectives, who had gained inches on his waist as he'd lost his hair, looked speculatively at Isabelle, then at Crowther. 'Am I missing something here?'

'Such as?' Crowther said belligerently.

Isabelle laughed raucously. 'I'm just old-fashioned enough to want a man and not a mascot,' she said callously.

A ripple of laughter went round the room.

'Can we get on?' Banham shouted angrily. 'We are having to work with Bow Street on this one, and I want to stay on top of things. Col, what's in that forensic report?'

Crowther angrily pulled more paper from the fax machine. 'Unless he changed his clothes before jogging home last night, Finn is in the clear,' he snapped. He swept a glance round the whole room, letting his eyes rest on Isabelle. 'There's nothing to link Brian Finn to Susan Rogers. Not from any of the tests that Pen did.'

'Why would he change his clothes?' Alison said. 'He had no reason to expect us.'

'Unless he was tipped off,' Crowther suggested more calmly. 'A lot of people on that estate knew we were Old Bill.'

'Uniform are checking all the bins within a mile of Susan Rogers's shop,' Banham said. 'They're searching for the weapon, and they'll let us know if they find any clothing. The murderer would have blood on him, that's definite.'

'Or her,' Alison corrected. 'I'll get them to widen the search to Finn's estate. They could check for CCTV too.'

Crowther was still reading the forensic report. 'The clothes you took from the two women have no traces of Susan on them either. But Penny *has* found a pubic hair on the knickers left in Shaheen's mouth.' His face brightened. 'There's a faded initial too. She's working on that.'

'Terrific,' said Banham. He looked across at the older detective with thinning hair and expanding waist. 'Get the FME to take a pubic hair from Brian Finn.'

'Guv.'

'Any updates on Shaheen Hakhti?' Banham asked.

The family liaison officer raised his hand. 'Her husband reported her missing on January thirty-first when she didn't come home. We have CCTV footage of her, arriving at St Pancras. She was wearing the same clothes she was found in.'

'Judy Gardener said she was planning to stay with Susan Rogers,' Isabelle added.

'So how did she end up down here?' Banham mused. 'Crowther, get a search warrant before I have to release Finn, then go and turn his mother's flat over. You're looking for the videos and the hundred grand cash. Better still, red G-strings.' He looked across at Isabelle. 'How is the research going on the knickers?'

Isabelle shrugged. 'They're over twenty years old. No one manufactures them here – they came from China. The sex shops I tried all said they look like old stock, but no one was a hundred per cent on a photo; they need to see the real thing.'

'That'll have to do for the moment. Isabelle, you and Alison go and talk to Kenneth Stone. Use that feminine charm of yours.' Alison looked at him, the dark flecks in her eyes growing. *She's in a strange mood again*. He carried on, 'Stone met Olivia at that club. He has a lot to lose if those videos ever made it to the *News of the World*. Get him to account for every second of his movements last night. Assure him it's all off the record, or he'll clam up. Then bring him in. Looks like we need a sample of his pubic hair – tell him it's to eliminate him from our enquiry.'

He continued to brief members of the team for a few more minutes, and they began to drift away.

'I've got today's best job,' Crowther said with a cheeky grin.

'Only if you find the videos,' Isabelle said grabbing her coat and making sure it hit him in the face. 'You never know, there might be one with instructions on how to keep it up!'

A whole morning ahead in Isabelle Walsh's company. Alison's heart was already sinking into her shoes.

Isabelle munched on a large packet of Maltesers on the way to the Stones' house, talking all the while into her mobile phone. Her washing machine had broken down, and the constant crunch of the chocolates and endless dialogue explaining the problems she'd had with the spin began to get on Alison's nerves. She gritted her teeth and accelerated noisily away from the traffic lights, shaking her head irritably as Isabelle pushed the inviting smell of chocolate under her nose. She needed to lose three or maybe even five pounds, then her tiny bust wouldn't look quite so bad against her wide hips. Yesterday, apart from black coffee, she had fasted, so the smell of Isabelle's chocolate was the last thing she needed.

It wasn't that she disliked Isabelle; sometimes she was fun to have around, and she was an excellent source of gossip. But she irritated Alison, who knew her well enough to know the young DC would sell her own soul – or anyone else's – to get what she wanted. And at the moment that was promotion.

Isabelle had moved into CID after a brief affair with a very senior, very married officer. She cultivated the right people as friends, and she was clever and astute. That made her a good detective, which Alison admired – although she didn't admire the way Isabelle made use of her detective skills to discover people's weaknesses. She had found out about Alison's disastrous date with Banham; when Alison asked her how, Isabelle had tapped her nose and replied, 'Woman's intuition.' A more likely answer was eavesdropping – and it hadn't stopped Isabelle from flirting with Banham under Alison's nose. Banham didn't even notice.

Until recently, the flirting wouldn't have worried Alison; Banham had given her every reason to believe he wasn't interested in a relationship with anyone. But of late things had changed. He had started to look at pretty women in a different way. He couldn't take his eyes off Katie Faye. Isabelle too was very pretty, despite her loud, coarse mouth; and Banham was naïve when it came to women. Alison couldn't bear the thought of him being with Isabelle, with her twenty-two inch waist and skin clear as purified water. How unfair was that? Alison lived on Ryvita and black coffee and spent her spare time in the gym, working off the excess on her hips and thighs to compensate for having no bust. Isabelle had great boobs, and said she got all the exercise she needed chasing criminals; her diet consisted of chocolate and milky lattes and butties dripping with bacon and ketchup. Life was a bitch sometimes.

Isabelle finally fixed her washing machine repair

appointment and clicked her phone shut.

'Can we forget our domestic problems now, please, and concentrate on the case?' Alison snapped.

Isabelle crumpled the empty Maltesers bag and dropped it on the floor. 'Oh dear. You're in one of your "I'm the sergeant" moods,' she said dryly.

'I *am* the sergeant, as it happens,' Alison replied. 'So here's what I've decided. When we get there, I talk to the women and ask them to come in and give a DNA sample, while you take a statement from Kenneth Stone and tell him we need some pubic hair from him. Use your charm; he's a difficult man, and a potential suspect. We need to get him into the station, but we can't arrest him till we have something on him.'

Isabelle nodded. 'Sounds good to me.'

'You need to push him for everything you can about the Scarlet Pussy Club. Banham asked you to deal with Stone, because he knows you're good at getting what you want out of men.'

'Hey, I resent that.'

'I'd take it as a compliment if I were you.'

Alison turned the car into an unmade road. A painted sign saying "CHERRY TREE WALK" was nailed to a large tree; its branches swung out into the road, partly blocking the view ahead. The car bumped its way over the potholes.

'What's going on with you and Crowther?' she asked Isabelle.

'You mind your own!' Isabelle joshed.

'Damn! Look at that!' A stone flew out from under the

front wheel and smacked into the bodywork of Alison's green Golf.

'I hope the DI hasn't used up too much of the budget on blow-up dolls from the sex shop,' Isabelle said sarcastically. 'You're going to need some for car repairs.'

'I'll send Ken Stone the bill,' Alison retorted, pulling up at the bottom of the Stones' vast U-shaped driveway. She decided against driving up to the house, parking instead beside a bush by the gate. From here she could observe the house and most of the drive, where there were already four cars parked: Katie Faye's BMW, a shining silver Mercedes, Olivia Stone's brand new royal blue convertible Mini, and another, older BMW.

She teased Isabelle as they walked up to the house. 'Is Crowther not good in bed, then?'

Isabelle ignored the remark and stopped to examine the cars. 'He must get a deal with BMW,' she said. 'One of the perks of being a Right Honourable.'

'If I see you driving one, I'll know who your next conquest is,' Alison teased again.

'You're the one who'll need a new car,' Isabelle retorted.

They reached the Mercedes with its personalised registration: KS 001. 'Do you think that stands for marks out of ten?' Alison joked.

Isabelle laughed crudely. 'Crowther's got a beat-up Cadillac with zero-zero-zero on the plate. Does that answer your question?'

Olivia's son Kevin opened the door. 'Sergeant. Hello again. Mum and Auntie Katie are still upstairs. Come in and I'll give them a call.'

'Your father too, please,' Alison said, wiping her feet on the doormat. Isabelle ignored it and walked straight into the wide hall regardless of the mud on her boots. 'We'd like to see him first. He is expecting us.'

'Oh.' Kevin looked surprised. 'Dad's not here. He's gone to the House.'

'Isn't that his car in the drive?' Isabelle asked.

Katie Faye appeared at the top of the elegant curved staircase which snaked across the hall. She hurried down as fast as her Moroccan-style mules would allow, pushing her arms into a dressing gown that matched her long, royal blue silk nightdress. 'Please don't say something else has happened?' she said, pulling the sash around her trim waist.

Her hair was uncombed and she wore no make-up. Dark rings under her eyes hinted at lack of sleep. Alison noticed a small pimple on her chin, and wondered if Banham would have found her quite so irresistible this morning.

'No, nothing else,' Alison reassured her. She introduced Isabelle and explained the reason for the visit. 'We came to talk to Mr Stone too,' she added.

Fear clouded Katie's eyes. 'Why do you want to talk to him?'

'We need to ask him a few questions, that's all.'

'And we need a sample from him too,' Isabelle said.

Alison glared at her. 'For elimination.'

'He's not here,' Katie said.

'His car is,' Alison pointed out.

Katie's eyes flicked in the direction of the drive, then back at Kevin.

'He often gets picked up by a driver,' he said quickly.

Katie was clearly edgy. She walked to the front door and opened it.

'The driver parks outside, does he?' Alison asked.

Kevin nodded.

'It's just that there are no fresh tyre marks in the gravel.'

Katie closed the door. 'Thank you for your concern,' she said in the soft, sweet voice she used on television as Staff Nurse Penelope. 'Do have some coffee before you go. Olivia and I will make our own way to your station as soon as we're dressed. Kevin will stay with us.'

Alison gave up. 'Please tell Mr Stone we'll come back this evening,' she said. 'We'll expect you and Mrs Stone at the station in a couple of hours.' She put a hand on the door handle and was about to open it when voices sounded from upstairs. 'Has your mother got guests?' she asked Kevin pointedly.

'I think that's the radio,' Kevin answered quickly. 'And my sister is upstairs.'

Alison blew out a sigh. 'Miss Faye, we're concerned for your safety,' she said. 'We will find whoever killed your friends, but we'll do it more quickly with your help.'

Katie wrapped her arms round her body and shivered. Alison had to admit she was good at the vulnerable look.

Kevin slipped his arm around her. 'It's all right, Auntie Katie, I'll look after you and Mum. I won't leave either of you alone. Not even with Dad.' He looked at Alison.

'I'm retaking my A-levels,' he told her. 'I can study anywhere. I'll drive Mum and Auntie Katie to the police station this morning.'

Alison opened her mouth to ask him how he planned to defend them against a knife-wielding maniac whose intention was probably to kill them. Then she closed it again, and dug in her pocket for a card with her mobile number on it. She handed it to Katie. 'We'll expect you both in a couple of hours,' she told her. 'And if anything happens, either of you can call me, night or day.'

'What about Theresa?' Katie blurted. 'Who's looking out for her? She's got Brian Finn's daughter, but she won't talk to him ... Bernadette's mentally handicapped...'

'At the moment we have Brian Finn in custody,' Alison told her. 'And by lunchtime you'll all be under twenty-four hour police protection.'

'Doesn't Theresa live with her mother?' Isabelle asked.

'Have you met her?' Kevin said disdainfully. 'She's a liability – always drunk. I'll phone Theresa. She can stay here too, with Bernadette. I grew up with Berny. I used to babysit her. We're the same age, but ... well, you know. I've done self-defence classes, I'll look after you all.'

'He was definitely there,' Isabelle said a few minutes later as they clicked their seat belts. Alison started to do a u-turn, backing the car over flying stones and cursing as a wheel hit in a large pothole.

'Careful,' Isabelle shouted as Alison reversed angrily. 'There's a big bush behind you.'

'I've seen it,' Alison snapped, reversing into it.

Isabelle laughed. 'Only one more scratch, no one will

notice. What kind of bush grows to that height and colour in the middle of February?'

'I didn't have *any* scratches till I started to drive down this road,' Alison snapped. 'And with the kind of money they've got, they can afford a gardener to come in every day.' Isabelle was being really irritating. She raised her voice. 'And I know he's bloody well there.'

'Some gardener, to get it that big.' Isabelle realised what she'd said and burst out laughing.

'You've got size on the brain,' Alison told her. 'The question is, why doesn't he want to talk to us?'

Her mobile buzzed, and she pulled the car into the side of the road before glancing at the number display. 'Well!' she exclaimed. 'Would you believe it?'

CHAPTER EIGHT

Olivia faced the dressing table mirror and pulled the brush through her hair. Kenneth was perched on the side of his bed, phone to his ear and plastic charm fully stretched.

'Hello, Inspector, I'm so sorry ...' There was a brief pause. 'Oh ... Sergeant? Surely not? I really thought you were the one in charge.'

Olivia rolled her eyes and went on brushing her hair.

'I must have just missed you,' Kenneth continued. 'I was in a meeting.' His lips stretched into a false smile as he listened. 'To the station? Well, of course, to eliminate me from your enquiries, why else? It will be a pleasure. I have meetings all day, but for you I'll fit it in.' He turned angry eyes on Olivia. 'Yes, this morning if possible, or as soon as I can. Many thanks. I'll see you later.'

He clicked the phone off with a sharp snap and stood up, his face like thunder.

Olivia knew that look, but decided to brave it out.

'It's only a DNA test,' she soothed. 'You heard what they said to Katie; we're all doing one, just for elimination.'

His face grew redder as his temper bubbled up. 'I'm a respected government minister. If this gets in the papers ... you said there would be a storm in a teacup when Finn came out, and now we're involved in murder, blackmail and God knows what else.'

'You should have seen it coming.' Olivia tried and failed to keep her voice level. 'If you hadn't refused to pay Brian off in the first place, none of this would have happened.'

'Haven't I already paid out enough? And why the hell didn't you tell me the bastard was blackmailing you? I had to hear it from bloody Dixon of Dock Green last night.'

'I didn't tell you because I knew how you'd react!' She turned back to the mirror and lowered her voice. 'Look, it won't make the papers, and it won't wreck your career. The police don't want to ruin their case.' She picked up a hairbrush and started to pull hair out of it. 'There are people more influential than you around,' she added almost in a whisper.

Suddenly he was upon her. He grabbed her by the upper arm, pulled her up and twisted her round so she had to look at his face.

'Stop it, you're hurting…'

His nails pinched the thin skin on her arms, then his grip loosened. As she pulled her arm away, his clenched fist whacked her in the eye. Her hand flew to the spot; the edge of his thick gold signet ring had caught the skin under her brow and a trickle of warm blood ran over her fingers.

Footsteps galloping up the stairs were followed by urgent rapping on the door. 'Mum? Mum, are you all right?'

Ken's temper vanished as quickly as it had erupted. 'It's all right, Kevin,' he called. 'Everything's fine.' He pulled a clean handkerchief from his pocket and held it against Olivia's eye.

'I'm fine, darling,' she confirmed, controlling her voice with an effort. 'I just bumped into the wardrobe.'

'I'm so sorry,' Ken whispered. 'I don't know what came over me.'

'No. You never do, at least not when you're sober.'

More banging on the door was followed by Katie's and Ianthe's voices.

'Livvy, are you sure you're OK?'

'Mummy, has Daddy hurt you again?'

'Open the door! Open the bloody door! Dad, if you've hurt Mum, I'll bloody kill you.' Kevin's voice drowned out the sound of Ianthe crying.

Olivia snatched the handkerchief from Ken and pushed him away. 'It's all right, Kev. I'll be down in a minute. I can't let you in, I'm getting dressed. We've all got to go to the police station.'

Judy Gardener was cutting slices of pink beef with an electric carving knife. Two plates balanced upside down on the cooker to warm, and beside them were two bubbling saucepans.

As Kim walked into the kitchen, the phone on the table started chirping. The two women looked at the phone, then each other.

'Shall I answer it?' Kim asked nervously.

Judy stopped carving and wiped her large hands on the navy and white striped apron tied around her waist. 'No, I will.'

It was Isabelle Walsh. As Judy listened to what she had

to say, Kim's small-boned face grew more and more anxious. Kim was in her usual choice of attire – a fawn tracksuit – and today the neutral colour wasn't doing her any favours at all. She looked pale and thin, and there was a red, angry eruption of acne around her nose and cheeks. Her big brown eyes reminded Judy of a terrified rabbit facing a hunter's gun.

She replaced the phone on its cradle. 'Nothing vital,' she said. 'They'll need a hair sample from you at the station, that's all. We'll go as soon as you've eaten this meal.'

'It smells great,' Kim said flatly. 'I only wish I had an appetite.'

'Please try,' Judy said, conscious of a little more irritation in her tone than she wanted to show. 'You need to eat.' She opened the fridge, filled a glass from a carton of apple juice and handed it to Kim. 'Nothing will happen to you, Sausage. I'll protect you.'

Kim took the drink and sipped it, then set it down and picked up one of the saucepans to drain it. 'What exactly does this hair sample entail?' she asked.

'Just let the FME take some of your pubic hair, that's all.'

'The who?'

'Forensic medical examiner. It'll be over in a couple of seconds.'

Fear clouded Kim's eyes again.

'It won't hurt,' Judy reassured her. 'They've found a hair, and they just need to eliminate all you girls.'

'I don't understand.'

Judy sighed. 'If the knickers are the real thing, from your strip club, anyone who wore them could have left a stray pube on them.'

She pointed at the table, and Kim obediently sat down. Judy put a plate of roast beef and vegetables in front of her, picked up the knife and fork and put them in Kim's hands. 'Early lunch,' she said gently. 'Eat. Please.'

'Couldn't *you* do the test?' Kim said.

Judy didn't move. 'No, I ... can't.'

'But you just said you'd protect me.'

'I will,' Judy insisted. 'I'm staying by your side night and day.'

Kim began to cut her meat into tiny strips. Judy sat down at the table and fixed her eyes on her partner. 'I went up into the loft last night.'

'What for?' Kim's fork stopped halfway to her mouth.

'You know what for. I needed to see if there were any red G-strings in the costume trunk.'

Kim's knife fell with a clatter, and Judy leaned towards her. 'Kim, I love you, and I will protect you – but you haven't told the police everything, have you?'

Kim looked down at her plate. 'What do you mean?'

'They don't know we bought some of the club costumes when they auctioned all that old gear off.'

'I didn't get them all. Someone else bought the other trunks ... I didn't want to put the cat among the pigeons, that's all.'

Judy looked at her.

'I didn't get the red G-strings.'

'Not all of them, no.'

Kim shook her head vigorously. 'We bid for the trunk with the sequinned bikinis and the feathered showgirl stuff, remember?'

'Yes, I remember.'

'It was you who saw the advert for the auction,' Kim reminded her. 'You suggested we might get the costumes very cheap. You even signed the cheque.'

'I remember.'

'So what else is there to tell?'

'I don't know, Kim. You tell me.'

It was nearly lunchtime. Theresa McGann ran up the twelve flights of stairs to her flat. Graffiti covered the walls around her, fast food containers and old papers blew about in the February wind, and a used condom squelched under her cheap boots.

They had kept her waiting longer than she had hoped at the police station, and she needed to get back before the valium she had given Bernadette wore off – and before her mother woke up and needed a gin to start the day.

When the police had rung and requested a hair sample from her, for elimination, she almost laughed. Hers would have been instantly recognisable. Nineteen years ago she had long hair, naturally bright red. Now it was cut like a boy's and almost completely faded to grey. Both then and now, her hair was quite different from the other girls'; three of them were blonde, all courtesy of a bottle, and Shaheen was naturally dark, although also faded to grey now. Kim was the only one with natural hair untouched by chemicals, and hers was dark brown.

The interview had been unnerving. When they told her they were holding Brian in custody and he had admitted blackmailing them, she had played naïve, and pretended she knew little about it. She had felt herself blush when the young detective told her Brian could go back to prison.

Now, bounding up the stairs, she feared the consequences of what she had done. A month or so ago Olivia had told her Kenneth was going back on his word, refusing to give her and Brian the lump sum they needed to start a new life. Getting Brian to blackmail Katie and Olivia had been her idea. Brian had agreed; he was an innocent, too nice for his own good; he'd do anything for her and Berny. And the police were clever enough to realise that. If they found out she was behind it, she could go to prison, and then what would happen to Bernadette?

She had spent nineteen years watching Olivia and Katie have it all. She'd had no choice but to accept their handouts – but now Brian was out, she wanted to start again. And they couldn't do that without money. It hadn't seemed such a crime at the time, seeing that Brian had gone to prison for them. But now it was different; there was a murderer on the prowl. Someone who knew about Ahmed Abdullah's death, it seemed.

So who knew about their secret? It was just the six of them, wasn't it, apart from Brian. It certainly wasn't him. He was as thick as a sledgehammer, and he would never hurt a woman.

She ducked under the washing lines that blocked the walkway to her flat and quietly unlocked her front door. There was no sound of crying or shouting; her mother's gin-soaked night and her daughter's valium were still working. She breathed a sigh of relief; she had peace and quiet for a little longer.

She stared miserably at her face in the kitchen mirror. She was thirty-eight years old and she looked fifty. Her skin was prematurely lined, her wild red hair was now colourless and dull and disgracefully cut with the kitchen scissors. Her tracksuit and trainers had more than had their day.

And Olivia Stone and Katie Faye drove around in top of the range cars, and were groomed like Hollywood idols. They had been good to her; they'd kept her mum in gin and been very kind to Bernadette – but so they should've. If Brian hadn't done a nineteen-year stretch and kept schtum, they certainly wouldn't be living the high life. She and Brian deserved that hundred grand.

But where was it? The police said the money was missing.

Her hands were shaking. The police had promised twenty-four hour protection, and she was glad, because she was very scared.

She hadn't really believed Shaheen's death was anything to do with the club. They'd never got on anyway, and Shaheen was responsible for the whole thing kicking off that fateful night at the Scarlet Pussy Club. She had just walked away and let Brian take the rap; she hadn't even done anything for Bernadette, who was born without a father because of her. Theresa had no intention of mourning her death.

But Susan Rogers had remained a close friend all

through those nineteen years. She'd visited Brian regularly, and had always looked after Berny, even when she had very little herself. And now she had been murdered! But by whom? The young detective had said it had to be someone who knew about the club, and the dirty videos they'd made.

The videos were here in the flat. She had kept them since Brian went down, as security, in case the flow of money from Olivia dried up. She was in two of them herself: in one she was giving Ahmed a blow job, and in the second she was sitting astride him while he smacked her bare bottom with a horse's whip. She didn't want Brian to see them, and she certainly didn't want to explain why there was more than one.

Perhaps she should dump them. The police had said Susan's killer had taken the money, and it was unlikely Olivia and Katie would come up with another hundred grand.

She knelt in front of the cupboard and reached into the back for the videos. If the police were going to be around she needed to get rid of them, and quickly.

But where?

CHAPTER NINE

Banham was on his computer, searching the criminal records programme. Katie Faye wasn't listed. He was pleased about that. Olivia Stone too was squeaky clean, and so were Shaheen Hakhti-Watkins and Susan Rogers.

Theresa McGann was next. Banham wasn't surprised to read she had been charged with shoplifting three times, and once with causing affray. He double-clicked on her name for more details.

She and her mother, Sarah McGann, had been in a fight with the manager of an off-licence. The police had been called, and the pair were arrested and charged after threatening the shop manager with a broken bottle.

He was pretty sure Kim, the nervous, mouse-like girlfriend of PC Judy Gardener, would have previous. The list of petty drug offences proved to be as long as one of her skinny arms, right to the bird tattoo that decorated her shoulder. It was all very minor; it wasn't as if she'd been a dealer.

Banham pushed his fingers through the front of his curly, flyaway hair. It kept falling over his eyes, a reminder that Lottie had told him to get a trim. He should have listened; she knew that when his hair reached his collar it started to curl, reminding him of his hated school nickname – Girlie-whirly.

Brian Finn was next. He had been in front of a magistrate many times for brawling, before he was found guilty of the murder of Ahmed Abdullah.

There was a knock at the door. Colin Crowther stood there, looking despondent. Banham had to fight to keep a straight face; the turn-ups on Crowther's sleeves really did resemble a roll of carpet.

'Finn's flat is clean, guv. We turned the fucker upside down. There ain't a single pornographic video there.' He shrugged. 'We've nothing to hold him on, and time's pressing on.'

'What about his DNA? That pubic hair?'

'Not his, guv.'

Banham rubbed his mouth. 'Has Penny finished with the G-string that was left with Shaheen Hakhti's body?'

Crowther nodded. 'It's in a plastic exhibit bag in the incident room.'

'Show it to Kim Davis when she comes in. See if she can tell us if it's from the club.'

'Guv.'

As Crowther turned to go Banham's face broke into a grin. 'Alison and Isabelle rang in,' he said. 'They're running a bit late. They've got a puncture, and Alison isn't in a good mood.' He became serious again. 'They had a wasted journey too. Kenneth Stone wasn't at home.'

Crowther smiled back but made no comment. Banham knew he was on his best behaviour at the moment; a sergeant's post had become vacant, and Col was taking great care not to fall out with anyone.

'Stone did ring Alison,' Banham added. 'He said he'd

been in a meeting and was on his way in to give us his DNA sample, as are his wife and Katie Faye.'

Crowther scratched the back of his gelled hair. 'Let's wait and see if he turns up. If he doesn't, can I arrest him, guv?'

'You can certainly have that pleasure,' Banham told him. 'And if he comes of his own accord, I can't think of a better person to interview him.'

The smile that lit up Crowther's face was short-lived as Banham added, 'And when Isabelle and Alison get back, you and Isabelle can take Olivia Stone's statement. And yes, I know you and Isabelle aren't exactly best buddies at the moment.' Crowther said nothing. 'But if you're going to bed all the women on the team then drop them, you have to learn to work with them afterwards.'

'Not all of them, guv. Only two,' Crowther said quietly. 'Isabelle was a moment of madness. I'm back with Penny now.'

Banham studied his favourite DC. 'Can't have moments of madness if you want to be a sergeant, son. Patch up your differences. We're a team, remember.'

'I'll remember, guvnor.' Crowther turned to leave. 'You'll be interviewing Katie Faye, will you, guvnor?' he asked casually, his back to Banham.

Banham wasn't aware anyone had noticed that he was attracted to Katie Faye, but Crowther obviously had. 'Yes,' he said curtly.

'What about Finn, guv?' Crowther turned back to face him, the remnants of a smirk on his lips.

'What time is the twenty-four hour protection for the

women scheduled to start?' Banham asked.

'I'm told around lunchtime. But we don't know to the minute.'

'OK.' Banham nodded. 'After Katie and Olivia and Kim have given their statements, check none of them will be on their own, then let Finn go.'

As Crowther left the room, Banham enjoyed a few seconds of amusement at the thought of Alison's reaction when she got the puncture. He half-wished he had been with her to change the tyre, but she was too independent to allow that. She was a stubborn Taurean, and never gave in. He was afraid that same stubbornness would work against him; now that counselling had given him hope and things were finally beginning to work for him, he wanted nothing more than to take her to dinner again and ask if they could start over. But that stubborn streak would never let her agree.

He reached for the phone and dialled his sister's number. *Engaged again.* He picked up his polystyrene cup of sweet, muddy coffee and walked to the window sipping from it. A dark blue BMW pulled up with Kevin Stone in the driving seat. He watched him drop his parents and Katie Faye, then drive off to park.

Banham drained his cup and tossed it in the bin.

'Crowther!' he called as he passed the incident room.

They were at the front desk to meet them as they walked in.

Crowther took them all to separate interview rooms. As Banham stood at the front desk leaving word for Alison, Kevin Stone walked in. 'I'd like to speak to someone about a domestic violence issue,' he said to the desk sergeant.

'I'll deal with this,' Banham interrupted. He put his hand out to shake Kevin's. 'Shall we go somewhere more private?'

Kevin refused tea or coffee and sat opposite Banham, looking very nervous.

'You saw my mother's face, Inspector,' he said hesitantly. 'The bruises, and the cut on her forehead. Mum wouldn't admit it for the world, but I'm sure my father did it.'

'Has it happened before?'

'They're always rowing. Mainly when he's been drinking, though it seems to have got worse recently. I suppose it's the stress – these murders are a bit too close for comfort.'

'And he's often violent, is he?'

Kevin didn't reply.

'I know it's difficult, but if I'm going to help you…'

'OK, OK. Yes, he gets violent.'

'With all of you, or just your mother?'

'Put it this way – I failed my A-levels last summer. I didn't dare pass, because that would have meant going away to university and leaving Mum and Ianthe alone with him. Ianthe's having nightmares again. Dad picks on her, and Mum sides with Dad because she's afraid of him. If I'm not there, Ianthe will have no one. He doesn't have a go at me any more – not now I'm taller than him.'

Banham's jaw tightened. Kenneth Stone had a wife and two children, and this was the way he treated them. He studied the nervous teenager, who was trying hard to be grown-up. His features were so like his mother's; his eyes were the same unusual violet as Olivia's. He had fine-boned artist's hands, with long nails that looked dirty against his bright white shirt.

Banham leaned his elbow on the desk, and chose his words carefully. 'You're saying he's always been violent?' he asked Kevin.

The boy shrugged. 'It goes in phases. It had stopped recently. A couple of months ago he went too far and knocked Mum unconscious. But then it started again this morning.'

'This morning?'

'Dad was upstairs in the bedroom with Mum. He saw your two women detectives coming up the drive and told me to say he wasn't in. I did as I was told and they left. After they'd gone I heard a thump, and Mum cried out. The door was locked and I couldn't get in to help her.'

The boy grew more and more distressed. 'Did he hit her with anything?' Banham asked him.

'No. I don't think so. He's always been jealous because Mum is so attractive. And he doesn't want the press to find out she was a whore.'

'A whore?' This was news to Banham.

'Well, a stripper. A club hostess. It boils down to the same thing.'

'I see.' Banham interlocked his fingers under his chin. 'Who told you that?'

'What, that Mum was a stripper? Dad did. And he calls Mum a whore every time he hits her. Ianthe and I try to stop him.' The boy was clearly traumatised. He dragged his hand down his face. 'He keeps on about Mum working at that club. Says it could ruin our lives.' He looked at Banham. 'But if it was such a dreadful place, why did he go there? That's what Mum always shouts at him.'

'What do you want me to do, Kevin?'

'Stop him hurting my mother and sister.'

'Will your mother back you up, do you think?'

'No, never. She's much too loyal.'

Banham lowered his eyes, trying to stay calm. He would have liked to get hold of Kenneth Stone and knock him senseless. He abhorred men who hit women – and as for hitting children, Banham couldn't allow his mind to go there.

'Can you persuade your sister to give me a statement?'

'I can't.' Kevin leaned across the desk. 'He'd really hurt us. This has to be in confidence. I can't write anything down, or sign a statement. And you can't ask Ianthe. She's only thirteen – she'd never sleep again.'

A muscle in Banham's face began to twitch. 'What about Katie Faye? She's your mum's friend. Would *she* make a statement?'

Kevin shook his head. 'She'd never go against Mum's wishes. They're really close. Mum and Aunt Katie used to do a lesbian act. Not that they're ... you know. It was only an act.'

The feelings aroused by the thought of Katie Faye and Olivia Stone together took Banham by surprise. But that did nothing to dampen his anger. 'Kevin, I'm glad you've told me all this,' he said, getting to his feet. 'But I have to work within the law. I can't do anything unless one of you is prepared to make a statement.'

Kevin stayed in his chair. 'I can look after myself,' he said, 'but I won't put my little sister or my mother at risk.'

There was a notepad on the table. Banham took a pen from his pocket and put it in front of Kevin. 'You'd be protecting them in the long run,' he said, walking towards the door. 'Think about it. I'll be back in twenty minutes.'

Alison was back at her desk drinking black coffee by the time Banham returned to the incident room. Her eyes had that close-set, squirrelly look, and her eyebrows seemed thicker than ever. She was dressed in brown corduroy trousers and a short tan calfskin jacket, and both bore evidence that she'd been lying in the wet road. Her khaki scarf was wrapped around her neck several times. Her feet were bare, and her boots and thick socks stood by the radiator drying out. There were small bits of twig in her loose, wild hair.

Banham had trouble keeping a straight face when he saw her, although he knew she would be in one of her famous tempers. She looked up, the black flecks shining out from her eyes. This wasn't the time to enquire about the health of her car.

'I hear you're releasing Finn,' she said.

'We have to. Nothing to hold him for, all the forensics came up negative on him.'

Crowther appeared in the doorway. 'Katie Faye and Olivia Stone are waiting to be interviewed,' he told Banham. 'Isabelle and I have taken a statement from Kenneth Stone. He was with friends at the time of Susan's murder. It checks out, if you believe anything a politician says. The FME took a hair sample from him.'

'I've just been talking to his son,' Banham said. 'He's too nervous to put it in writing, but he says Stone is violent to his wife and children. He's terrified for his mother and sister.'

'They'll be under twenty-four hour surveillance before long,' Isabelle reminded him. 'If he gets violent, he'll be arrested.'

Banham picked up Kenneth Stone's statement and read it. He put it on his desk, and rubbed his hand over his mouth. 'Right, Alison, you might want to put something on your feet. We're going to take Katie Faye's statement. Crowther, you and Isabelle can interview Olivia Stone.' He looked at Isabelle and back at Crowther. 'And since you've got such a way with women, try and persuade Mrs Stone to tell us about the bruises on her face. Ask her what Ken Stone is really like to live with.'

Alison was trying to flick twigs out of her hair and slide her feet back in her boots at the same time. 'Katie Faye,' she said, her tone a mixture of ice and venom.

Crowther was making the most of the moment. He was pleased that Isabelle was sitting beside him, even gladder that her face was like thunder, as they watched the lovely Mrs Olivia Stone remove her elegant faux-fur coat and hang it over the back of the chair. Her scarlet nails and shiny red mouth matched her silk blouse, and strands of her glossy, perfectly cut pageboy-style hair stuck to her glossy lips. Crowther watched as she fiddled with it and flicked it back, then tilt her head and sigh heavily.

Crowther sat back in his seat. He could read these signals. The woman was trying to hide her uneasiness.

'Can I smoke?' She fumbled at the buckle of her leather handbag and brought out a gold lighter followed by a packet of Dunhill Menthol.

'Course.' Crowther picked up the lighter and held it out, ready to light her cigarette. 'You'll be under police protection from this afternoon. We're going to keep you safe,' he assured her, watching her ample bosom rise as she inhaled deeply on the smoke.

'Thank you.'

'And we will catch this killer,' Isabelle added, though not very reassuringly, Crowther thought.

One of Olivia's eyes was swollen and puffy; she noticed Crowther looking and gave a small smile.

'Your husband must be nervous too,' he said.

She nodded, and flicked the tip of the cigarette over the ashtray he had taken out of the drawer. 'If this gets into the papers he could lose his job.'

'At this moment we're more concerned about your life,' Crowther said.

'So, as precisely as you can, can you tell us your movements last night, until you discovered the body of Susan Rogers,' Isabelle said.

'I've been through all this with Inspector Banham.'

'We know,' Crowther said sympathetically. 'But you're a material witness. And you'd had a bad shock last night; things might have come back to you since then. So as much detail as you can give us. Every moment you can remember. Please.'

His eyes dropped to her bosom, which rose with another nervous sigh.

Alison felt like a scarecrow. When she flicked her hair behind her ears, a puff of dust flew out and a small twig fell free. She shook her head as discreetly as she could. Her clothes smelled of rubber and oil from the tyre she had changed, and more tiny particles of evidence were distributed about her hair.

Banham's full attention was on the lovely Katie Faye, who sat opposite them looking fresh and pretty and smelling of expensive perfume.

On the table in front of Katie lay a transparent plastic evidence bag containing the stained, torn remnants of the G-string left in Shaheen Hakhti's mouth. Katie pushed her knuckles against her mouth and stared at it. Then she looked up, and those huge, wide-set blue eyes stared helplessly at Banham from under her fringe.

His voice was gentle as he asked, 'I realise how difficult this is for you, but do you think this is one of the G-strings from the club you worked in?'

Katie swallowed hard and nodded. 'They look the same.'

'There's an initial on this pair. We think it may be an S. Would that be S for Susan?'

Katie's face crumpled. She squeezed her lips together, then nodded again.

Banham turned to Alison. 'Could you take these next door now?' he said. Crowther and Isabelle were with

Olivia Stone in the next interview room.

As Alison stood up, he gave his full attention to Katie Faye again.

Crowther placed the evidence bag containing the knickers in front of Olivia. 'Could they be the same ones you wore during your stint in that Scarlet Pussy Club?' he asked.

Isabelle was surprised to see Olivia blush as she stared at the knickers. She nodded. 'They've got that same cheap, shiny finish ...' She paused and swallowed, then blushed again. Her voice was barely audible as she continued, 'Even though they're so filthy and ... bloodstained.'

'There's an initial,' Isabelle said. 'It looks like an S – for Shaheen, perhaps? Did you each write your initials on your own?'

Olivia shook her head. 'We didn't use our names. We were only teenagers, but we weren't stupid. We didn't want to leave behind anything that said we'd ever worked there. We all used pseudonyms.'

The perfectly kept hands with long manicured nails rubbed the base of her neck. 'There was a big bag of those G-strings in the dressing room.' She shook her head. 'Well, the tip we changed in.' She seemed to grow distressed. 'Susan was in charge. She told us to take two pairs each and write a name, or an initial, on them. We took them home with us and washed them ourselves.' Her bosom heaved again, and her eyes began to fill up. She blinked the tears back and went on, 'To be honest I really don't remember what names we were using then. We changed them a few times. I do remember Theresa was called Cherry, for a while anyway. I can't remember the others, though.'

'Not even your own?' Isabelle asked sharply.

She blushed again. 'Katie and I did a double act. Sometimes I was Candy Floss and sometimes she was. I don't think either of us knew or cared.'

'What was the other called?' Crowther asked.

Olivia paused. 'Strawberry,' she said after a few moments. 'That was it. Strawberry.' She gave Crowther a quick, nervous frown.

'But which was which?' he insisted.

'They were interchangeable. It didn't seem important.'

'But you said you kept your own G-strings and initialled them,' Isabelle pushed. 'What initial did you mark on yours?'

Olivia lifted both her hands. 'You know, I really can't remember,' she said.

When Banham walked back into the incident room, Isabelle was sitting on the edge of her desk, legs crossed, swirling the froth of her over-sweetened cappuccino with a straw and sucking the toffee toppings from it.

Crowther was at the next desk, on the phone to Penny about the forensic tests.

Alison was feeling desperately in need of a shower, but for a moment she forgot how embarrassed she'd felt, looking like a scarecrow in front of the lovely Katie Faye. She was almost sorry for Isabelle, sitting next to the man she wanted, watching him engrossed in another woman. Alison knew just how she felt.

She couldn't work out whether her dislike of Katie Faye was jealousy or copper's instinct. For the time being she decided to keep her feelings to herself.

'OK, what have we got?' Banham asked.

'Ask Know-All Col,' Isabelle said sourly. 'He's got everything.' She uncrossed her legs, jumped down from her desk and threw her paper cup in the bin.

Crowther's nickname had been Know-All Col since he first joined the force. His connections in the East End meant he always knew the right person for the job; in fact he seemed to have useful contacts just about everywhere, and made a point of letting everyone know he had.

He replaced his phone on the cradle. 'Fax coming through from forensics,' he told Banham. 'This morning's DNA test on the hair won't be back until tomorrow morning, but…'

'Yes, we know,' Isabelle said loudly. 'They normally take three days. Penny is doing you a favour!'

Crowther flicked an irritated glance in her direction but made no comment. 'A few more notes from SOCO,' he said, pulling the papers from the fax machine and handing them, still warm, to Banham.

Banham scanned the notes. 'There was another letter beside the S on the G-string. It's very faint. Penny couldn't make it out – it could be an H, a B, a P, an F, or possibly an R.'

'Rogers,' Alison said immediately. 'Susan Rogers.'

Isabelle shook her head. 'That was her real name. Olivia said they used their stripper names to mark their G-strings.'

Alison looked at Banham. 'Katie said they used their own names.'

The room went quiet.

'Isabelle, get the file out on Ahmed Abdullah's murder,' Banham said. 'If the knickers are still there in the evidence bag, check if there was an initial on them. We're getting somewhere now!'

CHAPTER TEN

The large gin and small valium Theresa had given her mother with her cornflakes had done the trick. She was still in the bedroom, snoring like a donkey in labour. Bernadette, thanks to another valium, was fast asleep in the living room.

Theresa still wasn't taking any chances. She crept around the tiny flat in stockinged feet. She wasn't proud of herself, but what choice did she have? She hadn't been able to find a babysitter, and if she'd left her mother in charge, the old bag might have given Bernadette a good clout.

While they were both still asleep there was time to get rid of the videos. But where to hide them?

She was dead tired herself, hadn't slept a wink since Brian came out of jail. She decided to have a coffee while she turned over a few ideas.

She picked up the kettle and filled it with water, gazing out of the window but seeing nothing. They had planned all this for years, she and Brian; it had kept them going during the long prison years. They would ask Olivia and Katie for a lump sum of money to give them a new start, then move away, out of London, to somewhere quiet and pleasant. But Kenneth Stone had decided to pull the plug; he'd come to the flat, ranting about all the money he'd paid out over the years, and declaring that they wouldn't get another penny out of him.

But they'd earned that new start. Theresa didn't enjoy resorting to blackmail, but if it was the only way, that's how it had to be. It wasn't as if anyone would get hurt; Katie was happy to give them the money, and Ken had plenty even if his mean streak had come out. And they'd all get their videos back, and the sordid episode would finally be over.

At least, that's what Theresa had thought.

But now everything had changed. Shaheen and Susan had been murdered and, in a way, that meant it had to be connected with the other dreadful business.

She plugged the kettle into the wall, and rinsed a breakfast cup from the table. The detective had shown her the G-string that had been left on Shaheen's body. It was disgusting – smeared with Shaheen's blood and goodness knew what else. Theresa shuddered. It meant the murderer had to be someone who knew how Ahmed had died, so it could only be someone who had been there that night. She couldn't believe Brian was capable of killing someone, but prison did change people.

Besides, who else could have known? And where did they get the G-string? It was identical to the ones they all used to wear. Seeing it had brought back so many memories. They had each written their name or initials on their own, so they didn't muddle them up. The detective had said there was an S on that one: Susan? Shaheen?

But hadn't they used their stripper names or initials, rather than their real ones? Hers was Trixie. It was Cherry at first, because of her red hair, but Ahmed changed it to Trixie because he said she was good at turning tricks...

She put her hand on the kettle. It was still cold; she had forgotten to turn it on. She flicked the switch nervously, telling herself to get a grip; she had a disabled child and a drunken mother to care for. The detective had told her that by lunchtime she would be under twenty-four hour surveillance; she would be safe, and no one would hurt her.

But she had to dump those videos before it was too late.

The question churned round and round her brain: who knew they killed Ahmed?

Was she missing something here? As the years had gone by, Brian had grown to hate Shaheen. She had caused the problem in the first place, and had simply run away.

But Brian would never hurt Susan. She had been a good friend to them both; she had even visited him in prison, and was always kind to Bernadette.

She opened the cupboard and felt around on the top shelf for the jar of Nescafé. As she prised the top off the jar, a sudden thought struck her: *Ken Stone*. He used to go to the club; he was certainly a nasty piece of work. But did he know the truth about Ahmed's death? *And why would he want to avenge him?*

She spooned coffee into the chipped mug. *If not Ken, then who?* Could there be someone else, someone she didn't know about, someone who held a grudge and had waited until Brian came out, to put the blame on him and get even? She poured the boiling water over the coffee granules, pulled out a plastic chair and sat at the table.

Ahmed had a daughter ... no. She was in America, and she hadn't even come to the funeral. She'd sold the club about six years ago; why would she reappear now?

A half-eaten bowl of cereal, a bottle of gin and a brown teapot full of cold tea cluttered the table. She picked up the overflowing ashtray and tipped its contents in the bin. The milk hadn't been put back in the fridge, but it smelt OK. She poured some into her mug, leaned her elbows on the table and sipped the hot coffee.

Then she sat bolt upright. *Suppose Brian tells the police that the blackmail was my idea* ... no. He cared for Bernadette too much. He wouldn't play such a dirty trick.
Would he?

At first she didn't hear the quiet knocking. Brian knocked quietly; he knew not to wake anyone who might be still sleeping. She put her mug down and went to open the door.

She hardly had time to register recognition or surprise. A gloved hand grabbed at her face, covering her mouth. Strong fingers squeezed her cheekbones, pushing her back into the kitchen. Her back thumped against the wall by the table, sending crockery crashing to the floor.

Something cracked, and a volcano of pain erupted inside her head. She fought for breath and tasted the nauseous slime of blood as it ran up her nose, and down into her throat. She clawed her assailant's hands to relieve the pressure, but it was useless; she was no match for the other person's strength. She was lifted off her feet by that vice-like hand over her face, and her head slammed hard against the wall behind her. Everything exploded into stars, but she fought to keep her eyes open, pleading with them, but in vain.

The attacker smiled. That was when she saw the knife, glinting in the light from the window. She sent a last prayer to her God as her assailant turned her round and the razor-sharp blade touched her throat. As it entered her neck and ripped into her artery she heard a noise like tearing paper. Then, in slow motion, she saw the bright red blood arc like water from a garden hose. It puddled on the blue plastic table cloth and splashed the surrounding walls and floor.

She wasn't conscious as the knife slit across the rest of her freckled neck, or as the intruder released her lifeless body and let it slump across the table.

Or when the killer's gloved hands dug into a pocket and pulled out a red G-string.

Banham was still waiting on reports, and decided to take a very late lunch break. He was still getting the engaged tone on Lottie's phone; she lived less than five minutes away, so he picked up his jacket from the back of his chair and decided to pay her a visit.

Everything was moving along as it should. Theresa McGann had rung to say she was back in her flat with her mother and daughter. Katie Faye had just phoned too; she had arrived safely back at the Stones' house, and Olivia was there with her children. Judy Gardener would take good care of Kim Davis.

So he was content to leave the station for an hour or so. It was half-term, so Madeleine and Bobby would both be at home.

He turned into the small side road and saw Bobby sitting on the wall outside the house eating a sandwich. He pulled up beside him and lowered the window. 'Where's your mum?'

The boy shrugged. 'Inside, on the phone. She's always on the bloody phone.'

Banham chose to ignore the language. He stepped out of the car and flicked the lock.

'Tea's going to be late again,' Bobby added sulkily.

A large football sat in the gutter just in front of the car. 'Want to play footy?' Banham asked his nephew.

That cheered the boy up. They kicked the ball around for a few minutes, then Bobby shouted, 'Where's Alison?'

'At the station,' Banham replied. 'Working.' He took aim, missed the ball, then made contact and sent it in Bobby's direction.

'Are you going to marry her?'

'You always ask me that,' Banham said. 'And the answer's always the same. She's my sergeant, not my girlfriend.'

Bobby stopped dribbling the ball and looked up at Banham. His mouth shaped itself into a crooked grin. 'Yeah,' he said, his eyes deadpan and his tone far too grown-up. 'Like I'm supposed to believe you don't fancy her knickers off.'

Banham was shocked. 'Hey, you watch your mouth. I don't know where you picked that expression up, but don't use it to me. Or your mum for that matter. Especially not in front of your sister.'

He picked the ball up and walked toward the house. Bobby followed.

'That ain't nothing,' the boy protested, right behind his uncle. 'Mum says it all the time, on the phone.' He went into a bad impersonation of a sexy woman. 'Do you fancy my knickers off?'

Banham stood still and turned to look at Bobby, at a loss for something to say.

'That's what she says,' Bobby insisted, hands held wide.

A penny began to drop in Banham's head.

'Wait there,' he said to Bobby. 'Like your mum said. Sit on the wall. I'll be back in a moment.'

'It's cold out here. I want to come in.'

'In a minute. I need you to be the man of the family and wait there for a bit. OK?'

'OK,' Bobby agreed reluctantly.

Banham pushed open the front door and stood for a moment outside the lounge. His sister was talking on the phone, and he could hardly believe the stuff she was coming out with. So that was why the phone was constantly engaged – and that was where Bobby had picked up his colourful way with words. He knew her ex had missed some of the children's maintenance payments, but he hadn't realised Lottie was so desperate for money. He had a sudden urge to hit Derek hard for leaving his children wanting.

He opened the kitchen door. Madeleine was sitting on the floor, dressing her favourite doll for bed, and changing its nappy. The thought of this little innocent hearing her mother on the phone tore at his heart. He stood quietly in the hall, and when Lottie replaced the receiver he put his head round the door – just in time to hear the phone ring again.

Olivia Stone was in the kitchen peeling vegetables, and Katie Faye was blending fruit into a smoothie. Katie wore a comfortable grey tracksuit and house slippers, and Olivia had changed into trousers and a sweater.

Kenneth was sitting at the kitchen table slurping from a large glass of ginger wine and port. Beside him on the table was a bottle of each. 'Are we *ever* going to get any lunch?' he demanded petulantly.

Olivia didn't answer. She glanced nervously at Katie and ran the tap over the colander of peeled carrots.

'I don't even get an answer to a question now,' Ken snapped. 'No one answers me in my own bloody house.'

'You don't deserve an answer. You're drunk.'

'I am not bloody drunk!'

'I'll make some coffee,' Katie said peaceably, reaching for the cafetière.

'Oh, that's right, side with your friend,' he scoffed. 'One harridan in the house was bad enough. Now I've got two.'

'Stop it, Ken!' Olivia snapped. 'Insult me, if you must. I'm used to you having too much to drink and behaving like a pig. But leave Katie out of it.'

Katie shook her head warningly, but Olivia had reached breaking point. 'There's a lunatic out there, for Chrissake,' she shouted. 'Two of our friends have been murdered. And there are police at the bottom of the drive following our every move.' She looked at Ken, a little fearful, but he didn't shout back as he normally would. He was glaring at her, but for once he was actually listening. She started to cry. 'I hate being prisoners in our own home.'

'Only because you have to stay in,' he said coolly. 'You can't go off with your toyboy.' He looked her up and down contemptuously.

Katie and Olivia exchanged glances. Katie turned away and filled the kettle.

'Oh, here we go again.' Olivia scrubbed her eyes with a tissue and swallowed back the sobs. 'I've told you a thousand times, I don't play around. Don't judge every one by your own shabby standards.'

Kenneth didn't answer. He twisted the stem of his wineglass and stared at its contents. Then, moving so fast that she had no chance to escape, he stood up and grabbed Olivia by the throat, slamming her back against the corner of the kitchen unit. 'The shabbiest thing I ever did was taking you on,' he yelled into her face. 'This whole sordid business is your fault.'

'Ken, don't,' Katie pleaded, trying to pull him back. 'Please, Ken, come on, I've made some coffee.'

'Piss off out of it. This isn't your row.' He elbowed her away.

'Stop it, for God's sake!' Olivia pushed him away. 'Ianthe's next door doing homework, and Kevin will be back soon. I have to feed them.'

'Oh, yes, feed the children! Never mind the poor husband who pays for everything!'

Katie lost her temper. 'Leave her alone,' she shouted. 'You've already marked her face.'

Ken slapped Olivia across the face. She hit him back, but regretted it immediately as punches landed all over her head.

'Stop it! Leave her alone!' Katie shrieked, terrified that he would do her real damage.

Suddenly the kitchen door burst open. The sound of Ianthe screaming at the top of her voice stopped everyone in their tracks.

Ken let go of Olivia and sat down at the table. 'All right, nothing to get upset about,' he said, careful to avoid Katie's blazing eyes.

Ianthe ran to her mother and Olivia cuddled her close, fighting back tears. The front door slammed, and a moment later Kevin appeared in the doorway. Kenneth put out a hand and stroked his daughter's arm. 'It's all right, darling. Your mother and I were only playing.' His smile reminded Katie of a crocodile she had seen in the zoo.

Kevin walked slowly up to the kitchen table and leaned across it until his face was less than an inch from his father's. 'Well, next time, play nicely,' he said through gritted teeth. 'Ianthe and I are getting fed up with you.'

Kenneth shrugged. 'Fuck off,' he slurred.

'Don't talk like that in front of your daughter,' Olivia pleaded.

'How do I know she is my daughter?' Ken demanded. 'With your generosity, she could be anyone's.'

Katie, still trying to calm things down, held out a mug of coffee to Kenneth. Ianthe burst into tears and flew at her father, screaming, 'I hate you, Daddy. You're always hurting Mummy.'

The mug flew out of Katie's hand and the scalding liquid landed on Kenneth's trousers, seeping through and burning his leg. He jumped up with the shock, and raised his hand to hit Olivia again, but Kevin and Katie grabbed at him and forced him back into his seat.

'Take Ianthe upstairs,' Katie said in a low, urgent voice. 'Please, Kevin. Get her out of here before she gets hurt.'

Ianthe was cowering by the door, hands over her face. Kevin flung a venomous look at his father and did as Katie asked.

As the door closed behind them Kenneth stopped scrubbing at his trousers. 'I've given you everything,' he said to Olivia in a low voice. 'I put up no objection when your sleazy stripper friends came here. I even supported that brat of Theresa McGann's. And now you're asking me for fifty thousand pounds to ensure that your murky past doesn't wreck my career. I ask, is that really fair?'

Olivia threw Katie a nervous glance.

'He knows about the blackmail?' Katie said 'I thought ...'

Olivia shook her head.

'Your little secret, was it? And she's blown it? There, now will you believe she's not to be trusted?' Ken said triumphantly.

Katie looked at Olivia reproachfully. 'I thought we had all sworn to keep this between ourselves. Now it turns out Kim has shared it with Judy, and Ken knows too. Who else is in on it?'

Olivia didn't answer. Katie could see how upset she was, but she was furious. She raised her voice. 'Who else?'

'I didn't tell him. The police did.' Tears poured down her face, and Katie's anger melted.

'Never mind,' she soothed. 'We'll get it sorted.'

Ken stood up and pushed past her. 'Just for the record,' he snarled, 'I know exactly – exactly – what's on that video. And I'm starting to wonder why Ahmed Abdullah chose that particular scenario for you two.'

'Lottie, what's going on?' Banham asked.

'Please, Paul, don't start.' Lottie cradled the phone and stood up. 'I've got to get the kids something to eat.'

Banham blocked the doorway. 'Tell me,' he said gently. 'I care about you.'

She stared at the carpet, too ashamed to look him in the eye.

'I needed a job,' she said quietly. 'Something with hours to suit me – not some nine-to-five thing. I know it's a bit seedy, but Derek's stopped paying the kids' maintenance. I have to be here for them, you know that.'

'I told you I'd help out.' Banham felt anger rising. *Why should she be reduced to this?*

'I don't want your money!' She covered her face with her hands and sat down abruptly. 'I don't want to have to rely on someone else.'

'You're my twin sister, for God's sake!'

'I want a job of my own, so I can earn our keep.'

'Does it have to be a sex chat line?' He was shouting, but he couldn't help it. The current case invaded his head: those innocent women with their throats slashed and G-strings stuffed into their mouths. 'Lottie, you have no idea how dangerous this could be, what it could lead to...'

'A pay cheque,' she shouted back. 'Get out of my way, Paul. I need to make my kids some food.'

He swallowed down the conflicting emotions. 'Please, Lottie. You and the children are all I have. Please let me give you money. I'll sort Derek out too; he'll pay all the maintenance you want after I've seen him. But till I can do that, let me give you something to tide you over. What else have I got to spend my money on?'

'Spend it taking Alison out for a really nice meal,' she said with a small knowing smile. 'Now, do you want some tea?'

He blew out a long breath. She clearly wasn't going to listen. 'Yes, please. But I haven't got long.'

Lottie patted his cheek and went to the kitchen. She smiled at him and said, 'I'll make you a deal. Madeleine wants a banana and soldiers. You make that for her, and I'll cook us bacon and eggs. And while we eat it we can talk about whether you're going to ask Alison out.'

He looked at Lottie's tired face. 'I don't want to talk about Alison. She won't go out with me, so there's no point. I want to talk about you and the kids, and I want to help.'

'Good.' Lottie pulled a carton of eggs and a packet of bacon out of the fridge. 'Then feed your niece.'

That was when Banham's phone rang.

CHAPTER ELEVEN

'Brian Finn made the 999 call?' Banham asked, taking in the narrow concrete balcony leading from the graffiti-clad stairway to the open door of Theresa's high-rise flat.

Alison nodded. 'He was going mental when we arrived. Shouting and ranting like a wild animal. He kept saying she wasn't cold, so he thought she was still alive. Now his DNA is all over her.'

'Surveillance saw Finn approaching the flats?' Banham put his hand to his head. A wave of guilt overtook him; he should have been able to save Theresa.

'They were just arriving for duty,' Alison confirmed. 'They saw him approach, but didn't see anyone else leave.' She dug into her pocket and pulled out a piece of paper. 'We found this in the kitchen, near her body.'

On the paper were the words "Ken Stone" – *in Theresa's handwriting*, Banham assumed. His eyes lit up. 'Bring him in,' he said.

'With pleasure.' Alison took out her mobile and passed on the instruction to DC Crowther. 'And if he makes any kind of excuse,' she added, 'Just arrest him.'

Banham stroked his mouth with his hand. 'So we have the exact time that the call was made? And the exact time surveillance came on duty?'

Alison nodded.

'Do they match?'

'To within fifteen minutes.'

Banham read the concern in Alison's eyes, and a surge of panic went through him. He was about to face another female corpse, and if she looked so worried it meant it was going to be a bad one. He felt a sudden sympathy for Brian Finn. If he was innocent, he had just come home and found the love of his life murdered, and he hadn't been there to prevent it. Banham knew exactly how that felt.

Alison was looking at him. He blinked and pulled himself together.

'Surveillance are parked over there,' she said, leaning over the balcony and pointing to the car park. 'They had a clear view of all the entrances and exits. They saw Brian Finn arriving as they pulled up at two forty-five. They saw a gang of four youths, and an older woman with a shopping basket, but no one leaving the estate in a hurry. Finn's 999 call was logged at one minute past three.'

'Giving him enough time to kill her,' Banham said.

Alison nodded agreement. He moved toward the door, and she tactfully blocked his path.

'Could someone could have left the block without them noticing?' Banham suggested. 'Their brief was to check on people arriving, and keep an eye on Theresa.' He knew he was putting off the moment when he'd have to go into the flat, and saw that Alison realised it too. He met her eyes and lowered his voice. 'Is it as bad as the last one?'

'I'm not sure any corpse will ever be as bad as the last one,' she replied quietly. 'But you don't have to…'

'Yes, I do.' As he pushed open the door to the flat he

heard her say, 'Take a deep breath.'

The small kitchen smelt of boiled milk and blood.

Banham hovered inside the doorway. Heather Draper the pathologist was examining the body. She had her back to Banham, blocking his view.

'Evening, guvnor, glad you could join us.' Max Pettifer's public school voice rose from the floor. The forensics chief was crouching on the cheap lino, scraping up coagulating blood. 'Not a pretty sight, I'm afraid, and rather a confined space here, old boy. If you're going to throw up, can you try to do it outside?'

Banham caught sight of the blood-soaked red satin G-string which lay on the table. He quickly turned away. 'Time of death?' he asked, praying he wouldn't make Max's day by vomiting up the bacon sandwich Lottie had made him.

'I can only hazard a guess, but I'd say a couple of hours ago.' Heather Draper suddenly moved sideways, revealing Theresa's body. Her throat had been opened. Banham looked away.

'It's ten past five now,' Heather went on.

Banham's eyes settled on Max, still on all fours, carefully picking up a fragment of something pale with a pair of tweezers. He held it to the light before dropping into a see-through evidence bag, and gave one of his irritating hoots of laughter. 'The tooth, the whole tooth and nothing but the tooth.'

Banham became aware of Alison standing beside him. 'Finn's in the next room,' she said, raising her eyebrows.

Banham took the hint and followed her, leaving the

scene-of-crime team to their work.

Brian Finn had his head buried in his hands. He was sitting on a worn, rust-coloured armchair that would have looked more at home on a dump. Stained, grey carpet covered the floor and childish scribble decorated the beige painted walls. Alison nodded to the woman constable to leave them.

Finn puzzled Banham. He didn't have the bouncer down as very bright, nor had he seen any sign of real violence in the big man. Most lifers Banham had met never seemed to feel sorry for anything they had done, but Finn did. He had a vulnerability about him that worried Banham. He found it hard to see this man as a convicted killer, but the fact remained that he was. He decided to play carefully.

Finn spoke first. He looked up at Banham and said, 'I didn't kill her.'

'So why wait nearly twenty minutes before you called 999?' Banham replied.

'I didn't kill her,' Finn repeated. 'She's my world. I'd have died for her.'

'That wasn't the question.'

Finn shook his head. 'The front door was open and I walked in.' He hesitated and his forehead crumpled. 'Then I ...' Now his voice rose. 'I ... tried to revive her. I didn't want to believe ... I hoped she wasn't ... then I rang 999.'

'You must have seen her throat had been cut,' Alison said.

Finn looked at her helplessly. 'I thought maybe she'd wake up for me.'

'How did you try to revive her?' Banham asked. Finn's clothes were covered in blood.

'I pumped at her heart, like they do on TV. Then I pulled the knickers from her mouth and ...' His voice broke. 'That was when I knew she was ... dead. So I called 999.'

'The knickers?' Banham recalled the G-string on the kitchen table. 'They were in her mouth?'

'Yes.'

Banham exchanged glances with Alison, who immediately started writing in her notebook.

'What else did you touch?' Banham asked.

His voice rose almost to a shriek. 'My kid! I went to find Bernadette. She's been drugged, and so has Sarah.'

'Brian, you need to calm down,' Banham said.

'I didn't kill her,' Finn shouted. He opened his mouth and a long wail came out.

Banham closed his eyes. Guilty or innocent, Finn was in no state to answer questions. He gestured to Alison to follow, and left the room. She sent the uniformed female officer back to sit with Finn, and pursued Banham out on to the concrete passageway outside the flat.

'We'll take his clothes, of course,' she said, 'but he's cradled her, so it won't prove anything either way.'

'Let's give him a minute.' Banham stared unseeingly over the balcony.

'Do you think he killed her?'

'I honestly don't know. We'd better take him to the station and keep him there, while they pick up what forensic they can. He was in the area when Susan was murdered too. If it's a coincidence, it's a big one.' He shook his head to clear it. 'Why did Theresa write Ken Stone's name on a piece of paper? If she *did* write it, of course. When her mother wakes up, you'd better check it's her handwriting.'

'Guv.'

'And why the G-strings? Brian Finn and Ken Stone both have a connection with them. We need to keep pushing them both.'

'What about Olivia Stone and Katie Faye?' Alison said. 'They've got a lot to lose if those videos come to light.'

'You'd better talk to their surveillance officers. Check what time surveillance started.'

'I already did, guv. They're outside the house in Cherry Tree Walk, have been for two hours, and the women are in the house.' She flicked her eyes up at Banham and added, 'I hope they don't get a puncture!'

Banham ignored the comment. 'They all left the police station separately this morning,' he said. 'Ken went to a meeting. Olivia went home and Katie went to pick some stuff from her flat in Chelsea.'

'So they all had time to come here and kill Theresa after they left the station this morning, and then get back to the house before the surveillance team arrived.'

Banham nodded. 'We need a time of death, and as precise as possible.' He blew out a long breath. 'And you'd better get another statement from Judy Gardener and Kim Davis.'

Alison looked puzzled.

'There's no surveillance on them,' Banham reminded

her. 'Gardener particularly requested to look after Kim herself, with no surveillance back-up. Why?'

Alison nodded slowly. 'All those women have strong motive.'

Crowther was standing at the front desk in the station waiting for the duty sergeant to finish checking Ken Stone in. The front door opened and Brian Finn walked in, flanked by two uniforms. He was wearing a grey towelling dressing gown which belonged to Theresa, and his feet were bare; he had refused the regulation plastic flip-flops and seemed oblivious to the February weather.

'Well, thank the Lord!'

Kenneth Stone's upper-class accent irritated the hell out of Crowther, and the reek of alcohol made it worse.

'I hope this time they throw away the key,' Stone drawled.

'That'll do, Mr Stone!' The "Mr" stuck in Crowther's throat.

But Finn seemed so immersed in his own thoughts that he hadn't even heard. Crowther was glad of that – but he wasn't expecting what came next.

Finn, fast as a cheetah, turned, lifted his arm, curled his hand into a fist and laid it fast and hard in the side of Ken Stone's face before anyone had a chance to stop him. Then he raised his knee and with perfect aim landed it heavily in Stone's balls.

Stone crumpled in a heap on the floor. Crowther struggled to keep a straight face as he moved to pull the man to his feet.

But Finn was there before him. Before the two

uniformed police officers could restrain him, he dodged Crowther and swung another hard, fast punch, knocking Stoneon to his back again. He began to pummel him, giving him no option but to keep moving his arms defensively from face to groin and back again.

'That's for hitting your wife and kids,' Brian yelled. 'And if you've touched my Theresa, consider yourself dead meat.'

Crowther stood back, allowing Finn to get in another punch to Ken's chin, before two more uniforms who had heard the rumpus ran to help. It took all four of them to pull Finn back. It was left to Crowther to help Ken Stone.

'I'll sue you,' Stone said, sitting up gingerly. 'I've got plenty of witnesses here. You'll regret that.'

'You think I fucking care?' Finn struggled to break free of the officers who held his arms behind his back. 'Be a man – hit me back. Go on, I dare you.' Finn lifted his chin and jabbed it forward at Stone.

'Shut it!' Crowther shouted. 'Both of you shut up!' The four uniformed officers kept hold of the big man with an effort. 'Lock him up, and leave him to cool down!'

Finn was dragged off by two of the uniforms, and Ken Stone rose painfully to his feet. He brushed Crowther's upper arm. 'Quite right, animals like that *should* be locked up.'

The pint-sized cockney stared, half-amused, for a second or so, then turned to one of the remaining officers. 'He's right. Lock him up too.'

Stone started to protest, but Crowther pointed a finger in his face and added, 'If you don't put a lid on it, I'll get the bloody national press on the phone.'

Alison stood at the coffee machine watching Isabelle fill a mug with frothy hot chocolate. When she had finished, Alison pressed the button marked 'Black Coffee', as Banham walked up to the machine.

'Go with Crowther, will you, Isabelle,' he said. 'I need a statement from Judy Gardener and Kim Davis about their movements today. You'd better check it out when you've taken it.'

'Guv.' Isabelle looked from Alison to Banham and back again, a little smile playing around her lips.

'Now would be good,' said Banham sharply.

Isabelle tossed her hair back and walked off.

'What's with her?' he asked Alison.

'No idea, guv. Am I interviewing Ken Stone with you?'

'Yes – as soon as his solicitor arrives.' He hesitated a moment, then leaned towards her. 'Um, are you doing anything tonight?'

Alison's face flushed warmly. 'Guv?'

He was feeding coins into the machine.

'I don't know what time the solicitor will get here, of course.' He kept his back to her. 'You are free tonight, are you?'

She was always free. Why would she not be free? The only man who interested her was standing right here in front of her. She was more confused than ever, but decided to put it down to his need for company in the wake of another G-string victim.

'Yes, as it happens, I am.'

'Good.' He looked at the plastic cup in her hand. 'Would you like another coffee?'

'No, thank you.' She tried to be brisk and businesslike but knew she wasn't making a good job of it. 'Why do you suddenly want to know if I'm free?'

'I need a favour.' He ran his hand through his hair and took his own plastic cup of coffee from the machine. 'Ah. I'm sorry. I don't know what you must be thinking.' He turned away from her again and fiddled with the buttons on the machine. 'I'm not making a pass at you, Alison. I wouldn't dream of it.'

Adding insult to injury or what, she thought.

'It's just that ... well, I'm worried about Lottie, and the kids. There's something going on. It needs a woman's point of view and you're ...' He paused obviously trying desperately to choose the right words. 'I know you're more like one of the boys, but you are still a woman...'

It had been a very long day, and she had spent some of it under her car, lying on the dirty road changing her tyre. She was uncomfortably aware that she looked at her worst; no man in his right mind would fancy her, especially not with someone like Katie Faye on the horizon. At that moment her dearest wish was that for just one hour of her life she could look like Katie.

But the humiliation hadn't finished.

'I thought we'd have a takeaway. At your place, if that's all right. If it makes you feel better, you can pay half. But please, help me out here. I really need to talk to a woman about this.'

She reminded herself that this was a particularly

difficult case, and it had been a long day for him as well. But all the same, who did he think he was? Her eyes dropped to his waistline. It had definitely widened in the seven years she had worked with him, and the beige and green checked shirt and dark brown cords he was wearing were hardly a fashion statement. His face was nice in a boyish sort of way, and his blue eyes sort of hooked into you, but Hugh Grant he wasn't. What was the attraction? She really wished she knew.

'Oh, there's certainly a woman in here somewhere. So my current date tells me.' She watched for his reaction. 'And yes, as it happens, I am free tonight.' She sipped her coffee to give herself time to gather her confidence. 'He works nights, sings in a rock band.' Shock passed over Banham's face, but she was on a roll. 'And I may not have Olivia Stone's boobs, or Katie Faye's fringe, but I do have a brain, and you're welcome to pick it. So feel free to pay for the whole of the takeaway, which you can eat yourself, to add to your expanding waistline. Then you can bend my ear with your problems. That's what mates are for.'

He looked at her strangely, but she found she couldn't stop. 'Of course I'll help you sort out Lottie's problems. I like her a lot.'

She flicked her empty cup toward the bin, and for once it went straight in. She smiled smugly and turned and walked towards the toilets. She pushed the door of the Ladies, then looked over her shoulder at Banham. 'Nah. I'm one of the boys, isn't that right?'

She walked into the Gents.

Banham understood the strain she was under. This third

murder had got to all of them. He waited outside till she emerged from the loo.

'Why don't you call it a day?' he offered. 'I think I may do better with Ken Stone if I take Isabelle in with me. The man's a womaniser, and she's probably more his type.'

'She's going to interview Judy Gardener,' Alison reminded him. Her tone confirmed she wasn't in a good mood.

'I can change that.'

'No need. I'm fine.'

'Are you sure?'

'Oh, for heaven's sake!'

The black specks in her eyes had expanded and were shining so brightly they looked as though they might catch fire. He followed as she walked back to the incident room.

Crowther was wearing his Know-all Col look.

'I know it's after hours but I've found a judge to sign a search warrant,' he told Banham. 'So while you're interviewing Ken Stone, and before I pay Judy Gardener and Kim Davis a visit, I'll take a team round there and turn the Stones' house upside down.'

'Well done!' Banham said enthusiastically. He knew exactly how difficult it was to track a judge down after court hours. *Trust Crowther*. He really was on a mission to make sergeant.

Banham called in his office before following Alison to the interview room, and found a fax on his desk. One of the older detectives on the team had tracked down the people who had bought the lease on the Scarlet Pussy Club. A Mr and Mrs Diante.

Ahmed Abdullah's daughter had sold the club as a going concern many years ago. That was of no particular interest to Banham; the sale which had caught his attention had taken place six years ago, when the club's fixtures and fittings had been auctioned.

Now DC Downs had tracked down the auctioneers. Once he came up with the paperwork, they would have names and addresses of anyone who had bought costumes.

Kenneth Stone's solicitor was tall and thin, with a head shaped like a cricket ball. He wore bifocal glasses, of which Banham had a great dislike; they meant he couldn't read the wearer's eyes.

The lawyer had the same over-educated, over-articulated accent Max Pettifer suffered from. Banham decided he disliked the man even more than his eyewear.

'What exactly are you charging my client with?' he demanded brusquely, staring angrily at Banham over the top of his glasses.

Banham decided to play the courtesy card. 'Nothing at all, sir. He is helping us with our enquiries. For the moment I just need to ask him a few questions.'

He was taking no chances; no matter how heavy the solicitor got, he wasn't letting Kenneth Stone go until he was certain the man wasn't involved. He was certain Theresa's death could have been avoided, and determined it would be the last. But he had nothing concrete to justify keeping Stone in custody, since his son refused to provide a written statement about the domestic violence. All Banham had left was humility, at least for now. It wasn't easy after seeing Theresa's mutilated body, but it was a small price to pay to nail the killer.

'You could have asked me questions at home,' Stone said.

'I was protecting you. I'm sure you didn't want the neighbours talking.' *That's true, at least*, Banham thought. 'I decided the best solution all round was to bring you in, in an unmarked car.'

It seemed to work. Both the solicitor and Stone sat back in their chairs and relaxed.

'I want Brian Finn charged with assault,' Ken said defiantly.

Banham leaned back in his chair and interlinked his fingers. He had heard about the fracas in the reception area earlier, and was sorry he had missed seeing this fat bully of a man get a good clump. He would have given a lot to dish it out himself.

'I would ask you, under the circumstances, to reconsider that,' he said politely. 'Brian Finn found Theresa McGann's body.' He looked straight into Stone's flabby face and added, 'Her throat was carved open and the floor was awash with her blood. It wasn't a pretty sight.'

'My God!'

'So you'll reconsider an assault charge?'

Stone was visibly flustered. He gave a quick nod. 'Under the circumstances.'

'When was the last time you saw Theresa McGann?' Alison asked him.

Stone's cheeks reddened. 'She was at our house, a couple of days ago.' He rubbed his face. 'My wife has known her for years...' He looked at his solicitor, his embarrassment plain. 'Brian Finn is blackmailing us...'

'We know about the videos.' Banham leaned back in his chair and folded his arms. 'So Theresa was round at your house a couple of days ago. Why was that?'

'To talk about Finn's release from prison and the blackmail note my wife received from him.'

'This whole thing must be very uncomfortable for you,' Alison said.

Ken nodded and looked at the table. Alison continued, 'The press are like vultures. You couldn't let them get hold of those videos.'

Ken's head flew up. 'I didn't murder her, if that's what you're insinuating.' He turned to his solicitor. 'My wife and Theresa worked together when they were students. They both got pregnant at the same time. I married Olivia, but Finn went to prison. My wife felt sorry for Theresa. Her child...' He lowered his eyes. 'Well, she's not right. She's...'

'Mentally handicapped,' Banham prompted.

'Whatever.' He shrugged. 'We had a healthy son, and then a daughter, Ianthe. Theresa had no one, and her mother is a drunk. Olivia and I helped her bring up the child.'

'Very benevolent of you,' Banham said flatly. He held eye contact with the man.

Stone stared back, then flicked another embarrassed glance at his solicitor.

'You were a regular at the club where they worked as students, the Scarlet Pussy,' Alison said. 'In fact, I understand you were there every night.'

Stone reddened again. 'That was twenty years ago,' he protested. 'I was twenty years old, and single.'

'Where did you go when you left the station this morning, before you arrived at your house?'

'I told you. I had a meeting.'

'Who with?'

'I'd rather not say.'

'I'm afraid you're going to have to,' Alison said.

Stone looked at his solicitor again. The man's skinny head nodded like a plastic dog in the back of a car. 'With me,' he said. 'I can vouch for Mr Stone's whereabouts.'

Banham looked speculatively from one man to the other. Then, as if on cue, his phone rang. He excused himself and went into the corridor.

It was Crowther. He had just left the Stones' house with a large collection of pornographic videos he had found in Ken Stone's study. They were all labelled 'Scarlet Pussy Club'.

Banham returned to the interview room. First he glared at Ken's solicitor. Then he settled back in his chair, enjoying the moment. 'I'm so sorry, sir,' he said with icy civility to Kenneth Stone, 'but I'm going to have to detain you for a few more hours. My team have just completed a search of your house, and they've found what appears to be a collection of pornographic videos. I'm sure you know that certain kinds of porn are illegal. I'm sure these won't turn out to be those kinds, but until we have sorted through them all and checked the contents, we won't be able to let you go.' With growing satisfaction he watched Ken Stone slump back in an embarrassed heap in his chair, looking desperately at his solicitor. 'Hopefully,' he finished, 'we won't need to keep you too long.'

From where Isabelle sat on the sofa beside Crowther she could see into the kitchen. Judy was busying herself making tea in a large, bright yellow china pot. It was one of those modern open-plan houses where the lounge and kitchen ran into one; wherever you were on the ground floor, you could see everyone else. Kim sat with her feet up on the floral armchair opposite the one Crowther had settled in. She wrapped her long arms around her legs. Isabelle thought Kim had grown even thinner in the few hours since she last saw her. Her baggy jumper looked way too big for her, and the black leggings finished a good couple of inches above her thin ankles, revealing red blotches and flaky dry skin on her pale legs. Her short dark hair was uncombed and stood on end; she looked as if she had just climbed out of bed. She wore no make-up, and pimples decorated her pallid complexion.

'Sorry to be the bearer of that news,' Isabelle said to break the silence.

'We need you to account for your movements for the whole of today,' Crowther added. 'I'm sure you understand it's standard procedure.'

Isabelle watched Judy squeeze the tea bag. The policewoman's back was to them, but she answered before Kim had a chance to speak. 'Yes, of course we understand the procedure. We were here, together, weren't we, Sausage?'

Kim nodded, her eyes vacant. 'Yes, all day,' she said, her voice barely audible.

'Can anyone confirm that?' Isabelle asked.

Kim shook her head. 'No. It was just us.'

Judy came in with the tray and placed it on the table in front of them. She heaped sugar into one of the mugs and handed it to Kim.

While Isabelle sipped her tea, Crowther explained that surveillance would be in place that evening. 'It's extra security,' he told them. 'Under the circumstances, the guv thought it was best.'

Isabelle couldn't help but notice the glare Kim shot at Judy.

'I wasn't here at all this afternoon,' Kim reminded Judy after Crowther and Isabelle left. 'Why did you lie?'

'It was for the best, Sausage.'

'I was only at the school, sorting costumes for the end of term show.'

Judy picked up the tray and made for the kitchen. Kim shouted after her, 'They only have to ask at the school. Anyone will tell them.'

'They won't ask, though.' Judy clattered the crockery in the sink. 'I'm a copper. They'll take my word. Don't fret, Sausage.'

'Where were you, then?'

There was a silence, then Judy swung round to face Kim. 'Outside in the car, reading the paper, waiting for you.'

'That's not true.'

Judy stared at her. 'Kim, you're upset.'

Suddenly Kim burst into tears. 'You bet I'm upset,' she shouted. 'Theresa's been murdered. It could have been me. You said you'd look after me.'

'Oh, Kim!' Judy rushed to take her in her arms, but Kim jumped up and backed away and against the wall. 'You weren't reading the paper. You weren't there at all. It could have been me lying in the morgue.'

Judy sat down, her eyes never leaving Kim's face. 'Come on, Sausage. You're upset and confused.' She put her hand out but Kim turned away. 'You said you needed time on your own in the studio to sort out costumes. I was outside in the car.'

'I needed to find that trunk that we got from the club auction,' Kim said, suddenly calm again. 'I needed to see if there were any more red G-strings in there.'

'Now, listen, Sausage.' Judy stood up and grabbed Kim's upper arms. 'You're not well. You're still having bad dreams. And I am going to protect you, just as I promised I would. But you must do as I say.'

'OK.' The fight went out of Kim, her body went limp.

'Do not tell the police that there were red G-strings in that trunk. When they ask, which they might, you say there weren't any.'

Kim nodded meekly. 'There weren't.'

'That's OK, then. The murder investigation team will go after Ken Stone now. He's a ghastly individual. He beats his wife and children. He should be locked up, whatever he has or hasn't done. That's a favour we can do for Olivia.'

'All right,' Kim said quietly. 'If you say so, Judy.'

CHAPTER TWELVE

It was nearly one in the morning by the time they'd finished at the station. DC Crowther, living up to his nickname, knew a Chinese takeaway that did good food and stayed open most of the night. He gave Banham and Alison clear directions, suggesting, with an expectant raise of the eyebrows, that it wasn't far from Alison's flat. Banham seemed oblivious, but Alison glared at Crowther, and in return received a Know-all Col wink.

Alison claimed she wasn't hungry. The truth was she would never consider lining her stomach with anything so fattening, so late at night. The lasting effect it would have on her hips was unthinkable to someone who had flirted with anorexia throughout her teenage years. At any *normal* hour, a takeaway was laden with calories, and would be a rare treat. The guilt associated with enjoying food had never left her.

Banham was annoyingly indifferent to her protests. He ordered two portions of sweet and sour chicken, and when she said she absolutely would not eat that any of it, he promptly told the assistant to add chicken fried rice to the order.

The smell wafted into her nostrils as she stood beside him in the takeaway. All she had to look forward to was a large black coffee and the hope of being a pound lighter by the weekend. *I must really care for him,* she told herself, *to put up with this level of temptation*. If only the food didn't smell so inviting! She had been up since six and hadn't eaten a thing all day; it was enough to make anyone want to eat the paper package and all.

She reminded herself that she still carried three extra pounds from Christmas, and her metabolism was nothing like Isabelle Walsh's. That woman ate anything she liked, and had a gorgeous figure, slim and curvy. Alison had to work out in the gym for hours to keep herself toned, or every morsel she swallowed migrated to her hips.

Isabelle boasted that the only exercise she indulged in was sex. That wasn't on offer for Alison. The nearest she'd got with Banham was a kiss and *then* he'd run away fast enough to give any girl a permanent complex. He wasn't interested; he had made that very clear. But, judging by the way looked at Katie Faye, he was certainly interested in women. He had given Olivia Stone's cleavage more than a passing glance too; perhaps he was a bosom man, in which case she had no chance at all; she needed padding in a A bra cup.

She prayed she had gathered up her smalls from all over the flat; she left them drying in every nook and cranny, without a thought for discretion. She couldn't bear Banham to see her heavily padded Wonderbras and thongs spread all over the radiators. She crossed her fingers as she unlocked the front door.

It wasn't her lucky day. Her undies were on display on the radiator by the front door. She quickly scooped them up with the pile of mail on the mat, blushing furiously as she hugged the bra cups, all as flat as three-day-old champagne, to her chest.

When she looked up Banham was standing there, holding the Chinese takeaway and smiling. He hadn't noticed. Or had he? He gave nothing away. He walked on ahead into the kitchen, giving her time to hide the underwear in the drinks cabinet.

There was more embarrassment in the kitchen. The sink was full of unwashed coffee mugs. Banham put the brown paper bags of food on the worktop, turned the oven on, then rolled his sleeves up and started washing up.

He shook his hands and patted the mugs dry with the kitchen roll, hunted for plates in the cupboards and turned them upside down on top of the oven. 'Glasses,' he said, looking round, but didn't wait for an answer.

It took a second for the penny to drop. By the time Alison realised where he was going he had reached the drinks cupboard and taken out two champagne flutes. He completely ignored the underwear; she couldn't decide if he hadn't noticed or was too polite to comment.

He walked back into the kitchen, smiling at her blushing face as he passed her. He rummaged in one of the brown paper bags and brought out a bottle of champagne.

'I've warmed two plates,' he said, beginning to uncork it, 'and I think you should have a tiny bit of this food. You know what they say about champagne on an empty stomach.'

'No. What do they say?'

He turned to face her, and those blue eyes gazed into hers. 'Well, if you don't know, I won't be responsible for …' The cork flew in the air, cutting him off in mid-sentence.

'What's this in aid of?' she asked, a little bemused.

'It's Valentine's Day. Had you forgotten?'

'Yes, I had.'

He poured champagne into both glasses and handed one to her. 'Didn't the new fella send you roses?'

She coloured with guilt and looked away. 'Not his style,' she said feebly, knowing full well lying to a detective inspector was a waste of time. 'Stop staring at me. I'm your sergeant, not a suspect.'

'Sorry.' He clinked her glass with his. 'Here's to lovers everywhere,' he said, still looking her straight in the eyes.

She held his gaze for a few moments but was first to look away. After a few more seconds, he put the bottle down and walked through to the lounge. She stayed where she was for a moment, then picked up the champagne and followed him. She settled on the sofa beside him, but he jumped up and went back for the food.

The mood had changed.

She sipped her champagne while he munched on his supper. Every now and again he held a spoonful of food in front of her, but she always shook her head. There were enough calories in the champagne, but she couldn't resist that.

'Tell me about Lottie,' she said.

He told her about the sex chat line job, and how it was affecting the children. 'And of course she won't take any money from me,' he concluded.

Alison could see Lottie's point of view. 'She's a grown

woman and a mother, and she won't take kindly to you telling her how to run her life. She's trying to be independent. I can see she needs help, but you'll have to do it another way.'

'What if I tell her about this case we're on? Those murdered women were naïve students who ended up getting involved in pornographic videos. And now, after all these years, someone is killing them, all because of something that didn't seem at all threatening at the time.'

He's such a compassionate man, she thought. Eleven years as a murder detective hadn't killed that; he'd held on to his compassion and sensitivity. She had a sudden urge to put her arms around him, but fought it. It was the champagne, knocking her defences down.

The reason he was here at one in the morning, she reminded herself, was to talk through Lottie's problems; no more than that. 'No,' she said. 'Coming from you, that'll only put her hackles up more.' He looked bewildered, and she smiled. 'You're exactly the same, you and Lottie – stubborn.' She paused, her mouth watering at the scent of the food still in the foil dishes. 'Look, I'll talk to her if it'll help,' she offered. 'It'll be better coming from another woman.'

His face seemed to light up. 'Would you really do that for me?'

'Course I will. You can chase Derek for the maintenance he owes her.'

Suddenly he leaned towards her. She thought he was going to kiss her, but he lifted the spoon full of chicken fried rice to her mouth. 'Please eat something,' he said. 'I worry about you. You look half starved.'

The champagne had melted her defences. She accepted the food. 'I'll pay Lottie a visit and make her see sense,' she told him as she munched on the delicious rice. 'She just might listen to me.'

He fed her again and she leaned back, enjoying the flavour. Then she picked up the chopsticks that he had discarded and carried on feeding herself. Next thing she knew, the plate was empty.

'You're tired,' he said tenderly.

'Do you want to stay?' It was out before she could stop herself.

They stared at each other. 'Yes, please,' he said after a few seconds. 'I don't want to get done for drinking under the influence. The sofa will do fine.'

There were another few seconds of silence. Alison broke it. 'Fine, good.'

'I'll drive you to the garage in the morning before work. You can leave your car there, get your wheel sorted and the suspension checked. Then I'll take you back to pick it up later.'

'Thank you.' She stood up, consumed with humiliation. With any other man, a bottle of champagne would mean something. If she lived to be a hundred and eighty she'd never understand him. The only good thing was, she was drunk enough to fall asleep quickly.

Isabelle must have been watching out the window as Alison arrived at the station in Banham's car the next morning. She was washing her hands over the basin as

Alison walked into the locker room.

'You look tired,' she said, with a cat-like narrowing of her eyes.

'I am,' Alison said coolly. "We've got another G-string victim, just in case it had slipped your mind.'

Isabelle tossed her head. 'Nothing to do with you arriving in the guvnor's car this morning?'

Alison wasn't in the mood. 'Oh, do give it a rest, Isabelle. He picked me up because I had to leave my car in the garage to get the suspension checked. If you remember, I caught the silencer going over the potholes in Kenneth Stone's road. And that was before I got the puncture, which also needs fixing.'

Isabelle moved to the hand drier and shook her hands up and down. 'And the garage is on his way to work, is it!' she persisted.

'He owes me a favour,' Alison sighed.

'Did him one last night, did you?'

'If you invested as much effort on catching criminals as you do on other people's private lives, this squad would get spectacular results!'

She turned her back on Isabelle and dug in her brown leather shoulder bag for a comb. She could still see Isabelle in the mirror. The other woman lifted her hands defensively.

'OK,' she said apologetically. 'I'll mind my own. You didn't have a go about my embarrassing little fling with Know-all Col.'

'Yes, that did come as a surprise,' Alison said. She started to comb the end of the long plait she'd tied her brown curls into. 'I'd have thought the Borough Commander was more your type.'

Isabelle burst out laughing. Alison had to admire her for that. The woman was ambitious and a man-eater, but she didn't lack a sense of humour.

'He must be one hell of a good lay,' she added.

'I've had better,' Isabelle confided. 'Anyway, he's back with Penny now, so what the hell.'

Her hand was unsteady as she applied her lipstick, and Alison detected a glimmer of sadness in her eyes.

'I only slept with him because there's a rumour of a promotion in the offing.'

'Really?' Alison said. 'I haven't heard anything. Someone leaving?'

The foxy eyes flicked towards Alison. 'The DCI, according to the jungle telegraph. Keep it under your hat, though. The word is Banham will get DCI, you'll go to DI and it'll be between me and Col for sergeant.'

'I hadn't heard a word.'

'He doesn't talk in his sleep, then?'

'Where did you get it from?'

Isabelle examined her fingernails. 'Let's just say you were right. The Borough Commander *is* more my type.'

Banham clapped his hands for silence from the twenty-strong investigation team who were all talking noisily amongst themselves. The face of Theresa McGann, eyes terrified and staring, throat covered in coagulating blood, was stuck to the whiteboard beside Shaheen Hakhti-Watkins and the unrecognisable Susan Rogers.

'We've now got twenty-four hour surveillance on Olivia Stone and Katie Faye, and, from the end of today, on Judy Gardener and Kim as well. Our killer has already claimed three women, and the three remaining ones could still be in grave danger. We have Kenneth Stone and Brian Finn in custody, but we'll have to charge them or free them by the end of the day. We desperately need some evidence. If forensics can't come through, we have no choice but to put our possible suspects back out there.'

'Unless one of them is our murderer,' Alison said.

'Unless we can *prove* one of them's the murderer,' Banham countered.

'The super is giving us a lot of grief about releasing Ken Stone,' Crowther said. 'Some of us have been up all night watching the blue films we confiscated from his home…'

'Oh, what a hardship for you!' Isabelle called sarcastically.

'I've seen it all before, love!'

Banham was already edgy. 'Can we keep our minds on the case, please?' he snapped.

'Sorry, guv,' said Crowther. 'None of the films marked Scarlet Pussy Club had any connection with the Scarlet Pussy Club, or any of the six women. Not a red G-string in sight. They're obviously his own private collection. Nothing illegal, no children or anything like that. So he hasn't broken the law.'

'So, unless forensics turn something up,' Banham said, 'we'll have to let him go. We can't even hold him for domestic violence; the son won't play – he's afraid Stone will hurt his sister.' The DI rubbed his mouth. 'If we get no joy from forensics, we have to release him – but we'll put him under twenty-four hour surveillance. And we won't tell him. See to that, will you, Crowther?'

'Guv.'

'He may lead us to something. And if he does, we'll bring him in again. Now, what else have we got?'

'Penny is a hundred per cent sure that the letter on the G-string left with Theresa is a single S,' offered Crowther.

'Theresa's stripper name was Trixie or Cherry,' Alison reminded them.

'There must be something in that,' Isabelle said. 'All the G-strings are marked with a letter S. Are we missing something? Is the killer trying to tell us something?'

'If he was, wouldn't it be consistent?' Crowther suggested.

'Isn't it?' asked Banham.

'There's another faint letter beside the S on the other two. And Shaheen and Susan both begin with S, but Theresa doesn't.'

'But they marked the G-strings with their stripper names,' Alison pointed out.

'And Susan didn't have a stripper name,' Banham added.

'So maybe someone wrote the S on them for a different reason,' Isabelle suggested. 'Olivia Stone has an initial S too.'

Banham shook his head. *Too many maybes*.

The team tossed the idea around for a few more minutes, but it was plain it was going nowhere. Banham lifted his hand. 'Have we got the visiting records back yet, from Finn's time in prison?'

'They're promised today,' Isabelle told him.

Banham closed his eyes. 'For goodness' sake, what have we got? We have to report back to Bow Street – I'd like to be able to say we've made some progress. What about the weapon? Anything on that yet?'

Archie, the oldest member of the team, was leaning against the wall smoking a roll-up. He lifted his hand. 'We've searched every bin for a mile around the murder scenes of all three women. Nothing's turned up, but uniform has widened the search, and the door-to-door is still ongoing.'

'Heather Draper is pretty sure the same knife was used on all the girls,' Alison said. 'So we're not holding our breath. The killer has still got it.'

'That means he intends to strike again,' Banham said quietly.

Silence descended on the room.

'It still has to be somewhere,' Crowther said eventually. 'In the killer's house, or his car.'

'Or her,' Alison said quietly.

'Guv, we do have something,' said Isabelle. 'Surveillance report a tallish woman wearing a headscarf and pushing a shopping trolley coming out of the flats within minutes of Theresa being killed. We're trying to trace her. If she was on her way to the shops, it's highly likely she lives in that block. And she might have seen something.'

'At last!' Banham punched the air. 'Keep me posted on

that one. Anything else?'

'Can Alison claim for her car repair?' Isabelle said with a cat-like glint in her eye. 'The underbelly got caught in the potholes in the Stones' road. She's had to take it in, and she's relying on lifts.'

'Later,' Banham snapped. 'Isabelle, I want you with Crowther this morning. We have an appointment with Mr and Mrs Diante, the couple who bought the lease of the strip club and turned it into a café. They have found receipts and paperwork from the auction they held of the club's leftovers. See if you can retrieve anything relevant.'

'What about Ahmed Abdullah's family?' Alison asked.

'The wife died of cancer,' tall Archie said. 'Left everything to the daughter. She was the only child. She emigrated to Canada two years after her father's death, and didn't even come back for her mother's funeral. The club carried on for a few years, but she hasn't set foot on English soil since she left. The sale was arranged by lawyers.'

'Why does every door on this case lead to a wall?' Crowther said thoughtfully.

Archie gave a burst of laughter. 'Don't let that get you down, son. You can get over a wall. Rumour says there's nothing you can't get your leg over.'

Isabelle's face seemed to crumple. For the first time ever, Alison felt sorry for her.

Finn sat at the table, head buried in his hands. He looked up as Alison and Banham entered the room. Alison turned the tape on and murmured the formal words of introduction.

'I didn't kill her,' he said.

Banham was beginning to believe him.

'Did Theresa keep the G-strings from her time at the club?' he asked.

Finn's eyes were full of pain. He looked from Banham to Alison and again. 'Search me,' he said.

'You don't know?' Banham persisted.

'No, sir. How would I?' His eyes kept flicking back and forth. 'I've just done a nineteen-year stretch. I've hardly ever seen the inside of her flat.'

'You saw it today,' Banham said flatly. 'Have you seen any red G-strings there since you've been out?'

Finn was looking worried now. 'You don't think my Theresa killed them other girls, do you?'

'At the moment I don't know who killed them.' Banham hadn't taken his eyes off this man since he sat down. 'But I'm going to find out.'

'Do you remember any other strippers at the club with the initial S?' Alison asked. 'Besides Shaheen and Susan, I mean.'

'What, real names, or stripper names?'

'Either. Both.'

He screwed up his eyes thoughtfully. 'S is a common initial. Could have been a lot of them.'

Alison had been leaning her elbow on the table. She slowly moved her arm so it lay flat in front of her, and leaned a little closer to Finn. 'Enlighten us.'

'Let me think a minute. Shaheen was Brown Sugar. Kim Davis was Dusty Springfield, I'll leave you to work out why. And either Katie or Olivia was Strawberry.'

'Which?' Banham asked quickly.

Finn lifted a hand. 'I don't know, sir. Those two were interchangeable. It could have been either.'

There was a knock on the door. Alison stopped the tape. Outside was the new Indian CID officer, Mandi Patel. She handed Banham Brian Finn's prison records. He quickly scanned the list of visitors then handed it to Alison.

One name caught her eye.

Mr and Mrs Diante's café, once home to the infamous Scarlet Pussy Club, was in a small street off the main thoroughfare. It was a busy street in what was still the red light district.

As Crowther and Isabelle walked down the street, they passed young women in leather miniskirts, snake-patterned tights and stiletto-heeled shoes with ankle straps, standing in doorways. Most of them were smoking; all of them, Isabelle could tell from the haunted and vacant look on their faces, were addicted to hard drugs.

A young black girl, who couldn't have been more than thirteen, stepped out as they approached. 'Business?' she said to Crowther. 'It's happy hour,' she added invitingly. 'Buy one of us and another comes free.'

Despite the February chill, the girl wore a flimsy see-through blouse with a scarlet bra clearly visible underneath. It revealed a large expanse of tattooed and studded midriff. Isabelle dug in her pocket for her CID card, but Crowther put his hand over hers. 'Sorry, love, I prefer white,' he said to the girl. Fury suffused her sunken face. He added, 'Stockings, I mean.'

'I'm very surprised at you,' Isabelle said as they continued up the road. 'You've got your faults, but I never had you down as racist.'

'If you want to make sergeant, you'll have to wise up, darling. Her pimp will arrive in a minute; you'd better be prepared. I'll lay odds the bastard's a dealer, as well as a fixer for under-age girls. So we'll have learned something else while we are here. We'll know who runs this street.' He bobbed his head to the side knowingly. 'If we're going to talk about colour, I think you're still a bit green, sweetheart.'

No smart answer came to Isabelle's lips. She hated the way he made her feel. Normally she was completely sure of herself. She could pull anyone. She had only gone after Col to get him on her side; once she'd slept with a man she reckoned she knew his weak spots, and she needed to know his so she could beat him to the sergeant's post. But it hadn't worked out quite as she planned.

'Why did you dump me?' she heard herself ask, in a small voice that revealed her vulnerability. 'Most men would give anything for a night with me.'

Crowther didn't look at her. 'That's 'cos they haven't had one,' he said. 'One's enough.'

That floored her. He had turned the tables on her, and had her exactly where he wanted her. And she didn't like it.

Before she had time to gather herself, a brand new, shiny silver Mercedes mounted the pavement beside them.

The driver jumped out, followed by the passenger, a heavier, older man with a crowbar in his hand.

'Take the number,' Crowther hissed, and flashed his ID. 'Not a good idea,' he said. 'I advise you not to get on the wrong side of us.'

The men swiftly retreated into the vehicle and drove off.

'That,' said Crowther thoughtfully, 'is who runs this street.'

She couldn't help admiring his bottle. If only admiration was all it was. But Isabelle Walsh was falling in love.

The café was a family business. The Diantes were an Italian couple in their early sixties. They told Crowther and Isabelle that they had bought the lease six years ago as an investment for their old age. Downstairs was now a café, and upstairs was a flat where they lived.

The man gave Crowther a pile of bills. They included receipts from the auction they had held, and a list of names and addresses of purchasers.

The list was handwritten and almost illegible. They settled at a table to attempt to decipher it. Isabelle ordered herself a large cappuccino and Crowther spaghetti bolognaise.

She had to fight to concentrate. Crowther was an arrogant, know-all but, surprisingly, she had enjoyed her night with him. She hated to admit it, but he knew how to pleasure a woman, and she wanted more. She watched his hands flicking through the papers and remembered the way they had felt on her body. She wanted him like crazy.

And she was furious with herself. She had fallen into her own trap. And even worse, Crowther's girlfriend Penny Starr was a senior SOCO, not someone an ambitious detective constable like Isabelle could afford to offend.

Suddenly she was aware he was looking at her.

'What?'

He tapped the piece of paper he had just put in front of her. It read: "4 wardrobe skips @ £50 each. Kim Davis" and an address she recognised as the house Kim shared with Judy Gardener.

'My God,' she breathed. 'Do you think Judy knows?'

Crowther shrugged, then dropped another piece of paper on the table. She read: "Miscellaneous items of clothing – £25. Two dozen videotapes – £30. Kenneth Stone" followed by the address in Cherry Walk.

CHAPTER THIRTEEN

Banham sat down again and Alison clicked the tape back on. Finn's eyes darted nervously from one to the other.

'*You* were popular in the nick,' Alison said, dropping the visiting records in front of him.

His Adam's apple moved up and down as if he was trying to digest his fear. 'What d'ya mean?'

'You had more visitors than you told us.' She paused to rack up his discomfort level. 'Either you've got a bad memory, or you have something to hide.'

'I've never said nothing wrong.'

'You withheld evidence,' Banham said. 'That's not just wrong. It's an offence.'

Finn leaned across the table. 'You've got the wrong man.' He flung his hands in the air. 'Lock me up, then. I ain't got no fucking life now, anyway.' His voice grew deeper and more menacing. 'You'd better. 'Cos if you don't, I *will* commit murder. I'll top the fucker who killed my Theresa.'

'That's enough.' Banham spoke loudly and firmly.

Finn subsided into his chair, still glowering. Alison gave him a few seconds to calm himself. 'I didn't have you down as a friend of Ken Stone,' she said conversationally.

'You're right. I ain't.'

'He visited you regularly in the Scrubs,' she pointed out.

Finn didn't answer.

She leaned in toward him. 'Well, he did. Didn't he?'

Finn's eyes flicked away. He still said nothing.

'Answer the sergeant, Finn.'

Finn looked nervous now. 'Yeah. Yeah, he did,' he said quickly.

'What for? Hardly a social visit if he isn't a friend. Why did he come?' Alison probed.

'That's my business.' Finn scratched his forearm.

'Not any more,' Banham told him.

Finn shrugged.

'Was it because he wanted to get those videos back?' Alison asked.

'Yeah, that was it.'

'And you wouldn't tell him where they were, so he kept coming back.'

'You've got it.'

'Is that what Olivia Stone wanted too? She visited you more than a few times.'

'That's right, yeah.'

'And the other girls?'

Finn sat up. 'No.' He looked Alison in the eye. 'Theresa came because she's my girl.'

'And Susan?'

'We were mates.'

'You don't blackmail your mates for a hundred thousand pounds,' Banham said.

Finn hesitated. 'I wasn't asking for money from her.'

'You were,' Alison said. 'Indirectly.'

'Where are the videos now?' Banham asked.

Silence.

Banham spoke a little louder. 'Where are the videos now, Mr Finn?'

'Under the sink.' Finn dropped his voice.

'At your mother's?'

'At Theresa's.'

Banham looked at Alison.

'Long story,' Finn said.

'We have plenty of time,' Banham said. 'Tell us.'

'It doesn't matter now.' Finn closed his eyes. 'Nothing matters any more.'

Banham's tone softened. 'Tell us,' he repeated.

Finn seemed to have shrunk. It was several moments before he spoke, and when he did, he sounded defeated. 'We wanted to start our lives again. We were gonna to buy two of those beach huts in Canvey Island. One for us and Berny and one for the mums.'

'Who's idea was that? Theresa's?' Alison wasn't sure why she was asking.

'Mine. Am I going back to prison?'

'Depends,' Banham said. 'If Katie Faye and Olivia Stone press charges you will. If you murdered those three women you definitely will. That's what interests me. I don't give a stuff about the blackmail.'

Finn shook his head. 'You're wasting your time. I'd never kill anybody.'

'Well, somebody did, and it's my job to find out who. Could Katie and Olivia have known the blackmail was

Theresa's idea?'

'I don't know. I don't see how, unless she told them.'

'Think very hard,' Alison said. 'Olivia and Katie. Who was Candyfloss and who was Strawberry?' Something told her this was important.

Finn became flustered. 'I don't remember. Really I don't.'

Ten minutes later Alison was outside the station, organising uniformed officers and a detective to go to Theresa's flat to look for the videos. As the officers set off, Judy Gardener and Kim Davis pulled up in their car. Judy wound the window down. 'We've been asked to come in again,' Judy told Alison. 'Do you know what it's all about?'

'We need to know about the costumes Kim bought when they auctioned the club property,' Alison replied. 'If you'd mentioned it before, you'd have saved us a lot of trouble.'

'I'm sorry,' Judy said. 'We didn't think it was relevant. They were for Kim's dance school. There were no red G-strings in the skips.'

'You still should have told us before.'

Judy parked the car and Alison escorted them back into the station and took Kim to an interview room. Judy tried to follow.

'No, just Kim,' Alison told her.

'I've promised her I'll stay close to her. I'll wait outside.'

Alison didn't try to hide her impatience. Judy knew the procedure. 'She'll be safe with us,' she said curtly. 'Wait in the canteen, please.'

'I'm Kim's surveillance officer,' Judy protested. 'My brief is not to let her out of my sight.'

Alison called Isabelle to take her to the canteen. Judy looked furious but stopped arguing. As she walked down the corridor, Alison noticed how tall and broad she was.

Crowther was with Kim in the interview room.

'How are you feeling?' Alison asked.

'OK.' Kim's tone implied the opposite.

'We are putting twenty-four hour surveillance on you and Judy too, for added protection, as from this evening. We're going to keep you safe.'

Kim pulled her face into a tight smile. 'Thank you.'

'This way we'll all sleep easier in our beds.'

Kim managed a nod, but was clearly uncomfortable.

'Kim, why didn't you tell us you bought some costumes from the club?'

Kim stared wide-eyed at Alison. 'I didn't think it mattered. Ken Stone bought some skips too, and he hasn't even got a dance school. Have you talked to him about it?'

'Oh, we will,' Alison assured her.

'There were no G-strings in the skips,' Kim said firmly.

'You're absolutely sure?'

Kim's cheeks reddened. 'Of course.'

'Did any of the costumes have names or initials on them?'

'No, but we didn't use our real names.'

Crowther had been taking notes. He looked up. 'What was yours?'

'Dusty Springfield.'

'I think my mum was a fan of hers,' Crowther said. *The soul of tact as usual*, Alison thought.

'She was a gay icon,' Kim told him. 'Ahmed Abdullah gave me that name. He hated me because I'm gay.' She looked away. 'And the feeling was mutual.'

Alison couldn't let go of the 'S' connection. All the girls shared that initial in some way, except Candyfloss. And Theresa, of course; her nickname was Trixie or Cherry.

Unless Cherry was actually Sherry?

She decided to have one more go. 'What was Katie Faye's stage name?' she asked.

'I can't be sure. I was on drugs for so long. Heroin takes your memory. Strawberry, I think.'

'So Olivia was Candyfloss?'

'I'm sorry, I really don't remember.'

Alison glanced at Crowther. 'Fair enough,' he said flatly.

'What did you write on your G-strings? Do you remember that? Was it Dusty, or just the initials?'

'DS – I think, but…'

'All right, it was a long time ago. Can you remember what colour ink?'

'Olivia was the only one with a biro, I do remember that. She always had one on her. We all used it. It was just an ordinary blue biro.'

'We'll pick up your car at the garage on the way, and you can drive,' Banham said.

'You want me to use my car again? In the Stones'

road?' Alison looked at the end of her tether.

'If you want to claim the repair on expenses, I have to justify it,' Banham said. 'The super wants photos.'

'But it'll get more scratches. And what if the sump gets damaged again?'

'Then we'll get it mended again. We'll get photos of the road, and bring Ken Stone back for questioning. By the time he gets hold of his solicitor to spring him, forensics may have turned something up.' He ignored Alison's pained expression. 'I'm going to enjoy bringing him in again. He'll know what police harassment is when I've finished with him.'

'If we could persuade his son to make a statement, we could get him locked up,' Alison said. 'And save my car in the bargain.'

'Better still if we could get his wife to lodge a complaint about domestic violence.'

'I don't trust any of those women,' Alison declared. 'What do you make of Judy and Kim not telling us they bought costumes from the club auction?'

'Maybe they were concerned about putting Gardener's job on the line,' Banham suggested. 'Ken Stone didn't mention he went to the auction either – or that he visited Finn in the nick.'

'You think he did it, don't you?'

Banham turned the car into the garage forecourt and stopped the engine. He rubbed his mouth and looked at Alison. 'I don't know for sure, but I'd feel a lot happier if he was locked up.'

'I think you're wrong.'

'You think it's one of the women? You don't trust Katie Faye or Olivia Stone, do you?'

He's noticed, then. 'No further than I could throw them.'

'I'm surprised at you.' Banham sounded like a teacher talking to a pupil. 'You're normally more astute than that. They are both very vulnerable.'

'Oh please!'

'Alison, neither of them had families, and they had to learn to survive. They were young and naïve, and they made mistakes. And now they're paying a big price.'

'You should get out more,' Alison snapped back. 'You're the naïve one. Olivia married Stone for his money, and I'll bet Katie Faye wasn't too particular who she used to get where she is today.'

Banham shook his head. 'You're wrong. She's a victim in all this.'

'You fancy her, and your judgement is clouded!' She knew she was overstepping the mark but she couldn't stop herself. Banham stared at her open-mouthed. She opened the door to get out of the car. 'And you haven't even noticed that Olivia's tits aren't real.'

She slammed the door so hard the noise reverberated in his ear.

God, that woman has a temper.

Kenneth Stone was in his study when the doorbell sounded. He was indulging in his favourite pastime – playing with himself. Normally he liked to watch a pornographic film to aid his wrist action, but now that the police had taken his collection away, he was reduced to studying the curves of a nude model in the men's magazine he had read a couple of days ago during a particularly tedious discussion in the House.

It was hard work, but he needed the release. He hadn't had sex with Olivia since this business began, and he knew that if he didn't relieve his pent-up sexual feelings, his cruel streak would come out again. He hated upsetting his children, and he didn't mean to hurt Olivia either, but the way she looked at him sometimes was enough to drive a saint to violence. Who did she think she was? He'd dragged her out of the gutter and this was how she repaid him.

She'd refused to wear the French maid's outfit he had bought her, with black stockings and no knickers. She said it made her look like a slag, and couldn't understand that that was the point – that it turned him on like crazy. His erection withered as he remembered the look of disdain on her face.

He needed sex. His collection of pornographic films were his life-saver. If he couldn't spill out those feelings, he had no control at all over his temper.

The doorbell rang again, and his erection wilted completely. Whoever it was could go to hell. He needed this; Katie Faye was staying with them and he didn't want her to witness him hitting Olivia again. He started to work his wrist, slowly and evenly.

The doorbell rang for a third time.

'Someone's definitely in, guv,' Alison said. 'There are lights on, and four cars in the driveway.'

A moment later, Kevin opened the door. Alison stepped

in the hallway without waiting to be invited. 'We need another word with your mother and father.'

'How are you?' Banham asked Kevin, keeping his voice down.

'I'm all right, but Mum's not. Dad's back, and she's in a real state.'

'Where is he?'

'I'll get him.' Kevin ushered them into the living room. Olivia was sitting on the pale leather sofa and Katie was cross-legged on a rug on the floor, hair newly washed and hanging damp around her shoulders. She turned her wide-set blue eyes on Banham, and Alison tried to ignore the jealousy that stirred in the pit of her stomach.

'Is anything wrong?' Katie asked.

'We need to ask Mr Stone a couple more questions,' Banham told her.

Olivia stood up. 'Can I get you something? A drink?'

Banham shook his head. 'You didn't mention that you visited Brian Finn in prison,' he said.

Katie still had those eyes fixed on Banham.

'It was only a couple of times,' Olivia said. 'It didn't seem relevant.'

'Actually that's not true,' Alison said crisply. 'We've got the visiting records. You visited him quite regularly. Why?'

Olivia shrugged. 'I thought if I befriended him he might give me those embarrassing videos back.'

Raised voices came from upstairs. Banham looked up at the ceiling, than back at Olivia. Her cheek was still bruised. 'What really happened to your face?' he asked her.

'I told you. I walked into a door.' She looked at Katie, but the other woman turned her head away.

The lounge door opened and Kenneth walked in, his shirt hanging out of his trousers. Kevin followed him.

'What do you want this time?' Kenneth demanded. 'This is beginning to look like police harassment.'

'We need a word, in private,' Banham said coldly.

Ken looked at Olivia. She didn't move. 'Take them to your study,' she said.

'I can't. There are confidential papers out. You'd better come through to the kitchen,' he said irritably.

'He's got *Big and Bouncy* open on the desk,' Kevin told them as they left the lounge.

Olivia followed them.

'I hope you've got a good reason for bothering me like this,' Kenneth said, shifting his eyes from Alison to Banham as he ushered them in the kitchen.

Olivia perched on the stool by the door. 'I presume I'm allowed in,' she said.

Banham nodded acquiescence. 'Why didn't you tell me you visited Brian Finn in prison?' he asked Kenneth.

'I didn't.' Kenneth narrowed his eyes angrily at his wife.

Banham folded his arms across his chest and leaned back against the wall. Alison stood by the table.

'Oh, for goodness' sake,' Olivia said. 'They've got the records – times, dates, everything. It says clearly Mr K Stone and Mrs O Stone. I've seen them. You might as well admit it.'

'I didn't visit him,' Kenneth said again.

'Do you want to get arrested for obstructing a murder enquiry?' Olivia said through gritted teeth. 'Tell them, or they'll arrest you again.'

'All right.' Kenneth threw his arms in the air. 'I visited Brian Finn regularly in prison. Satisfied?'

'So why deny it?' asked Alison quietly.

'Oh, for Chrissake!' He slapped his forehead. 'I've had a very long day and you're trying my patience.'

'Three women have been murdered,' Banham said, battening down the urge to shout. 'It's my job to find out who did it, before he does it again. I don't have time for patience.'

Kenneth's gaze settled on Olivia's cleavage. 'I visited him because my wife is a whore, and had embarrassed me by making pornographic videos. I need to get them back. If they get into the public domain, my career is down the tube.' He glared at Banham. 'Anything else?'

'Yes, as it happens. Why did you buy two skips of costumes at the Scarlet Pussy Club auction?'

Olivia's head shot up. 'I didn't know that.' She looked at Banham. 'I definitely didn't know that.'

'What auction?' Kenneth said wearily.

Alison sighed. 'Mr Stone, we have the receipts.'

'Then arrest me.'

'Ken, for goodness' sake, just tell them.' Olivia's voice sounded taut and stretched.

He took a step towards her. 'Are you calling me a liar?'

'What happened to your wife's face, Mr Stone?' Alison said.

Colour flooded Kenneth's face. 'Are you trying to set me up?' he snarled. 'I'm telling you once and for all, I didn't kill those women.' He flew at Alison, grabbing her arm and dragging her towards the door. 'Fuck off out of my house.'

Banham grabbed the shirttail, which was hanging out of his trousers and twisted him round. He grabbed his wrists and pulled them firmly behind his back as Alison pulled out handcuffs. She clicked them around Stone's wrists as Banham recited the caution: 'Kenneth Stone, I am arresting you for attempting to assault a police officer, and for withholding information that is vital in a murder investigation...'

Olivia started crying, and Katie and Kevin ran in to comfort her. While Alison marched Kenneth to the unmarked police car at the bottom of the drive, Banham stayed with the women. 'He did that to your face,' he said to Olivia. 'Why don't you tell me about it?'

'I *have* told you. I walked into a door.'

Kevin and Katie Faye exchanged glances. Kevin said, 'Mum, tell him what happened.'

Olivia shook her head.

'You tell him, Auntie Katie.'

Katie looked nervously at Banham, then lowered her gaze.

Banham pulled his wallet from his pocket and handed Olivia a card. 'If you change your mind and want to press charges, just give me a call.'

'Will you let him go?' she asked anxiously.

'We'll keep him overnight, at least.'

'Mum feels nervous when Dad's not here,' Kevin said. 'I have no idea why.'

'No need,' Banham assured them. 'There are officers keeping guard twenty-four hours a day. If you go out, they'll be right with you. And you can call me any time, night or day.'

The women seemed to relax a little. *Time to leave*, Banham thought. But something held him back. 'Can I have a private word with you?' he asked, with a quick glance at Kevin.

'It's all right, don't mind him,' Olivia said. 'What is it?'

'Your stripper names? Have you remembered who was who?'

Olivia answered quickly. 'Honestly, we can't. I think I was Candyfloss and Katie was Honeysuckle.'

'Honeysuckle?' That was a new one on Banham.

'Wasn't it the other way round?' Katie said.

'What about Strawberry? One of you was Strawberry, isn't that right?' Banham said.

'I don't remember,' Katie said.

Olivia shook her head. 'Why does it matter?'

'I'm trying to piece things together. If you do remember, you will call me?' He handed another card to Katie. 'Any time. Night or day.'

He turned to find Alison standing in the doorway. Her arms were folded across her chest, and the black flecks in her eyes shining.

'Are you OK?' Banham asked as they walked down the gravel driveway.

'I'm fine. Stone reeks of alcohol.'

'We'll leave him in a cell to sober up. Interview him later, even in the morning.'

'Good. That gives us time to visit Lottie. Shall I call her and say we'll pop by?'

'No point; she'll be on the phone. We'll just turn up.'

It was seven twenty by the time Alison had negotiated the rush-hour traffic. The low hanging branches in Cherry Tree Walk had again caught the paintwork on the roof of her car, and after they parked in Lottie's street she examined it for damage.

There was an excited squeal as seven-year-old Madeleine spotted her Uncle Paul, and clattered down the street to greet him in her mother's high-heeled shoes. She carried a doll under one arm and a burger in the other hand; between those and the oversized shoes, Alison was afraid she might fall over.

Banham obviously thought the same. He ran to meet her and scooped her into his arms. From one pocket he pulled a handkerchief, which he used to wipe the lipstick covering her mouth. From the other he took a packet of chocolate raisins, and offered them to her. Madeleine struggled out of his arms and sat on the edge of the pavement, discarding the burger and emptying the sweets all over her lap.

'It's too cold to sit out here,' Banham said, throwing Alison an anxious look. 'Let's go indoors.'

'Mummy says we're to eat our tea out here, then play out until bedtime,' the little girl told him.

'Where's Bobby?' Alison asked.

'Round the corner, playing football,' Madeleine answered through a mouthful of chocolate.

'Who with?'

'Shane and Leyton, I think.'

'Come on.' Banham held out a hand. 'Let's go and find him.'

The look on his face told Alison it was all he could do not to explode.

She waited till they had turned the corner, then walked up the path. The front door was on the latch.

'Lottie?' She put her head round the lounge door just as Lottie replaced the phone on its cradle. 'Hi. The front door was open, so I came in out of the cold.'

'Is Paul with you?' Lottie sounded wary.

'He's playing football with the children.'

Lottie looked sheepish. 'Do you want some tea? Or something stronger?'

'Tea's fine. I'll put the kettle on, shall I?'

The small, compact kitchen was decorated with children's drawings in brightly coloured crayon. On the fridge door was one of a green stick man marked "Uncle Paul", and beside that a pink stick woman, holding a telephone. That one was labelled "Mummy".

'You have observant children,' Alison said casually.

'I've got a telephone job at the moment,' Lottie said, reaching for the teapot. 'I need a job I can do at home.'

Alison looked Lottie directly in the eye. 'Tell me to mind my own business if you want, but I wasn't born yesterday.'

'I need a job I can do at home,' Lottie insisted. 'Derek

owes me back maintenance. I need to earn some money.'

'I understand,' Alison said, covering Lottie's hand with her own. 'But – telephone sex?'

'It's well paid.'

'And dangerous. Who knows what it might lead to?'

'What do you know about it?'

'Lottie, we're detectives. We see things. And Paul cares so much for you. He worries terribly, you know, about you and the kids.'

Lottie banged the milk jug on the worktop. 'It's none of his business.'

'Perhaps not. It's even less mine, but I'm still concerned about you. Thanks, but I don't take milk.'

'You're too thin. You shouldn't diet.'

'I'm not dieting. I'm allergic to milk. Look, Lottie, can I talk to you, in confidence?'

Lottie looked at her and her face softened. 'Sure.'

'We're on a very nasty murder case. The killer has tracked down a group of women who worked together nearly twenty years ago, in a strip club. They were just students at the time, and they needed money. But the job didn't stop at stripping. The girls got involved in pornographic videos, and now it's led to blackmail. It was all nearly twenty years ago, but three of the women have been murdered, and the other three are living in fear. That all started because they all needed a job that earned them quick and easy money. They all thought the sex trade would provide it.'

'What's the motive? Paul always says there has to be a motive,' Lottie said. 'Find that, and it will lead you to the killer. Don't they reckon that in two out every three cases the victim knows the killer?' She passed Alison her mug of black tea.

They were going off the subject. But Lottie was right. 'You've got it,' she said. 'We're stuck on motive. Maybe that's the key.'

She shook her head as Lottie offered her a tin of Rich Tea biscuits.

'What about the other three women?' Lottie suggested.

Alison laughed. 'You should be my twin, not Paul's. That's exactly what I was thinking.'

'Must be a woman's mind. We're devious.'

'And you're changing the subject. We were talking about you. Listen, I think I might have a solution for you.'

'I won't take money from Paul!'

'No, of course not. But surely you'll accept a loan.'

'How can I pay him back if I give up the job?'

'That's easy. Derek owes you big time – and that's something Paul can take care of. He'll enjoy going to see him, and he'll make sure he pays up. Then you can pay Paul back.' Lottie looked dubious.

'Think of the children, Lottie.'

For a moment, Alison thought she had won, then Lottie shook her head.

'OK. If you won't take a loan from Paul, how about from me?'

'You?'

'Yeah.' Alison winked. 'Then I get to have a go at Derek. Am I allowed to punch his lights out?'

Lottie smiled. 'OK, you win.' She laughed. 'It's a crap

job anyway. Though I was getting good at it, especially with the older men.'

'So if I need help getting someone to fancy me, I can come to you?'

'You certainly can. I've learned all the tricks of the trade.'

'You didn't talk to anyone with a fetish for red G-strings by any chance?'

'No. There was someone with a thing for older strippers, though.'

Alison's antennae were suddenly on alert. 'You haven't got that on tape, have you?'

'Of course. I have to tape everything. I get paid per call. But I'd die if Paul heard me.'

'He won't. You have my word. I'll listen to it myself, and if it's no use, I'll return it. Or destroy it.'

'Return it, please,' Lottie said with a grin. 'I haven't been paid for it yet. Are you two staying for supper?'

'That would be nice – but we'll have a takeaway, and my treat. You and I can fetch it while Paul puts Bobby and Madeleine to bed.'

Lottie went to get her coat. Alison went in search of Banham, who was playing football with the children.

'Sorted,' she told him. 'I'm lending her the money. Better for her pride. You get the job of sorting Derek out. If you think you might hit him, maybe better let me.'

'He deserves a smack.'

'Yes, I know. I want to do it.'

'Uncle Paul, it's your kick-off,' Madeleine shouted from across the street. She had joined in the football, wearing her mother's shoes.

Banham walked over and picked her up. 'It's bedtime. I'm going to tell you your favourite story – Cinderella and her Fairy Godmother.'

Alison couldn't help noticing Madeleine looked just like him.

'I wish Mummy had a fairy godmother,' Alison heard the little girl say to her plastic doll.

'She has,' Banham answered, with a glance over his shoulder at Alison.

Madeleine's little eyes lit up. 'Will she make Mummy's dreams come true?'

'Yes.'

'And will we have lots of money, and be able to buy school shoes for Bobby, and nappies for Molly-Dolly?'

'Oh, yes,' Banham assured her, taking the shoes from her and tucking her feet under his jumper as he carried her up the path.

'And do fairy godmothers only grant wishes to people who are good?'

'That's right.'

Bobby slouched up, his football under his arm, scowling to make sure they all knew he was too old for that silly stuff.

'No wonder we haven't got any money,' Madeleine said. 'Mummy is always saying bad words.'

Lottie was standing on the doorstep. Alison lowered her gaze as Banham locked eyes with his sister.

Then Lottie said, 'Mummy isn't going to say bad words ever again.'

CHAPTER FOURTEEN

Banham had been awake most of the night tossing thoughts around in his mind. He got up early, and rang Alison.

'Heather's doing the post-mortem on Theresa McGann this morning. I'd like you to come with me.'

There was a silence. Then, 'What about Ken Stone?' she asked.

'We'll give him a bit more time to cool down.'

'OK. Um ... you're sure about the post-mortem, guv?'

He wasn't, but had no intention of admitting it.

The mortuary technician pulled open the cold-drawer containing Theresa McGann's body. Her name was written on a label tied to her waxy white toe. As she was wheeled to the metal table in the middle of the room, Banham saw a look of concern pass between Alison and Heather Draper, the pathologist.

He felt in his pocket for the three clean handkerchiefs he had brought with him. He was determined to see this through.

The nauseating smell of disinfectant mixed with dead flesh suddenly hit his nostrils. He stared hard at the walls. He was coping. If he got through this, he would have made another leap forward. Maybe next time he would be able to look at a female corpse and not be reminded of his own tragedy. Sometimes he still believed that he'd come home and find Diane cooking supper, and Elizabeth, now eleven, doing her homework. At other times, the memory of that tiny broken body hit him so hard the pain made him want to cry out.

Something touched his arm. 'Are you all right, guv?' Alison asked.

He managed a nod.

Heather Draper shook her head. 'It's not imperative that you're here,' she told him gently. 'I'll have the report on your desk by lunchtime.'

He hesitated, but he had made a promise to himself. For better or worse he was staying put.

'Make sure you get the mouth and broken teeth from all angles,' he said to the exhibits officer.

The officer nodded, and moved in closer to video the wounds on Theresa's mouth. After a minute he stepped back. Banham felt in his pocket for handkerchiefs again as the cutting and the drilling and dissecting began.

He kept his eyes pinned on Theresa's mouth, frozen ajar and smeared with stale blood, but he was sickeningly aware of a sound like a nail being dragged across a television screen, which he knew was the stomach being cut open. He could see Heather out of the corner of his eye. She lifted the skin and went in with gloved hands to examine the contents. Banham forced himself to concentrate on why he had come. He now had a good idea who the killer was, but he needed evidence. And he hoped it might be here.

'I'm not sure I could eat anything,' Katie Faye said, watching Kevin dish scrambled egg and tomato on to her plate.

'You must try, Auntie Katie.'

'I expect they'll let Daddy out this morning,' Olivia said brightly.

Ianthe had been tucking heartily into her breakfast. Now she looked up at her mother and stopped chewing.

'Do they have to?' she asked Katie.

'He's frightened, darling. He didn't mean to hit Mummy. He won't do that again.'

'Come off it. He does it all the time,' Kevin protested.

'He hits me and Kevin too,' Ianthe said. 'I hate him.'

Katie looked at Olivia. She shook her head. 'They're exaggerating.'

'We're not,' said Kevin.

There was an awkward silence. Katie fiddled with her food, then threw her fork down. 'Come outside a minute,' she said to Olivia.

Olivia followed her into the lounge. Katie closed the door and leaned back against it, folding her arms across her figure-hugging lilac roll-neck sweater. 'What's going on, Liv?'

'You've never been married. You wouldn't understand.'

'I understand more than you think. Kevin and Ianthe are my godchildren; I have a responsibility to them. If Ken's been hitting them you should have told me.'

Olivia slumped on to the sofa.

'Look, it's pretty obvious that whoever killed Susan and Shaheen and Theresa knows what happened to Ahmed.' She watched Olivia. 'That really narrows things down. If Ken has a violent streak, you have to tell the police. Come on, Olivia, you must see you're putting all our lives in danger.'

Olivia looked away. 'My marriage is none of your business.'

'It's very much my business if my godchildren are getting hurt and my life is at risk.'

'Kevin stands up for us. He's bigger than Ken now – he makes him back down.'

Katie stared at her in disbelief. 'Olivia, he shouldn't have to do that! He's only eighteen.' She narrowed her eyes. 'How long has it been going on?'

'It comes and goes. He thinks I had an affair.'

'Did you?'

Olivia picked up a packet of menthol cigarettes from the table and shook one free. She pushed it into the side of her swollen mouth, and lit it with the heavy onyx lighter on the coffee table. 'No. Marrying Ken put a stop to all that. I'm not a slag, Katie, whatever he thinks.'

Katie perched on the arm of the sofa and put her arm around her friend. 'Livvy, I know it's hard. Deep down you still love him, but he can't be allowed to get away with this. You have to tell the police he has a violent streak.'

'It would ruin his career.'

'He's ruining your life! And Ianthe is terrified of him. He's a bully, and I can't understand how he's got such a hold over you all. Ianthe will never trust men, and Kevin will become aggressive himself. And if he keeps getting away with it, he'll only get worse.'

Olivia dragged hard on the cigarette, blew the smoke out and took another deep puff.

'Olivia, I'm sorry, but I'm not letting this go on. Here's the deal: either you tell the police Ken did that to your face, or I will.'

'You'll do no such thing!' Olivia sat bolt upright.

'So you do it.'

Olivia ground the end of the cigarette into the ashtray.

'I mean it, Livvy. There's too much at stake here.'

Olivia rubbed the back of her neck. 'You're right. I know you are. It's just ... he's my husband, Katie. I can't let myself believe he's a ...' She swallowed hard. 'OK. I'll talk to the police. But don't be surprised if he kills me.'

'Brave girl,' Katie said gently. 'I'll come with you if you like.'

'No, I'd rather go alone. I'll have to do it before they release him or I'll lose my nerve. I'll go this morning.'

After Heather Draper had examined the cornflakes, milk, and fruit juice Theresa had consumed for breakfast, she moved to the wound across the throat. Again Banham nodded to the exhibits officer, and the DC moved in with his video camera and photographed the wound from every possible angle.

'The pattern is the same as in the other two victims,' Heather said, pointing to the crusted, blackened blood on the neck. 'Same shape, same depth. I'd stake my reputation he used the same weapon.'

'Which we haven't found,' Alison added.

'You're looking for a knife about nine inches long,' Heather told her.

'What about any residue on the wound from the knife?' Banham asked her.

'Yes, I was going to mention that,' Heather said. 'The grit in this wound is consistent with what I found on the last victim, but not the same as the first one. Penny, do you want to…?'

She raised a hand, and Penny Starr stepped forward, a flat utensil in her blue-gloved hand. She scraped carefully at the tiny particles of grit edging the neck wound and slid it into an evidence bag. 'I'll make this a priority,' she said. 'I'll get back to you ASAP.'

Banham rubbed his hand across his mouth thoughtfully. 'The weapon was hidden. After the first murder he hid it, then put it back in the same place after the second. I'll bet he's put it back again, and it's there now.'

'Or she,' Alison said in a low voice.

'So wherever it was kept, it wasn't very clean. Heather, do we know anything else, other than a nine-inch blade?'

'It was sharp, maybe new. A butcher's knife, or one used for carving. Could be a good-quality kitchen knife.'

'Could the grit be soil? Perhaps it's been hidden outside, in a shed or a garage.'

'Crowther searched the Stones' house,' Alison said, 'but I didn't see anything in the report about the garden. I'm trying to remember if they've got a garden shed.'

'You can see the garden from that long lounge,'

Banham said. 'I didn't notice a shed. Just loads of different trees.'

'Very green and very well kept,' Alison added. 'The front ones, at least.'

'I can test for unusual foliage,' Penny offered.

'Good idea,' said Banham. His mobile bleeped for attention, and he pulled it out of his pocket. Alison followed him into the corridor.

'That was the DCI again,' he said, flicking it closed. 'Ken Stone's solicitor is claiming police harassment, and the DCI wants him either charged or released before we have the press down on our heads.'

'We can only charge him with assaulting a police officer,' Alison said. 'And we'll have to bail him.'

'Drop me back at the station,' Banham said. 'I'll try to stall for time. You pick up Isabelle and take one of Penny's team back to the Stones' to look at the garden. But try not to be seen. It will take at least two hours to get a section eighteen search through.'

'Even if your name is Crowther?'

'I'll get him on to it,' Banham said with a brief grin. 'Start a search of the grounds anyway. See if there's a shed, then scoop up some soil and foliage samples.'

Alison nodded. 'Katie Faye is staying there.'

Banham stiffened. 'What are you saying?'

'She's a suspect. So is Olivia Stone.'

'I think you're wrong. Those women are victims.'

They had reached the door. Alison pushed it open and took out her car keys. 'But you admit yourself, you're not very good at reading women.'

'I can read you.'

'Really? Go on, then. What am I thinking?' She smiled at him; that twinkle he found so attractive was back in her eyes. But he didn't have a clue what she was thinking. Of course he didn't.

Before he could think of something to say, she had climbed into her car and started the engine.

Judy had brought the large wooden skip of costumes down from the loft. She knelt on the floor on the landing, sorting through the feather boas, lacy body-stockings and other skimpy garments. Kim sat beside her, folding the costumes neatly and putting them into piles to go back in the skips.

'There are definitely no G-strings in here,' Judy said. 'I thought I remembered seeing some, in the boxes Ken Stone passed to us.'

Kim finished folding a white lace maid's apron and added it to the pile. It was a few seconds before she answered in a quiet voice. 'There were. They were with the bag of different coloured tassels. I took that box to the school, remember? We used them in the *Chicago* number we did in the Christmas show. That box of costumes is still there, in the props wardrobe.'

'Are they the boxes you were going through yesterday?'

'Yes.'

'Looking for red G-strings?'

Kim nodded. 'But they weren't the ones that we used when we worked at the club. We all took our G-strings home and washed them ourselves. We always did that, so we didn't wear each other's. That's why we initialled them.'

Judy watched her carefully.

'So,' she continued a little louder, 'the red G-strings in these skips wouldn't belong to any of us.' She paused for a few seconds. 'Because after we went home that night, we never danced again.' She laid the white aprons back in the skip and took a deep breath. 'We went back to the club on the Monday, because we had agreed to turn up and make it look as if everything was normal. But we knew it wasn't. He was dead, and the club would be closed and we wouldn't be dancing.' Her voice cracked. 'Because he was dead. We'd killed him.' She took a deep breath and seemed to calm down a little. 'So I didn't bring my G-strings with me to the club. I left them at home, and I assumed the other girls had too.'

'But you can't be sure?'

'No.' She looked at Judy, and repeated, a little more loudly, 'No. I can't be sure.'

'So what exactly are you saying?'

'That the red G-strings in the costume skips weren't the ones that belonged to us. 'They wouldn't have had our initials on them.'

'But there aren't any red G-strings in this skip, are there?'

'There don't seem to be, no.'

'And the ones left with the bodies did have initials on them.'

Kim couldn't look at Judy. 'Someone is trying to frame us.'

'Who?' Judy asked, struggling to keep her voice level. 'Do you mean Ken Stone?'

'I just don't know.'

'So what are you looking for?'

'Costumes. Our costumes, the ones we wore.'

Judy put a hand to her forehead. 'I'm not following this,' she said, trying to stay calm.

'If I could recognise any of the costumes, I might be able to ... but I can't, because my memory's shot to pieces by the drugs. And it's so long ago.' She stood up and clutched at the banister rail. 'The club was closed that night, when we came back to work,' she went on. 'There was no work. The police were there, asking questions. So all our costumes were left behind. They had our initials on them – that's what we did. If I could just see them again, I might remember who wore them, then I could check the initials. And I'd know who used what initial...'

Her voice trailed away and she began to tremble. Judy got to her feet and put a hand on her partner's shoulder. 'But you can't, Sausage. It was so long ago. No one expects...'

'I was called Dusty Springfield, I think.' She knuckled her eyes like a child. *She looks so tired*, Judy thought. 'But I can't rely on my memory. Dusty. But I'm sure he called me Rusty sometimes. He hated me,' she ended, a sob in her voice.

'There's a mix-up about Olivia and Katie's names. You can't clear that one up, can you?'

'You've asked me that already.' She ran her fingers through her hair and scratched her head. 'Katie changed her name. Ahmed made some disgusting remark about her pubic hair tasting of candyfloss, so she changed it to Honeysuckle.' She nodded thoughtfully, as if she was pleased she had remembered. 'That's it. Olivia was Strawberry, and Katie was Candyfloss but changed to Honeysuckle. And we wrote our initials with Olivia's red pen, and Olivia drew a strawberry next to her initial. Unless I dreamed it.'

'Red pen? Didn't you say blue before?'

'Did I? Oh, I'm not sure. Yes, I think you're right, it was blue. The costumes in the other skip are marked in red ink, but not with our initials. Someone else marked theirs in red.' She rubbed her temple. 'It's all a blur. I don't remember any of us wearing the French maid or the bunny rabbit costumes, and that's all there is in that skip.'

Judy put her arm round her. 'I'm going to make you some Earl Grey tea. You're tired, Sausage, and I don't think you're thinking straight.'

'I hate those police being outside spying on us. Can't they leave you to look after me? You will, won't you? Whatever happens?'

'Forget about them, Sausage. I will always look after you.' Her hand moved to cover her mouth. Kim was pale and thin, and that grey cardigan would have gone round her a dozen times. She ran her long fingers through her short brown hair, and looked around with nervous eyes before walking down the stairs. Judy threw the costumes back in the skip and followed her.

Crowther was out of his chair and heading for Banham as

soon as he walked in the incident room. Banham didn't let him get a word out. 'Yes, I know,' he said to the young DC.

Crowther spread his arms defensively. 'I haven't said a word yet!'

Banham kept walking. 'The DCI is on my case. Ken Stone's brief is having a field day, and is going to take me to the complaints board. And you've heard a rumour about a sergeant's job, so you're telling me before anyone else can.'

'OK, guv.' Crowther held up his hands. 'Just trying to help.'

'If you really want to help, get me a section eighteen for Alison and Isabelle, marked an hour ago. They're on their way to the Stones'.'

'I'm on it, guv.'

'You didn't notice a shed in the Stones' garden, did you?'

Crowther shook his head. 'There's an orchard at the back of the garden. I walked through it. It goes on for ever, but there ain't no shed.'

Banham pushed out his bottom lip.

'There's a small summerhouse,' Crowther offered. 'I looked in there; just a couple of chairs and a few motoring magazines.'

That was something. Banham flipped his phone open and called Alison.

'Any danger of me knowing why a shed?' Crowther asked as Banham closed his phone.

'The PM has turned up some grit on the second and

third victims, but not on the first. Looks like the weapon was hidden in the same place both times – probably outside.'

'Could it be a lock-up?' Crowther suggested. 'The killer could have rented a garage.'

Banham stopped, and turned to look at Crowther. 'Well done,' he said. 'It could be. Let's check Kenneth Stone's personals, and see if there are any extra keys are on his keyring. Then we'll talk to him just once more before the DCI knows I'm back and makes us bail the bastard.'

A voice boomed across the room. 'DI Banham!'

The DCI. For a moment Banham felt like a child whose hand had been caught in the biscuit jar. Then, to his relief, his phone bleeped. He put it to his ear, giving the senior officer a polite nod. As he listened to the voice at the other the end his face broke into a broad smile. 'We'll be waiting for you,' he said, giving Crowther a triumphant thumbs-up. 'Thank you, Olivia.' He closed his phone and beamed at the DCI. 'Mrs Stone wants her husband charged with domestic violence and kept away from her and the kids. She's on her way in to make it official.'

'Nice one, guvnor,' Crowther grinned.

'I'll tell the boss we're going to let him go within the hour. You can tell his brief the same. Then you get the pleasure of taking Mr Stone through to release him, and as he is claiming his possessions you re-arrest him for domestic violence. Meanwhile Alison and Isabelle are turning his garden over looking for a weapon. And we've now got another thirty-six hours to find it.'

CHAPTER FIFTEEN

Alison's newly mended exhaust was dragging on the ground as the car bounced over the potholes of Cherry Tree Walk. Every few seconds, stones flew from either side of the wheels, some hitting the windscreen. Isabelle was finding the experience highly amusing, which only served to wind Alison up further.

The police surveillance car was missing; one member of the team had driven Olivia Stone to the station. A solitary officer raised his hand in greeting as Alison drew the car to a halt. He pointed at the traffic cone reserving a space opposite the Stones' driveway, but Alison shook her head and lowered the window.

'No,' she said to the young DC. 'Katie Faye is in there with the children. We don't want them to see us from the window – we're still waiting for our search warrant.' She put the car in reverse and the wheels spun in a pothole, kicking up a stone which hit the paintwork. She cursed under her breath. 'I'm parking under that bush by the wall. We'll be out of sight there, from all sides of the house.'

The surveillance officer backed away, and for once Isabelle didn't argue. She pulled blue forensic gloves over her hands picked up the black evidence bag from the floor. 'You don't like Katie Faye, do you?'

Alison revved the car noisily as she reversed, drove

forward a few inches than back again, each time trying and failing to edge nearer to the wall. '*Like* has nothing to do with anything,' she said. 'I don't trust her, or Olivia Stone.'

'Nothing to do with the way our DI can't take his eyes off the lovely Miss Faye?'

'Who told you that?'

'You did.'

Alison slammed her foot on the brake. The car was still sticking out at an angle. 'Let's just concentrate on the job, shall we?' Realising how badly she had parked, she started moving the car backwards and forwards again, but to no avail. 'He's a useless judge of women, you said that yourself.'

Isabelle said nothing.

'If he fancies her, that's his lookout,' Alison added. She brought the car to a standstill and noticed Isabelle squeezing her lips together. 'All right, I'm the world's worst at parking. Don't rub it in.'

Isabelle swallowed the laugh. 'What are we looking for, sergeant?'

'Collect earth, foliage and stones.'

'Yes, ma'am.'

'I'll go round the back to check the summer house. If we're seen, say we have a search warrant. Know-all Col is on the case, so I have no doubt we'll have one soon.'

Alison opened the car door. 'And you don't like those women any more than I do.'

'I certainly don't trust them.'

'Woman's intuition.' Alison closed the door quietly.

'Ken Stone isn't the only suspect around here.'

'It's not looking good for him,' Isabelle pointed out. She took a leap and landed lightly on top of the fence, then disappeared over the other side, unhampered by her long black coat, or the pink and mauve scarf knotted around her neck. *She even managed to look gorgeous climbing a fence*, Alison thought. As usual, she had chosen practical clothes for the damp and frosty weather: khaki chords, brown flecked jumper over a thick green shirt, with her parka-style anorak over the top. Her hair was pulled back in a ponytail with a dull brown scrunchie, and on her feet she wore sensible brown walking boots. She would have loved to be naturally sexy and feminine, like the Katie Fayes and the Isabelles of the world, with tiny waists and button noses. But she preferred comfortable, sporty clothes, didn't like make-up except for special occasions, and her favourite sport was self-defence. No wonder Banham couldn't take his eyes off Katie Faye.

But she couldn't think about that now; she had a job to do. She was over the fence and standing in the driveway in a couple of seconds, and found herself face to face with Katie. The actress was wearing a sugar pink T-shirt tucked into ice-blue jeans, finished off with a thick black leather belt that accentuated her tiny waist.

'What are you doing, what's going on?' she asked looking from Alison to Isabelle, who was already on her knees and had started shovelling dirt from the ground into a plastic evidence bag.

'We need to check the grounds. Just routine.'

'And you shouldn't come out of the house,' Isabelle

added. 'It's not safe.'

Katie looked uncertain. 'I just came to see...'

Alison pressed home her advantage. 'If you see someone in your garden, you should ring the number you've been given.' She pointed at DC Holt, now sitting on a tree trunk at the bottom of the driveway, a newspaper open on his lap. 'No point having a policeman on guard if you don't make use of him.'

Katie turned those enormous blue eyes on her, and Alison pretended to be taken in. 'How are you?' she asked her.

'What do you mean, just routine check?'

Alison shrugged. 'We've just been asked to collect some samples, and check on you. Are you alone here?'

'Not for long. Kevin has taken Ianthe to see her pony, but they'll be back soon. And Judy and Kim are going to come over in a while, to keep me company.'

'Good.' Alison pointed at DC Holt again. 'Denis Holt is watching the house, and Charlie Mitchell will be back as soon as Olivia has given her statement.'

Katie's eyes wandered to Isabelle, clipping fragments from the base of the bush at the bottom of the drive.

'And I think you'll find Kenneth Stone won't be released just yet.'

Katie turned the vulnerable eyes on Alison again. 'Thank you,' she said softly, with a grateful smile.

Alison was more than ever convinced Katie was putting on an act. From her own days in amateur theatre, she knew it was the tough ones who got the best parts; given the kind of success she'd had, Katie Faye simply wasn't this vulnerable. 'You're welcome,' she said. 'All part of the service. I'll just go for a quick look round the back while we're here.'

It took her less than three minutes to find the summerhouse and turn the whole place upside down. She found nothing incriminating.

Katie was still standing in the driveway when she came back through the garden gate.

As she reached the bottom of her drive and came within sight of her car, her mouth fell open. 'Oh fuck!' she shouted, staring at her second flat tyre in two days. 'Fuck, fuck, fuck!'

'Something else for the expense account,' Isabelle said, right behind her.

'The bloody thing's only just out of the garage,' Alison said angrily, pointing her key at the boot to get the spare. 'Thank God I got the last one fixed.'

A chuckle from a few yards away made her turn. DC Holt was mightily amused.

'That is way above the call of duty,' Isabelle said, failing to keep her face straight.

Alison chose to ignore the fun both DCs were having at her expense. 'Tell you what, though,' she said. 'I'm glad that I don't do kitten pink T-shirts, arse-tight jeans and high heels.' She threw the spare wheel on the frosty ground and lifted the wheel brace and jack out of the boot. She flung Isabelle an angry glance. 'Do something useful,' she snapped. 'Go and collect some dirt from this side of the fence.' She gestured at a large bush that leaned, half in the road, and half in the Stones' driveway. 'To compare with the earth on the other side.'

Isabelle patted the earth below the bush. 'Hey, this is newly dug.' She prodded the bush. 'You know, I thought this didn't look real last time we were here. It's too green for this time of the year.'

DC Holt put in his fourpennyworth. 'It was only planted a few days ago. They wanted a bit more privacy.' He carried on reading his paper, and Alison and Isabelle looked at each other. Isabelle put her hand on the base of the bush.

Alison stood up.

'It's not very secure either,' Isabelle said.

'Holt? Over here,' Alison ordered.

The three of them dug down into the loose soil with bare hands and the small shovel, until Isabelle hissed, 'There's something down here, buried.'

Alison looked up the drive towards the house. Katie was nowhere in sight. By the time she looked back down Isabelle was dragging a bulky blue carrier bag from under the bush. She opened it and pulled out a long knife, then a dirty transparent plastic bag.

It was full of red G-string knickers.

The cuffs of Crowther's new jeans were turned up so much he looked as if he was wearing knee-high socks. He wore a blue jacket dotted with tiny flakes of silver, which might or might not have been an attack of dandruff.

Crowther was flattered that Banham had given him the job of taking Olivia Stone's statement. Where he came from, in the worst part of the East End of London, women often took a belting from their husbands when they stepped out of line. But it was something he hated. He treated women flippantly, but he liked them a lot. He'd sleep with them and move on, but he liked to think he made them feel good about themselves. He was old-fashioned that way; he looked after his girls, cherished and spoiled them, bought them nice dinners, liked them to dress up nicely for him. He was first to admit he was a bit of a chauvinist, but he would never hurt a woman, and he despised men who did.

So this wasn't about gaining brownie points for promotion. This was about the beautiful woman who was sitting opposite him, distressed, with a swollen, bruised face.

He placed a cup of coffee on the table in front of her. 'I've sprinkled chocolate flakes on the top,' he said. 'It gives it that extra flavour. I hope you're not watching your figure.'

Her full mouth stretched in an attempt at a smile. That told him what he needed to know – that he was winning her over. 'I made it warm, not too hot, in case your mouth is tender.' He smiled. 'It certainly looks it to me.'

'Thank you.' She smiled back. Even with one of those eyes puffy and shiny, she was a real stunner.

'I'm going to record this interview, just routine. No hurry and no pressure. Have your coffee first.'

Suddenly tense, she shivered and pulled her cardigan from the back of her chair. It was cerise cashmere trimmed with a fur collar the same colour. Crowther briefly wondered what animal it was supposed to be from.

He winked to reassure her.

'Can I smoke?' she asked.

'Course.' He took an ashtray from the drawer and put it in front of her.

She opened her bag and scrabbled around for her cigarettes and lighter. She laid them on the table, and Crowther picked up the lighter, waiting for her to put a cigarette in the side of her swollen mouth. When she did he lit it, and watched her blow the smoke out.

'You want to make a statement about the abuse you have suffered at the hands of your husband, Kenneth Stone,' he said, softening the formal words with an encouraging nod.

'It's for my children,' she said. 'I wouldn't be here if it wasn't for them.'

'They're afraid of him too?'

She paused. 'Yes, they are.' Her voice broke slightly as she spoke. 'He hits them as well.'

'He's a violent man, isn't he?'

She fought back the tears as she nodded agreement.

Crowther leaned towards her. 'Was he violent when you first knew him?'

'No, not violent. But he's always been jealous, and possessive of me.'

He tried to sound sympathetic. 'When did he start to show his violent side?'

Olivia flicked nervously on the cigarette. 'I can't remember exactly. What will happen? Will he get a warning? Or what?'

'That depends,' he said gently. 'He's also a suspect in a

murder enquiry.'

Olivia looked at him wide-eyed.

'Did he tell you he bought a skip containing red G-string knickers and a large quantity of sex videos at an auction when the Scarlet Pussy Club changed hands?'

She looked sheepish. 'That was because ... I made a video. We all did.'

'We know about that. Tell me about him. You met him there, at the club?'

'Buying those videos ... he was trying to stop them getting in the wrong hands, that's all. At the auction he bid for whole skips of stuff in the hope that the videos of me and Katie were in them.'

'But they weren't?'

'No.' She flicked the cigarette again. 'Kim was opening her dance school,' she told him. 'The skips had costumes in them; he thought she would be able to use them for her dance productions. He passed the skips on to her.'

There was a knock on the door and Banham's head appeared. Crowther turned the tape off and excused himself.

Banham quickly updated Crowther on what Alison and Isabelle had found. 'It's going to take a good twelve hours to check for DNA, or faded initials,' he said. 'We can't see any initials on pairs that we've just found, but there is a motif that looks like a strawberry. It's being checked at the lab as we speak. So delay that interview with Olivia Stone any way you can. Tell her something urgent just came up, and you'll have to ask her to wait. I want you to and Isabelle to have another crack at Ken Stone, and Alison and I will go for Finn. We'll keep pushing at them. I think we've got the killer here, but until forensics turns something up, I don't know which one it is.'

Finn was getting agitated. Gone was the nervous underdog; now Banham was seeing another side of this big man, and the undercurrent of anger running through him.

'If you're not charging me, let me go. My kid needs me.'

'She's with her grandmother,' Alison told him. 'And you're looking at another murder charge.'

'Where's your evidence?'

'You're strongly advised to co-operate and answer our questions.'

Finn sighed noisily. 'I want to see a brief.' He raised his voice. 'But I want out of here.'

'Why did Olivia or Katie change her name from Candyfloss to Strawberry?' Banham barked.

Finn shook his head. 'It was Olivia. Ahmed called Olivia Candyfloss because he said she got everywhere. She didn't like it, so she changed it. End of.'

'You've lost me,' Banham said. Alison threw him a despairing look.

Finn leaned back in his chair and put his hands behind his head. 'She put herself about. First Ahmed, then me, and then Fat Ken Stone came along. I wasn't rich, so she dumped me and went off with Stone.' He shrugged. 'No crime there. She was eighteen and beautiful.'

Banham's phone bleeped. He checked the number of the incoming call and switched it off.

'She was getting some attention for the first time in her life,' Finn said. 'Me and Ken Stone, we were both in love with her.'

'What did Theresa think of that?' Banham asked.

Finn laid his hands flat on the desk. 'Olivia chose Ken. I courted Theresa, and I fell in love with her.' He looked away. When he spoke again after a few seconds, his voice had changed and the aggression had gone again. 'I loved all the girls,' he said 'I made it my job to look after them.'

'Why did Ken Stone visit you in prison?' Banham asked.

Finn gave a puzzled frown. 'He didn't.'

'Oh come on, Finn.' Banham was losing patience. 'We have evidence that he did.'

'On my life, guvnor.'

Banham threw down a transparent evidence bag containing the prison record in front of Finn. 'For the tape, I'm showing Mr Finn exhibit 313, prison visiting records,' he said. 'It's there in black and white: Mrs O Stone and Mr K Stone.'

Finn shook his head again and met Banham's eyes. 'That don't say Ken came,' he said. 'That says Mrs O Stone and Mr K Stone. Olivia brought Kevin to see me.' He hesitated a moment before adding, 'He's my son.'

With difficulty, Banham kept his astonishment from showing on his face. This time the silence lasted almost half a minute. Then he asked, 'Does Ken Stone know?'

'Yeah. I couldn't marry her, could I? By the time she knew, I was doing time for Ahmed.' Finn looked away. 'She didn't want me anyway. And I loved Theresa, and she was pregnant too. It was a bit of a mess. But Ken wanted to marry Livvy, so it looked as if it might work out, for her anyway. Then when Kevin was about ten she brought him in to see me, and told him I was his father. They both visited me regular after that. At first Kev didn't want to, but then we got on, had a laugh, like. He told me about Ken, how he got violent with them.' He clenched his fists. 'After that I just wanted to get out and kill the bastard.'

'Is that why you blackmailed him?'

He looked at the wall. 'Wouldn't have been any need, if he'd coughed up like he said he would.' He turned round again and pushed his face into Banham's. 'It was tough on Theresa, you know. She had Bernadette, and it was ... tough.'

'Are you saying the blackmail was her idea?' Alison asked.

Finn made no reply.

'I thought Olivia helped her financially?' Alison pushed.

'Some. Enough to get by.' He blew out a breath. 'I was stuck in prison, Theresa had a handicapped kid, and Olivia had it all. Why shouldn't Mr Kenneth Bigshot Stone pay up?'

'What about Katie Faye? Where does she come into this?' Banham asked. 'She was paying half the blackmail. Didn't you feel guilty about that?'

'No, I didn't!' He slammed a fist on the table. 'If it weren't for me, she'd have nothing.'

'Now you've lost me.' Banham watched Finn's gaze

move nervously around the room.

'It doesn't matter,' he muttered, dropping his head into his hands. 'Oh Christ, what have I said?'

'If there's something you think we should know, you'd better start talking,' Alison said crisply. 'This is a triple murder enquiry, and one of the victims is the woman you love. If you withhold anything that could be relevant, you could be looking at another prison sentence.'

Finn looked at her like a man resigned to a fate he didn't want to imagine. 'All right. It looks like I've got no choice.'

'Do you think we've finally got the truth?' Alison asked Banham, outside the interview room twenty minutes later.

'Oh yes. He hasn't any reason to make that up; he's already served nineteen years for it. The question is, is he right about the stripper name? He pulled his phone from his pocket and switched it back on. 'And that strawberry motif on the G-string. Does that tell us who the killer's lined up next?'

He checked his phone. There was a string of missed calls made from the same number: one he didn't recognise. He quickly pressed 'Return', but the number was unobtainable.

'I'll get Katie Faye brought in,' Alison said, taking her car keys out and heading for the front door.

'Before you do, just run a check on that number for me.' He handed her his phone. 'It's called sixteen times in the last twenty minutes.'

CHAPTER SIXTEEN

Alison's arm was halfway into the sleeve of her anorak as she rushed back along the corridor to the incident room. She tossed Banham's mobile back to him and spoke at the speed of a Euro train. 'Grab your coat. The calls were from Olivia Stone's private line in her house.' Her car keys were already in her hand. 'I'll meet you at the car.'

Banham grabbed his coat and ran after her, pausing only to punch DC Holt's number into his phone.

'Have you got Katie Faye with you?' he asked the young surveillance officer.

Holt sounded out of breath. 'I needed the loo, so I knocked on the door. There were raised voices, so I followed the sound to the back of the house. Then I heard a car engine fire at the front, so I rushed back, just in time to see the BMW roaring off with Katie Faye at the wheel. I've already called for back-up...'

'Put out a warning not to approach her,' Banham said urgently. 'Give them the registration, but tell them to keep their distance. She may be armed and dangerous.'

He had reached the bottom of the stairs, opposite the station sergeant's desk. 'Get me a radio,' he said to the duty sergeant, 'and alert all areas. We're looking for a black BMW – DC Holt will give you the registration number. Warn them the driver may be armed.' He put his mobile back to his ear. 'Back-up's on the way, and so are we,' he told him. 'Stay at the house and keep us posted.'

Alison had the engine running and the door open as Banham tore out of the station, still talking to DC Holt. 'You said you heard voices at the back of the house? Whose? Besides Katie Faye?'

'I don't know, sir. A man, that's all I could tell. I didn't see any visitors arrive. If someone else was in the house, they got in without my knowledge.'

Banham climbed into Alison's car. It was moving before he had closed the door.

'Let's hope for a clear road,' she said.

She turned into the main road and jumped an amber light. She must have been driving at sixty miles an hour. Banham switched on the radiophone and asked the station sergeant for siren-led back-up. 'That'll help us cross London,' he said, 'and keep us in one piece.'

'Just pray we don't get a puncture. I've just changed the wheel and haven't had time to get it mended.'

They approached a T-junction, and she pulled out without waiting for an oncoming car to give way.

'I'll pray your driving doesn't get us killed as well, shall I?' he said, clutching the edge of his seat.

Katie slowed down to just under thirty miles an hour. Her eyes kept flicking toward the driver's mirror. She couldn't turn her head to the left. If she moved even a millimetre, the large, shiny, newly sharpened carving knife pressed against her throat would penetrate her skin. The side of her ear was already stinging from the small nick intended as a warning not to try to alert anyone.

That sting made her aware exactly how sharp that knife was, and the damage it could inflict. The fear of what it might do to her throat stopped her thinking straight.

A red G-string lay on the passenger seat beside her. Another warning, as if she needed it: she already knew she was next in the killer's sights.

The memory of the weeks working at that dreadful club soaked her mind. She'd been stupid. Stupid, and so desperate to earn the money to go to college and better herself that she put herself through the humiliation of rolling around naked on a filthy mattress pretending to have sex with Olivia, and having a huge dildo pushed up her anus by that pervert Ahmed. Taking her clothes off twice nightly in front of crowds of jeering drunks who pawed and mauled her young body, in the oppressive temperatures of the hottest summer in history. All because she had a dream – to become an actress, and make something of herself.

She slowed and stopped at a red light. Again she flicked a glance at the mirror, touching a finger under her eye to catch a tear, so that her vision wasn't blurred and her mascara wouldn't sting.

He was kneeling on the floor behind the driver's seat, an arm around her throat and a strange, twisted smile across his face. He could have been a stranger, not the child she had watched being born. She had held his mother's hand during the birth, and sworn to watch over him and protect him as his godmother. She hardly recognised her Kevin, with those mad eyes and a gun in his left hand in case the knife wasn't enough.

She lowered her eyes. Reasoning with him was out of the question. Her only hope was that someone would pull up beside them at the lights, recognise her and knock on the window for her autograph. But for that to work she needed to position her face closer to the window – and his grip was so tight she couldn't turn her neck.

'Where am I driving to, Kev?' she asked, failing to keep the tremble out of her voice.

'Keep going south, then turn left as soon as you can towards the river.'

Her body stiffened with fear. He obviously sensed it, because he began to laugh.

'I know you're afraid of water, Auntie Katie. You're going for a little swim.'

She took a deep breath and fought the tears trying to explode from her eyes.

'You won't be alone,' he told her. 'There'll be plenty of rats to keep you company.' He laughed again, a whining sound she heard never heard from him before. 'You won't see them, though. I'm going to cut out your beautiful blue eyes first. And feed them to the rats.'

The tears suddenly spilled out. She moved her head minutely as she tried to fight them back, and the edge of the knife caught her throat. First she felt the sting, then the trickle of warm blood as it tickled and slid down her neck. Then she heard that strange laugh again.

'Blimey, it's her. It's Nurse Penelope from *Screened*.' PC Garrad slammed his foot on the brake of the police patrol car. 'In front of us! Look – black BMW, number plate KAT. That's the car we're looking for.'

His partner, PC Tracey Alexander, spoke into her radio as Garrad crawled alongside them.

'Keep your distance, Jim,' Tracey said. 'There's someone in the back. He's got a knife to her throat.'

Katie saw the patrol car pull alongside them, praying that Kevin hadn't. But it was too much to hope.

'Go!' He pressed the heel of his hand against her throat, making her gag. 'Never mind the lights. DRIVE!'

She hesitated. He loosened his grip on her throat, and something stabbed her left hand, which was holding the handbrake.

'Do it! DRIVE!'

She did, without looking to see if they were about to be killed by the oncoming traffic. Cars swerved around her, hooting and shouting, verbal abuse flying out of open windows. *Surely the police car will come after us now*, she prayed.

But nothing happened.

'Keep your foot down. Keep driving.' The knife moved back to her throat, and his arm gripped her head and neck even tighter. She couldn't see the blood oozing from the cut on her hand, but she felt its warmth as it slid between her fingers.

'All units urgent!' The station sergeant's voice crackled out of Tracey's radio. 'Black BMW, registration KAT, heading south driving erratically. Do NOT approach, repeat DO NOT APPROACH. Armed and dangerous passenger in the car. Keep under observation but wait for back-up! Armed response is on its way.'

Alison, now sandwiched safely in between two patrol cars with sirens squealing, sped across red traffic lights. Banham clung to the edge of the seat and barked orders into his radio.

'Stay back. Do not get too close,' he shouted. 'Do not attempt to flag it down.'

Katie pulled up at the next traffic lights. Her eyes slowly focused on the driver's mirror. Kevin smiled that strange smile again. He drew the knife up her neck on to her chin and across her cheek, slowly sliding it toward her eye, grazing the soft skin of her cheek and angling the razor-edge so it was less than a millimetre from her left eye.

She froze.

He moved again, dragging the blade down her face over her already smarting cheek, and pushing the sharp edge in hard under her chin. Her heart was beating so hard it felt like a bomb about to explode. She closed her eyes, waiting for the agony as the knife penetrated her throat.

Nothing happened.

She opened her eyes again.

'I've got an erection, Auntie Katie. Do you want to feel it?'

This time she couldn't stop the tears. Mascara ran into her eyes, stinging and blinding her.

She had nursed him as a baby; bought him his first train set, and watched him grow up, hardly missing a week of it. In all those years she'd never seen a hint of this side of him. Had they been so busy feeling guilty for denying him a childhood with his real father that they had failed to see how disturbed he was? That he was a very sick boy in need of psychiatric help? Or was it a direct result of the violence Kenneth had shown him?

The traffic light turned green.

'Drive on,' he said casually.

She lifted her bloodied hand and tried to wipe the mascara from her eye so she could see clearly. Another prickle stung her shoulder like an angry bee. She couldn't move her head, but she felt the blood as it leaked on to her pink T-shirt. An uncontrollable sob burst from her mouth, and the car stalled.

'It's only a nip, don't be such a baby,' he said irritably.

She restarted the car and felt the heavy steel against the back of her head. There was a sickening, slicing sound, and she fought to keep the car straight as her body tensed, waiting for the pain.

He laughed, dangling his trophy in front of her. It was a large hank of her long golden hair.

Her first thought was that the studio would be furious. She had signed a contract agreeing not to change her hair in any way. She could get the sack. Then reality hit her. The job was the least of her worries; her chances of getting out of this situation alive were practically nil.

She lifted a trembling hand and wiped the smudged mascara from across her face. Blood from the cut on her hand stung her grazed cheek.

They were travelling at nearly eighty miles an hour, sirens

screaming at their front and rear. Banham spoke into his phone. 'The description fits Kevin Stone,' he told Crowther. 'Get Brian Finn into the back of a very fast unit car, and tell them to step on it. They are heading south towards the river. Bring a radio and I'll keep you updated. Time is at a premium.'

Alison's accelerator foot hit the floor.

Banham clicked his phone shut and heard himself praying aloud that they would be in time to save Katie Faye's life.

'We're doing everything we can,' Alison said quietly.

Katie slowed as she approached another set of traffic lights.

'Stop here,' Kevin said, looking around.

Where have all the police cars gone, Katie thought desperately.

He took the knife away from Katie's throat and sprang lightly over the top of the passenger seat.

The car was stationary. This was her only chance.

She opened the driver's door and launched herself towards the gap, but screamed with pain as he dragged her back by her hair. He grabbed the collar of her leather jacket with the other hand; he had obviously dropped the knife and the gun, so she resisted with all her strength. But she couldn't match his. He hauled her back into the car.

First his fist landed hard on her temple. Her head spun and she saw stars. Then he leapt out of the car and ran round to the driver's side; he pushed her legs in and slammed the door so quickly she had to pull her feet free.

As he climbed back into the passenger seat, terror consumed her; he grabbed her hair and turned her face towards him. His fist slammed hard into her face, and blood spurted from her nose and mouth. 'Now drive the fucking car!' he snarled.

She was dizzy but she drove on. Any hope of being recognised was gone; her face was a mess. She was losing hope.

Crowther and Brian Finn were in the back of a unit car, siren screaming, overtaking everything on the road. Banham's voice crackled over the radio. 'Kevin Stone is armed with a gun and a knife. An ARV is on the way. Stay out of sight until the ARV arrives. Katie Faye's life depends on it.'

'Let me talk to him,' Finn offered. 'He'll listen to me.'

'Not yet,' Crowther said.

'That bastard Ken Stone,' Finn muttered. 'He's responsible. No wonder the boy's like he is.'

Crowther glared at him.

'I'm your only hope,' Finn urged. 'If the police approach him, he could kill her. He'll listen to me. I'm his dad.'

'What do you think you're doing here?' Crowther sighed. 'A fucking joyride? When the time is right, you'll talk to him. But right now, shut the fuck up, will you.'

'Turn left at the lights,' Kevin said.

Katie still felt dizzy. She hesitated for a moment, trying to focus on the lights.

'I said, turn left.'

She felt another sting on her hand, and a trickle of fresh blood ran down her fingers. Her feet fumbled with pedals, then she put pressure on the accelerator and turned left.

'South! South!' The voice sounded in all fifteen police cars closing in on the BMW. 'Correction: target has now turned east and is heading towards the river.'

Brian Finn sat ashen-faced and silent, listening to every word.

The police car in front of Alison slowed, and the wailing siren went silent. Alison followed suit, and so did the car behind her. A voice came over Banham's radio. 'They're only a couple of streets away, guvnor.'

The familiar stab of guilt made Banham catch his breath. He hadn't been able to save his wife and baby, but he wasn't going to let Katie Faye die.

Katie tried pleading, but the words almost choked her. 'Kevin, I don't deserve this.'

'Yes, you do fucking deserve it! You let my father rot in prison.' His voice was cold and angry. 'For something he didn't do.'

'You've got it wrong. It wasn't like the ...' Another punch to the side of her head knocked the breath out of her, and hysterical sobs began to spill out. 'Please, Kevin, say you won't hurt your mother,' she begged. 'She loves you, and she wouldn't...'

The knife was in his hand again. He cut through her T-shirt and into her collarbone where the skin was thin. It was a shallow cut, but the pain was nearly unbearable and she had to fight for breath again. She opened her bleeding mouth, but only a strange animal-like sound escaped.

The voice came through the police radios. 'Target has turned left. The road leads to the docks.'

Alison slammed her brakes on. She reversed quickly, spun the car and headed in the opposite direction.

The blue lights on the other cars flashed silently.

She flicked a glance at Banham. He was staring out of the window, and she knew exactly what he was thinking. More than anything in the world, she wanted to save Katie too. She had misjudged her. And Banham would blame himself forever. If they didn't get there in time, he might never recover.

She approached the junction and slowed down.

Banham spoke into the radio. 'Any news on the Armed Response Vehicle?'

'Here, guvnor. Right behind you.'

CHAPTER SEVENTEEN

'Next left,' Kevin said, his tone chillingly casual. He ran a finger along the edge of the knife, pulling it quickly away to remind Katie how sharp it was.

The cuts on her body were reminder enough. Mascara stung her eyes, and her mind was growing hazy. It took her a moment to work out which was right and which was left.

'Next left!' he shouted, raising the knife.

She indicated left and out of the corner of her eye saw his hand drop. He started cutting at the G-string with the edge of the knife, carving little snips off the leather ribbon. The soft sound terrified her.

She turned the car into the side road, and her heart hit her boots. The road led to the water.

Banham spoke quietly but with authority into his radio. 'Keep your distance. No one, repeat no one, is to follow target vehicle. Armed Response van is directly behind us. We have a visual on the BMW, which has just pulled up by the edge of the river. Everyone else leave your cars, and very quietly, I repeat very quietly, move in on foot. Be very sure you are not seen. Crowther, take Finn with you, but stay out of sight. Armed Response officers are now moving in.'

Kevin placed the G-string on the end of the gun in his left hand. He opened the passenger door. 'Stay in your seat. I'm coming round to get you,' he told Katie.

Hysteria was overtaking her. The pain she was in and the sight of the water were proving too much for her. She grabbed his arm before he set a foot on the ground.

'Kevin, please, I'm begging you, don't do this. Your mother ...' She stopped mid-sentence. He turned towards her, the knife in his right hand. 'Oh God. No ...' Her arm flew up defensively, but not fast enough. The knife scored the side of her head above her ear. Blood ran down the side of her neck.

'Now get out,' he ordered.

Everything faded and all she could see was grey. A small, still-aware part of her mind prayed for the end to come quickly, before the deep, dark water swallowed her up.

He was standing by the open driver's side door when her vision returned. 'Out,' he commanded.

She obeyed. As he pushed a hand into her armpit and started to march her towards the river, she made a last appeal, slurring like a drunk as she spoke. 'Kevin, don't hurt your mother. Promise me ...' A ripping sound stopped her in her tracks. The knife cut through her leather jacket and continued into her back. All she felt was excruciating pain which took over her whole body. She gasped for air as the agony hit her lungs and shot up to her brain. Then her knees gave way, and she fell to the ground.

Banham saw it all. There was no time to wait for the

Armed Response team. Ignoring Alison's warning, he leapt from the car and ran down the middle of the road. He had no body armour, nothing at all for protection: just the overpowering urge to save Katie Faye.

'You're surrounded, Kevin,' he shouted. 'Drop your weapons, or we'll shoot.'

Within seconds a dozen armed police officers moved in behind him, their guns pointed at Kevin.

An ambulance had been hovering out of sight on the corner of the neighbouring street. Two paramedics armed with oxygen jumped from the back.

Katie was face down on the ground.

Banham slowed to a walk. 'Drop the gun and the knife, Kevin.'

Suddenly Alison was beside him. For a moment the world seemed to rock around him. 'Get back!' he shouted. 'Wait behind the AR vehicle.'

'I'm staying with you.'

'I'm giving you an order, sergeant. Not open to negotiation. Do as I say. Now.'

She hesitated and stopped. He kept walking.

'Drop the gun and the knife,' he said, his eyes on Katie.

She was struggling to her knees. Kevin pointed the gun at her head.

'Stand away from her,' Banham shouted. 'A dozen guns are aimed at you.'

'Guv, please.' Alison was beside him again.

'I told you to go back,' he said without taking his eyes off Kevin.

Kevin placed a heavy boot on Katie's back. Her body

quickly gave way and she sank to the ground. 'Go ahead,' he goaded. 'Shoot.' He raised his hands high in the air, one holding a gun, the other a knife.

Banham lifted a hand to halt the police riflemen, who were awaiting the order to fire. 'Alison, go back,' he said calmly.

'No,' she said, planting herself squarely beside him.

Kevin's hand dropped. He opened his flies, pulled his penis free and urinated over Katie. 'Sorry about that,' he shouted. 'It's the river. All that water. Couldn't stop myself.'

A voice boomed out from a little way behind Banham. 'Drop the gun, son.'

Brian Finn.

'Don't shoot her, son. Give the gun up. Do it for me.'

Banham heard footsteps, and glanced back to see Finn hurrying down the road towards his son. DC Crowther followed closely behind and stopped beside Banham and Alison. Finn hurried on.

Ten yards from his son he stopped and put out a hand. 'Give me the gun, son.'

'I'm going to count to ten,' Banham said.

'Shooting's too good for her,' Kevin retorted.

'Kevin, please, for me, for your dad, stop this. Give yourself up.' Finn moved forward again; now he was only a few feet from Kevin. 'Do it for me?' he asked again. 'Give the knife and the gun to me.'

'Nine. Eight. Stand away from him, Finn.'

Finn ignored him.

'Seven. Six.'

Katie stirred slightly, murmuring in pain.

Banham took another step towards Katie. 'Five. Four.'

Alison and Crowther moved in behind him.

'Step to the left, guvnor,' the head of the AR unit shouted as Banham raised his hand to give the signal.

'Paul, for Chrissake!' Alison screamed.

'Three. Two.' Banham's hand rose a little higher.

'Give me the gun,' Finn said urgently to Kevin.

'No.'

'One.'

Everything happened in an instant. Kevin lifted the knife to stab Katie. Finn lunged at Kevin to grab the gun. Banham moved to shield Katie Faye from the knife. Alison put out an arm to push Banham clear as a shot rang out.

Brian and Kevin, struggling with the gun, knife and each other, fell to the ground. Kevin dropped the knife. Finn tried without success to wrestle the gun from him.

Banham kicked the knife out of reach and stood over Katie, watching desperately for the right moment to wade in and grab Kevin.

Kevin and Finn rolled on the ground with Finn. Kevin had firm hold of the gun, his finger treacherously near the trigger.

The paramedics moved as close as they dared, waiting anxiously with a stretcher and emergency oxygen at the ready. The armed police officers closed in around Brian and Kevin, rifles pointed.

Then another shot split the air.

Brian Finn fell on his back, blood pumping from his

chest.

Kevin leapt up, waving the gun.

'Drop it!' Banham roared. 'Drop it now, or you're a dead man!'

Kevin obeyed. Crowther grabbed him and spun him round, clicking handcuffs on his wrists.

The paramedics came rushing past to the aid of Brian Finn and Katie Faye.

'You've killed him,' Kevin yelled at Banham. 'You've killed my father.'

Banham walked swiftly up to him. 'No.' He pushed his face into the lad's. 'No, Kevin. You've killed him. And you've killed three women. Maybe four.' He stood back and looked into the boy's eyes. 'Kevin Stone, I'm arresting you for the murders of Shaheen Hakhti-Watkins, Susan Rogers and Theresa McGann, and for the attempted murder of Katie Faye. You do not have to say anything...'

After he had finished reciting the familiar formula, he remained motionless, his eyes still locked with Kevin's. Crowther took his arm and pulled him away. But Banham was having none of it. He shook off Crowther's restraining hand and squatted beside Katie Faye's prone body. Alison was already there, alongside the young woman paramedic.

'How bad is it?' Banham asked quietly.

'Critical,' said the paramedic. 'She's haemorrhaging. We need to get her to hospital and into theatre as fast as we can.' She held a thick absorbent pad to the wound, applying pressure to try to stem the blood still pulsing out. 'The head wound looks pretty bad too, and we've no way of knowing about internal damage.'

Banham stood up and stepped back as a uniformed policeman came to help lift her on to the stretcher.

'Take care of her,' Banham said, a note of desperation in his voice. He followed them to the ambulance, and gently supported the stretcher as the two men lifted it inside.

A hand slid into his and gave it a squeeze as the siren sounded and the ambulance sped off. He turned to find Alison beside him.

'Modern medicine can work wonders,' she said quietly. 'Stay positive.'

He turned to face her. Those sludge-green eyes were swimming. He lifted her hand and gently kissed it.

Kevin's final victim still lay on the ground a few yards away. Banham and Alison walked towards Brian Finn's body in time to hear the other paramedic say, 'I can't help this one. He's gone.' He removed the plastic resuscitation tube from Finn's mouth.

'Was it the knife or the bullet wound?' Banham asked.

'You'll need the FME for that,' the paramedic said. 'But if you're asking me to hazard a guess, the bullet has only grazed his shoulder.' He pointed at the wound oozing blood through Finn's shirt. 'That's caused a bit of damage, but I wouldn't say it's enough to kill him. On the other hand ...' He pointed at the stab wound in the middle of the man's chest. 'The knife penetrated here. You really shouldn't take my word for it, but I think the post-mortem will confirm that that's what killed him.'

Banham stood up, his legs feeling suddenly weak. 'Alison, will you drive me to the hospital?'

'Of course. I'll bring the car down.'

Crowther was lighting a cigarette as Alison passed him. He offered the packet to her.

She shook her head. 'Thanks, but I've given up.'

'Never give up,' he said, following his cocky grin with a Know-all Col wink. 'If you really want something, you should never give up.'

By the time Banham and Alison reached the hospital, Katie Faye was in theatre undergoing emergency surgery. A young, exhausted doctor came to meet them.

'It'll be a long, uphill battle, I'm afraid,' he told them. 'And I can't promise you she's going to pull through. She had lost nearly six pints of blood, and though we've put it back, there may already be brain damage.' He knuckled his eyes, which were rimmed with dark circles from lack of sleep.

Alison flicked a glance at Banham. Guilt was surging off him in waves. She felt almost as bad herself, and it didn't help that all the good his therapist had done would be totally in vain if they lost Katie Faye.

It was no use telling him it wasn't his fault. A team of twenty-four had worked the case, round the clock in some cases. Three women had lost their lives before they found the killer. Banham would blame himself for the three deaths, and if Katie became the fourth, the emotional cost would be unthinkable.

She gave his arm a small squeeze, as if he was a grieving husband. He was, of course, and that lay at the root of what she knew he was feeling. He had never come to terms with his wife's murder, because her killer had never been found, and now the only way he could deal with it was to track down killers who preyed on women, and make himself responsible for every victim.

But this time there was more. *Had he really fallen for Katie Faye?*

To her surprise his hand covered hers and gripped it.

'When will we know more?' she asked the doctor.

'I'm afraid I can't answer that. The knife entered her back and ruptured a kidney, causing intensive bleeding. It's too early to say for sure, but we may be looking at a transplant.'

Banham's eyes were closed. Alison handed the doctor a card. 'We'll need to know the moment she comes round.' She flicked a glance at Banham and corrected herself. 'If she comes round. We do need to interview her.'

Banham followed her down the corridor, but she had the impression he was on autopilot. They came to a coffee machine, and she stopped and felt in her pocket for coins. 'Milk and sugar?' she said, feeding the silver into the slot.

He nodded, and seemed to come back into himself. 'I'm surprised you aren't champing at the bit to get out,' he said. 'We all know how you feel about hospitals.'

She waited for the muddy liquid to trickle down. 'I thought you needed a pick-me-up before we go back. You liked her a lot.'

Banham stared into the cup she handed him. 'I wanted to keep her safe,' he said quietly. 'It was her eyes. They were so like Diane's.'

So that was it.

She could see he was pretty close to breaking down. *He must really care*, she thought; *that's the first time in eight years he's admitted to real feelings*. He had fallen for Katie Faye. Well, that was life. Suddenly she felt her own emotions well up. She got a grip and started to walk on, leaving him to finish his coffee. Suddenly she felt his hand at her elbow. 'Alison, please sit down,' he said, guiding her to a seat in the A & E waiting area. She did, and looked up to find those blue eyes staring intently at her.

'Alison ...' He took a breath and looked down into his lap. 'I know we agreed that we wouldn't jeopardise our working relationship by becoming ...' He looked up, blushing.

'What?' she said. 'By becoming what?'

'Intimate.'

There was a pause, then she said, 'I agree.' Then, before she could stop herself, she added, 'And as you know, there is someone in my life.'

He stared at her, holding his breath. Then he let it go and sipped his coffee in silence.

'Who?' he asked after a long pause.

Why had she said that? Sometimes she wanted to kick herself. *You've blown it now*, said a small, insistent voice inside her head. She threw her hardly touched black coffee in the bin.

'No one you know.'

Banham slowly got to his feet. 'Katie has eyes like Diane's,' he said. 'But no one has eyes like yours.'

This time the silence seemed endless. Eventually she could take no more of it; she stood up and said briskly,

'We've got work to do. Let's interview Kevin Stone, before he has time to feign madness.'

As they made their way out they passed radio and TV crews and men in scruffy jackets who could only have been tabloid journalists. The hospital was fast filling up with media, all panting for news of Katie Faye. Alison wondered, not for the first time, how they had got wind of the story so soon.

'I hope she'll rally to see how much everyone loves her,' Banham said, climbing into the passenger seat and clicking his seat belt into place.

What a price to pay for the attention, though, Alison thought. But she decided, for once, to keep her mouth shut.

CHAPTER EIGHTEEN

Kevin Stone's smug grin made Alison want to pound his face to pulp. He lounged back in the chair across the table, next to the weak-mouthed, bifocalled solicitor who had represented Kenneth Stone.

Banham's fingers were interlocked and his knuckles were white. Alison could tell he was in danger of losing his temper, but was making a big effort to stay calm.

Kevin glanced, still grinning, from Banham to his solicitor and back again. He had ignored her from the start; *he clearly doesn't relate to women*, she realised. But as he wiped his hands surreptitiously on his beige Armani jeans, she saw that he was nervous too. *And with good reason*, she thought. Detective Inspector Paul Banham, the best cop in the business, had run him to earth, and now he would dig for every last drop of evidence to ensure this smart-alec boy was put away for the rest of his life. Three women had lost their lives and a fourth lay with hers in the balance; not forgetting a man who'd given his own life to save others.

At first Kevin had refused legal representation, even when Mr William Twig, whose flat, balding head made him look like a cross between ET and a used cricket ball, had turned up. Crowther, who was on a mission to get promotion and took every opportunity to impress his superiors, had talked him into allowing the solicitor into the interview room.

Alison had brought William Twig up to speed, and was delighted to see the complacent look on the man's face turn to grave concern. Twig was well known through his connections with Kenneth Stone's political party, and it took a great deal to knock him off balance; this time it was plain he gave little for his chances of getting his client off. When Alison told him they were waiting on news from the hospital, and Katie Faye could well be added to the list of murdered women, William Twig looked deeply worried.

Banham's penetrating eyes blinked. He unlocked his fingers and rested his arm on the table, then clasped his hands firmly together. He obviously didn't trust himself not to hit Kevin, and Alison understood why.

'You still want to stick with the "they had it coming" scenario?' he asked Kevin.

Kevin's smile widened. He pushed his tongue into his cheek and nodded.

Alison heard the intake of breath. Banham clenched his fists.

'How long had you been planning the murders?'

'They had it coming. All of them.'

'Answer the question,' Alison snapped, returning William Twig's glare.

Twig turned to Kevin and shook his head.

'We're impressed,' Banham said with a smile that didn't reach his eyes. 'You had us all fooled.'

Kevin nodded his head regally, but this time just one side of his mouth smiled.

'You rang Shaheen from your mother's phone, when she was on the train coming into St Pancras,' Alison said.

He nodded at them as if they were small children learning their ABC.

Alison pushed on. 'You told her you were coming to pick her up.'

He nodded again and said haughtily, 'When I got there, I told her there was a change of plan. I had been told to drive her to Judy and Kim's house; the meeting was to take place there because my dad was at home. Then I drove to a quiet lane, and I cut her throat. I put her in the boot. I had to break her legs to get her in, they wouldn't bend properly. I can't remember the make of the car. I think it was a Ford …' He turned his hands as if he trying to wind up his brain.

'A Mondeo,' Alison prompted.

'That's right. Aren't you the clever one?' *He'll pat my head in a minute*, she thought.

His expression darkened. 'The bitch peed on the seat. After she was dead, she peed on the seat. It stank. I wore overalls to do the job, but it still took me three showers to get rid of the smell. I wasn't happy about that.'

'I don't suppose her family were very happy either,' Banham said coldly.

Kevin's chin flicked up. 'What about *my* family? My real dad had no life. He spent nineteen years in prison because of her. And now he's dead. Shot down like an animal. I hope the man who shot my dad is going to hang. He deserves it.'

'That would be you,' Banham said, hands palms down

on the table. 'The gunshot only grazed his shoulder. It was the knife wound you inflicted on him that killed him.'

William Twig's face paled. Kevin looked at him for support, but he said nothing.

Banham continued, 'So when forensics confirm what I already know, I'll be adding manslaughter to the three murder charges. And we mustn't forget one attempted murder. "Attempted" for the moment, that is.' He raised his voice. 'You'll be spending your life behind bars, young man, and you'll deserve every minute of it.'

As William Twig opened his mouth to object, Kevin leapt across the table and flew at Banham's face. 'You set me up, you bastard.'

Quick as a flash, Alison was up and round the table, pinning his hands behind his back. 'Sit down,' she shouted, 'unless you want to add assaulting a police officer to the list. Or would you prefer we just locked you in a cell?'

Kevin obeyed, breathing heavily.

'My client needs a break,' William Twig said.

'Fine by me,' Banham said, straightening his shirt.

'I'm all right,' Kevin said, subsiding into his chair. 'I'm glad I killed those slags. I enjoyed cutting that brown woman's throat.'

'Because she was brown-skinned?' *Could he get any worse?* Alison wondered.

'No. Because she killed Ahmed Abdullah and let my real dad take the blame. She thought she was a cut above, but she was the worst of them all.' He pushed out his lower lip. 'She asked for it. My dad spent his life in prison because of her. And now he's dead too.'

'Where did you get the red G-strings?' Alison asked, more from curiosity than from any real need of the additional evidence.

'They were in the skips Kenneth bought at that auction. We were looking for videos of Mum and Auntie Katie, and I rooted through the other stuff and found the bags of red G-strings. Mum suggested Kim might like the other costumes for her dance productions, and sent me round to her house with the skips. I took the thongs out and gave the rest to Kim and Judy. Mum had mentioned that Auntie Katie's stripper name was Honeysuckle, so I wrote HS on them to make her the main suspect.'

'Did you write anything else?' Banham asked quickly.

He nodded. 'Nobody was quite sure which of them was Honeysuckle. Brian thought Mum changed hers from Candyfloss to Honeysuckle, and Katie was actually Strawberry. Then I realised there was an S in just about every name, so I drew the strawberry on a couple of them to throw the blame on Auntie Katie again. It was just fun really. Giving you lot a puzzle to solve.' He wiggled his fingers. 'Not that you were very good at it. You found the bag of G-strings I buried under the shrub with the knife, but you missed the others, under the lining of the boot of my car with the overalls. I still had enough left for the other three.' He shook his head sadly. 'Not now, though. I've blown it. I won't get the chance.'

'I don't understand why you wanted Katie to get the blame,' said Banham.

'She did a lesbian act with my mum.' He looked

vulnerable suddenly. 'That really turned me over. My mother, a dyke.' He shrugged. 'No matter really. I was going to kill her anyway. I was leaving her till last.'

Alison and the pallid William Twig made eye contact. Alison couldn't help wondering how he thought he would defend this one.

'Something's puzzling me,' Alison said. 'The day Shaheen was murdered a call was made to her from Katie Faye's mobile. Was that you too?'

He smiled. 'Yes. All part of my plan to make you suspect her. They were all waiting at our house. Katie's bag was with her coat; I took her mobile and dialled Shaheen's number.'

'You worked out every little detail, didn't you?' Banham said.

Kevin's grin was back. 'Clever, aren't I? I was going to use Katie's car too, to meet Shaheen at the station, but I couldn't find the keys. So I had to steal one.' He grinned again.

'What about Susan?' Alison said.

'What about her?' His face twisted with disgust. 'Fat slag. She smelt of cheap perfume and cat's pee.'

'Is that why you left her unrecognisable?'

He shook his head and looked serious. 'She was responsible for it all. She taught my mother to be a stripper. She was ghastly, and I hate cats.' His bottom lip turned down. 'Even her clothes smelt of them.' He laughed humourlessly. 'I enjoyed hacking her to bits. She was a piece of shit.'

'One thing I really don't understand,' Alison said. 'If

you were so fond of your real dad, why kill Theresa? He really loved her.'

Kevin hunched in on himself, drawing his shoulders together as if to protect himself. 'I saved him from her,' he said, almost apologetically.

'You broke his heart. She had his child. Your half-sister,' Banham reminded him.

He wiped his hands on his trousers again. He looked at William Twig and said in a low, confidential tone, 'He didn't know.'

Alison was running out of patience. 'What didn't he know?' she demanded.

His eyes narrowed. 'Bernadette's father wasn't my dad. She just said that to get money out of my mother.'

Banham and Alison exchanged glances.

Kevin continued. 'It was Ahmed Abdullah. She told me, last year. I was going to go to the social services about Bernadette; Theresa was always drugging the poor kid to sleep so she could go out. I told her I wanted to make sure she was properly looked after and, since she was my sister, the social services would listen to me.' He rubbed his face, and his eyes grew distant. 'The silly bitch said she wasn't my sister. She begged me not to tell Brian, because it was the only thing keeping him going in prison, and it would break his heart.'

He wiped his hands on his trousers for a third time. 'I thought he ought to know, but he died before I could tell him.'

No one spoke. Kevin stared at the table. After a few seconds he slowly raised his head and met Banham's eyes.

'She was a calculating, manipulative bitch and she deserved what she got. She would have used anyone to get money. Mum kept paying out because she felt responsible for the kid not having a father.'

'And now she hasn't got a mother either,' Banham said.

'She had it coming. I enjoyed cutting her throat and breaking her face with my fist and making her eat the G-string. She set my real dad up.'

'They all did,' Banham told him. 'Your father told us the truth. I think he was the only person who did.'

'He was a decent bloke. Not like all those slags. I did it all for him, you know.'

'Did Brian have any idea that you were carrying out these ... these revenge killings for him?' Alison asked.

Kevin shook his head. 'Dad wouldn't hurt a fly. He got beaten up in prison, and he wouldn't fight back in case he hurt someone. And in case it added to his sentence. He just wanted to get out and look after Theresa and Bernadette.'

'If you cared so much for your real father, how could you have planned to kill your mother?' Banham asked him. 'And what about your little sister? Didn't you think about her feelings?'

'I would have been doing her a favour. And as for Mum – she would have been better off dead than having to live with Kenneth Stone for the rest of her life. Ianthe and I have grown up with his violent temper. Every time he had too much to drink or had a bad day in Parliament, one of us got it. We lived in fear of him – but at least Ianthe and I knew that one day we could leave. Mum would never have left. What would she have done – become a stripper again?' His nose wrinkled. 'I'd have been doing her a favour. Putting her out of her misery. Wouldn't you do that for your mother?'

'Now it's up to the courts,' Banham said a short time later, as they made their way back to the incident room. 'That tape proves how intelligent and calculating he is.'

'And he's old enough to get four life sentences,' Alison added. 'I hope they don't ever let him out.'

Banham rolled his shoulders. 'I'm going back to the hospital. There are hordes of press gathered there. I'll make an announcement – take some of the heat off Katie.'

Alison nodded, looking at the floor. She realised she was wearing her brown lace-up boots – the most unfeminine footwear she possessed.

'Do you want some company?' The words were out before she could stop them.

He looked at her with those sad, dewy blue eyes. 'Yes, I do, very much indeed. Will you drive me?'

Olivia Stone was sitting in an empty interview room. Her right eye was still swollen from the punch she'd taken from Kenneth, and the bruising was growing more lurid. Black eye make-up had mixed with tears and crusted over her face, and she had had been chain-smoking for more than two hours.

The door opened and Judy Gardener walked in, followed by Kim. They sat down one on each side of her.

'You don't have to wait here, you know,' Judy said gently. 'It's all over now. You're free to leave whenever you like.'

'I haven't anywhere to go,' she said quietly. 'My husband is locked up because he's violent. My son has been arrested for the murder of my friends, and his defence is that we put his real father behind bars for a crime we should have paid for.' She dropped her cigarette in the ashtray and ground it out. 'The hospital says Katie's chances of pulling through are very slim. And Kevin was planning to kill me.' She turned to look at Judy. 'You know what? I wish he had.'

Judy put an arm around Olivia. 'Ianthe needs you,' she said. 'You'll get through this. You just have to take things one day at a time.'

'Tell that to Ken.'

Kim covered Olivia's hand with her own. 'You don't have to go home. You can come to ours. We'll go and get Ianthe, and you can both come home with us.'

Olivia didn't move. She picked up her packet of cigarettes and flicked another one out. 'Ken will lose his job,' she said. 'He'll blame me, and he'll probably kill me anyway. What will happen to Ianthe then?'

'If you have him charged with domestic violence you can get an injunction to keep him from coming near you,' Judy told her.

Olivia lit her cigarette and blew the smoke out. 'What about Ianthe? He is her father, after all.'

'She's offered to give evidence against him,' said Judy.

'Start your life again, you and Ianthe,' Kim said quietly.

'Won't I be charged?' Olivia asked. 'And Katie, if she

pulls through? You too, Kim. Won't we be charged with Ahmed's murder?'

'No.' Judy took her other hand and gave it a squeeze. 'It's too long ago. DI Banham has already told me he won't be following it up. If Kevin brings it up in court, it's his word against yours. His defence will go for an insanity plea anyway, so it wouldn't hold up. You've more than paid the price for that mistake.'

Olivia opened her handbag and took out a tissue. 'To be honest, I don't think I care any more,' she said, scrubbing hard at her cheeks. 'If it wasn't for Ianthe, I'd probably kill myself and save everyone a lot of bother.'

'Come on, Olivia,' Judy said sternly. 'Katie is fighting for her life and you dare to suggest ending yours?'

'I'm going to insist that you and Ianthe stay with us for a while,' Kim said.

'It's my fault Kevin turned out like this,' Olivia said, tears starting to flow again.

'Livvy, we were kids,' Kim said patiently. 'We didn't know we were playing with fire. And we didn't do it on purpose. It just happened.'

Judy squeezed Olivia's hand again. 'You're not the only one with a guilty secret,' she said sheepishly. 'I'm a police officer, and I lied too. I knew Kim had red G-strings in those skips, and I said she didn't, because I didn't want them to interrogate her. And it gets worse. I knew about Ahmed's death weeks ago, because Kim confided in me, and I kept it to myself.'

Olivia gave a watery smile. 'I guess no one's perfect,' she said.

'All we can ever do is try to hold it together,' Kim said.

'When I was a kid, shunted around from one foster home to another, I was determined to have it all when I grew up.' Olivia took another clean tissue from her bag. 'I really believed I could, too. And I might have, if I'd gone the right way about it. I was going to law school, remember? But I got it all wrong. And now look at me – I've got nothing at all.'

'You've got a beautiful daughter and you've got your friends.'

'What about Katie? I can't believe I may never see her again.' A tear dropped from Olivia's eye.

'Katie's tough,' Judy said encouragingly. 'She's a fighter. She could yet pull through.' She stood up and put out a hand to Olivia. 'Look, we'll go and get you a cup of something disgusting from the police canteen and, while you drink it, I'll go and pick Ianthe up from the stables and take her home to pick up some things. Then I'll bring her back here to fetch you and Kim, and we'll all go and visit Katie.'

'And then what?'

'One day at a time, eh? You can both stay with us, at least for a few days until the injunction is sorted. We can all go together to the hospital every day, and when Katie's better we'll all live together until things even out.'

Olivia smiled sadly. 'She's OK, your Judy,' she said to Kim.

'Yeah. I know.' Kim looked away, biting her lip.

'What?'

'No, you've had enough for the moment. This can wait

till later,' Kim said.

'Get it over with,' Olivia said flatly.

'OK. Social services turned up to see Bernadette, and Theresa's mother phoned us. We went round to help her out, and guess what she told us?'

'Go on.'

'Bernadette's father wasn't Brian. It was Ahmed.'

'Jesus!'

'Jesus would have been less of a surprise,' Judy said, 'seeing as she was an Irish Catholic, and Ahmed was an Arab.'

Olivia felt as if she'd been punctured. 'What would Katie say to that?' she wondered.

'We'll let you be the one to tell her,' Judy said. 'When she's well enough.'

CHAPTER NINETEEN

'My God!' Alison exclaimed as they approached the hospital entrance.

The building was surrounded. Fans, journalists, photographers, television crews, friends and well-wishers all stood waiting for news of Katie Faye's progress.

'There must be a thousand people here,' Banham said.

Journalists shivered in the February chill, notebooks hugged to their chests. Television cameras pointed at the doors, lights turning early evening into day, overhead boom stands connected. Everyone stood ready and waiting for the day's headline story: the nation's favourite soap star had been abducted by a serial killer, and lay unconscious and fighting for her life.

A host of fans had turned out too, some alone, some huddled together in groups, some holding large bouquets or single red roses, some crying, all waiting and wondering what would happen to Katie Faye.

'I hate the tabloids,' Banham said, digging in his pocket for his warrant card. 'They're like vultures, hovering and circling, waiting for a life to be extinguished so they can feast on the remains.' He held his card in the air. 'POLICE!' he shouted authoritatively. 'Clear a path.' He grabbed Alison's hand and skilfully manoeuvred through the multitude of people.

She wasn't sure if he held on to her so tightly because he thought she needed help getting through the crowd, or because he needed to hold on to her. Either way, she didn't object.

They stood in front of the hospital's glass doors and turned to face the crowd. Banham spoke in a loud voice, showing little sign of the emotion Alison knew he was feeling.

'There is no news at present. Katie Faye is still in the operating theatre. A man has been arrested and has now been charged.' He was briefly distracted by a young blonde woman in blue jeans and a floral overall, wheeling a garden trolley overloaded with bouquets and plants of every conceivable colour.

Alison noticed a blue van covered in enormous yellow and white daisies, parked illegally across an emergency bay in front of the hospital. Another woman was unloading more flowers from the back, while the woman with the trolley cut a path through the crowds to the door. Banham moved aside to let her through, and as she pushed the door open some fans rushed forward to add their own tributes to the pile.

'For Katie Faye,' she grinned, looking at Alison. 'And all those.' She waved an arm at the van.

Alison watched Banham taking advantage of the distraction to pull himself together. Someone in the crowd asked him how near a miss Katie had had. He opened his mouth to reply, but closed it again. Alison moved closer to him, ready to jump in and take over if necessary.

He's allowing himself to feel emotion, she thought,

even if he's not going to show it. This was a step forward for him; his counsellor was clearly getting through to him.

A cameraman walked toward Banham, a red light flashing on the top of his equipment: obviously a live news bulletin.

'That's all I can tell you at present,' Banham said, turning away. 'We will keep the media informed. If you're a fan, you might be better, certainly warmer, at home waiting for news by your television or radio.' He paused, and added quietly, 'Everyone is doing all they can.'

'That's the part of the job I hate,' he said as they walked through the revolving doors and towards the reception desk.

'You'll be doing a lot more of it soon,' Alison said briskly. 'If the rumours of promotion are true.' He looked at her with a puzzled frown, and she went on, 'Apparently you're going up to DCI and I'm going to be offered your job.'

'Who told you that?'

'Oh, the station jungle telegraph. I certainly haven't been offered promotion. But Isabelle Walsh said she slept with Crowther to put him off his guard, so she could beat him to my job.'

Banham slowed as they reached the glass reception counter, and turned to face her. His eyes creased with amusement. 'Strictly between you and me,' he said, 'the DCI's retiring and I've been offered his job.'

She said nothing, hoping he couldn't hear her heart thudding. He looked so attractive with those lines crinkling around his eyes. She couldn't bear the prospect of not working with him every day.

'I thought no one else knew,' he went on. 'You can tell Isabelle she wasted her time.'

'Crowther will be pleased.'

'I shouldn't think so. I enjoy the job I'm in. I turned the promotion down. So yours won't be up for grabs.'

'You don't want promotion?'

He shook his head. 'I like what I do. There's a new DCI starting next month, but no one is supposed to know yet.'

Alison struggled to keep the delight off her face. She wanted promotion of course, but perhaps she wasn't ready yet. Working alongside Banham, tracking down killers, was where she was happy.

The receptionist emerged from the back office and pointed them in the direction of Katie Faye's room.

'This one hit home with me, you know,' Banham said quietly as they walked down the corridor. 'I really wanted to save those women.'

There was pain in his voice. Alison had to squeeze her lips tightly for a second. 'You might still have saved Katie,' she answered. 'And all this exposure and publicity is what she thrives on. Remember what she said? She had no real family, and becoming famous was all she ever wanted.'

The skin around Banham's soulful blue eyes crinkled again, but he could only manage half a smile. He looked away, and she wondered if it was to stop her seeing his eyes fill up. 'She was already famous before all this began,' he said.

'But this proves how much the nation loves her.'

'I hope she lives to find out.' He stopped in his tracks and turned to look Alison in the eyes. There was such sadness in his eyes, she had to turn away. She'd broken one New Year's resolution; she was determined not to let herself start loving him again.

She turned back but still couldn't look at him.

'I desperately want her to pull through,' she heard him say.

Her own eyes started filling up. 'I do too,' she said, quickening her step and beginning to climb the stairs ahead of him. 'We all make mistakes when we're young. Those girls have spent their lives paying for theirs.' She looked at him over her shoulder. 'But you know, if she does pull through, we'll have to look at charging her with accessory to Ahmed Abdullah's murder.'

His face tightened. 'That murder has been paid for, sergeant. PC Gardener asked the same question and that's the answer I gave her. I certainly won't be following it up.'

'Kevin Stone's defence will use it.'

'It's his word against theirs. Brian Finn pleaded guilty and served his sentence. He isn't alive to retract that plea.'

'But it's our job to get to the truth. That's what we do.'

'We've got to the truth. It was manslaughter, not murder. Perhaps even accidental death. Those women have done more than a life sentence. I won't be pursuing it.' His tone held a note of finality, and she knew the discussion was over.

'You really do care about them, don't you?'

He stopped at the top of the staircase and put a hand on her shoulder. 'Six women made a big mistake when they were teenagers. They've paid a high price for it. Three of them were murdered because of it. Olivia Stone has survived, but what kind of life does she have to look forward to? Kim Davis was drug-dependent for years because of it, and if it came out now, Judy would lose her job and Kim might very well lose Judy. And Katie Faye's life is hanging by a thread, and she could end up with brain damage. Don't you think they've paid for what they did?'

'Oh yes. I do. I always did. I was just seeing how the land lay with you.' She tipped her head to one side. 'You've changed, Paul, and it's all good. You've stopped hiding your feelings. So is it the counselling? Or is Lottie having an influence on you?'

He looked straight into her eyes. 'Let me buy you dinner in that Italian restaurant where it all went wrong last time, and we'll talk about it.'

For a second, Alison was lost for words. 'I'm not sure,' she answered honestly.

'No, nor am I. The wine was good, but the pasta wasn't brilliant. What about the Indian in the middle of town?'

She stared at him quizzically. 'Business and pleasure don't mix, remember?'

'Nor do champagne and Guinness, but sometimes it makes you feel good.' Their eyes met, and the corners of his mouth curled, Alison sensed a little nervously. But when he spoke again, his voice was tender and sincere. 'I know I've mucked you about in the past. But I'm not going to let the past rule tomorrow.' He began to walk on.

'So will you come to dinner with me?'

She lengthened her stride and caught up with him.

'Will you?' he asked again.

'I'll think about it, OK? Let's see how Katie's doing.'

The corridor outside Katie Faye's room was a carpet of flowers. Alison and Banham trod carefully to avoid crushing them. He pushed the door ajar and they looked inside. Katie was back from the operating theatre. She lay still and pale in the bed, with more tubes going into to various parts of her body than the entire London Underground, it seemed to Alison. A monitor beside her flashed in a zigzag pattern, and bleeped every few seconds. To one side of the bed hung a clear plastic sachet of dark red blood, feeding into her through a tube attached to a needle in her hand. On the other side a container of clear liquid did the same job into the other hand.

A young nurse sat by her bed. Banham showed her his ID.

'How's she doing?' Alison asked quietly.

'Not great,' answered the nurse.

'Will she make it?'

The nurse shrugged. 'Not up to me to say, and it's much too soon anyway. If she does, I'm betting she'll be have some kind of paralysis, and her speech may well be affected. She's suffered a lot of internal damage; she lost nearly six pints of blood, and all her organs were starting to shut down by the time they got her into theatre. It's unlikely they'll ever be back to normal. That's if she pulls through at all.'

'On a scale of one to ten, what chance do you give

her?' Banham asked.

'You didn't get this from me – but no more than one,' the nurse said sadly. 'We all watch *Screened* when we can. It doesn't bear much resemblance to what really happens in a hospital, but we all love her to bits, and want to look like her. She's so pretty.' She swallowed hard and corrected herself. 'Was so pretty.'

Banham moved softly to the side of the bed and bent to speak into Katie's ear. 'It's all over,' he said, with more compassion than Alison had ever known him show. 'Kevin will go away for a very long time, and the Scarlet Pussy Club is history. You'll never have anything hanging over you again. So you have to get better, do you hear me? So many people love you, and you have so much to live for.'

Katie's eyelids fluttered. Alison touched Banham's shoulder. 'I think she heard you.'

They walked back along the corridor, in silence. After a few minutes Banham stopped. His blue eyes held hers for a few seconds, then he said, 'Please, let me buy you that dinner?'

It took Alison all her resistance. 'No. I'm sorry.' She shook her head a bit too hard.' No. My mind is made up. Detectives are notoriously unreliable. Their mobiles always ring and something turns up, and a five-course dinner turns into tea in a paper cup and a stodgy bun in the police canteen.' She didn't dare meet his eyes. 'And you end up eating both the buns and paying the one pound forty yourself,' she added.

He had stopped walking and was staring at her, smiling. 'It's not that big a deal,' he said. 'It's a "thank-you", for helping me out with Lottie.' Then after a pause and a sharp intake of breath he said at a rate of knots, 'No, it's not, actually. It's because I'd like to have dinner with you.'

She looked down at her brown cords and anorak. 'I'm not dressed,' she said, realising she should just have said 'no'.

'Go home and change. I'll come with you. While you're dressing, I'll ring the restaurant. You choose which one.'

She moved her head from side to side, keeping her eyes cast downward as if she was weighing up the options, but actually taking the seconds to curb her enthusiasm. Then she looked at him. He looked so vulnerable. Her resistance melted. 'OK, but it's just dinner.'

His smile looked so sincere, and those crinkles appeared at the side of his eyes, the ones she found so damned irresistible.

They left the hospital by the main exit. Banham made another announcement to the press, leaving out the news that Katie might not make a full recovery. 'She's out of theatre,' he told them, 'and the hospital will issue bulletins about her progress.'

'Can you confirm the rumour that Katie Faye was once a whore?'

The voice came from the back. Banham began to push through the crowd, fists clenched; Alison pulled him away. 'Let someone else deal with him,' she told him. 'It's time to forget work.'

He blew out a breath and she felt him relax. They turned and walked towards the car park, leaving the crowd behind.

She halted her in her tracks. 'I – do – not – believe it,' she said, staring at her car, all thoughts of their night out evaporating.

'What?'

'My car! Look! I've got another bloody puncture!'

'I'll change it for you.'

Her eyelids slowly lowered. Never in the seven years they had worked together had he once offered to help her with her car. And now, as well as a night out at her favourite restaurant, he was offering to change her wheel. But…

'The spare's in the garage being mended,' she said, trying not to let out a loud wail.

He rubbed his hand across his mouth. 'We'll phone the garage.'

'It's after six o'clock. They'll be shut.'

She looked at him, and their eyes locked. She squeezed her lips together. She didn't know whether to laugh or let him see her disappointment.

He lifted his eyebrows and smiled that smile again. 'The hospital canteen then? The tea doesn't come in paper cups and their buns are home-made. And I'll pay.'

Discover more from Linda Regan...

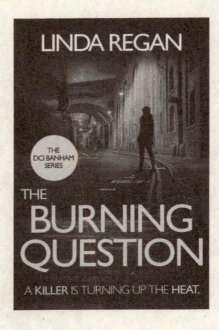

When an arson attack strikes in south London, leaving three people dead, it quickly becomes clear that the youngest victim, Danielle Low, was the intended target.

With no clear motive, and the killer at large, DCI Banham must act fast. But working with his partner, DI Alison Grainger, has its own challenges that threaten to stall the investigation. Then another body is found in similar circumstances and he knows that there is someone far more sinister at work.

As they begin to unravel a dark web of secrets, the case unexpectedly leads close to home and with time of the essence, and the killer always one step ahead, can DCI Banham and his team work together to put a stop to the depravity before another life is lost?

<u>Available to order now</u>

THRILLINGLY GOOD BOOKS FROM CRIMINALLY GOOD WRITERS

CRIME FILES BRINGS YOU THE LATEST RELEASES FROM TOP CRIME AND THRILLER AUTHORS.

SIGN UP ONLINE FOR OUR MONTHLY NEWSLETTER AND BE THE FIRST TO KNOW ABOUT OUR COMPETITIONS, NEW BOOKS AND MORE.

VISIT OUR WEBSITE: WWW.CRIMEFILES.CO.UK
LIKE US ON FACEBOOK: FACEBOOK.COM/CRIMEFILES
FOLLOW US ON TWITTER: @CRIMEFILESBOOKS